SHOOTOUT—
FOR A MAN WITHOUT A GUN

Ben Simmons was no gunfighter, and his death in a shootout with Bates was no less than cold-blooded murder in Quince Parker's mind.

Now Quince faced the dangerous man who had shot his friend, and the gunslinger returned his stare with pale, colorless eyes, a deadly smile fixed on his face. "Go for your gun," he said quietly, his hand poised for the draw. "*You* might just get lucky."

"I'm not wearing a gun," Quince said, looking Bates right in the eye.

"Then you had better *get* a gun, mister, 'cause I intend to kill you—with or without one . . ."

The Making of America Series

THE WILDERNESS SEEKERS
THE MOUNTAIN BREED
THE CONESTOGA PEOPLE
THE FORTY-NINERS
HEARTS DIVIDED
THE BUILDERS
THE LAND RUSHERS
THE WILD AND THE WAYWARD
THE TEXANS
THE ALASKANS
THE GOLDEN STATERS
THE RIVER PEOPLE

THE RANCHERS

Lee Davis Willoughby

A DELL/BRYANS BOOK

Published by
Dell Publishing Co., Inc.
1 Dag Hammarskjold Plaza
New York, N.Y. 10017

Dell ® TM 681510, Dell Publishing Co., Inc.

ISBN: 0-440-07485-1

Printed in the United States of America

First printing—March 1981

THE
RANCHERS

1

A RED BAND of color spread across the western sky, fanning out from the setting sun which had lost much of its heat and brightness, though none of its brilliance. Light and shadow played upon the Wyoming hills, while in the timbered draws the trees began to gather their night blankets of mist around them. The most prominent feature of the landscape was a mountain with three distinct peaks, called Three Crowns, from which the ranch took its name.

A young man stood on the porch of the bunk-house taking in the summer sunset. The bunk-house was about twenty yards from the main house, which the cowboys called "The Bighouse." The young man was lean and tough, and though his movements seemed relaxed, there was about him a controlled, graceful power, like the walk of a mountain lion. Even his hair was a sandy, tawny color, and his eyes, whose golden brown color and shining appearance were like the eyes of the big cat.

The man's name was Quince Parker, and he was the foreman of Three Crowns. Three Crowns was one hundred and sixty thousand acres of gently rolling grassland, surrounded by purple mountains and fed by the crystal waters of Indian Creek, a tributary of the Sweetwater River. Two dozen cowboys and ranch hands rode herd over thirty thousand cows. Quince was as proud of Three Crowns as its owner, Stuart Kendrake.

Kendrake was in the main house at this moment, sitting at a large rolltop desk, reading a letter. He was an Englishman, much trimmer now than he was when he arrived in this country five years earlier. He was a fine-featured gentleman with a full head of white hair and clear, blue eyes. He was actually a Lord, although he no longer used his title. He chuckled as he read the letter.

"Well, now," he said aloud, though there was no one in the room to hear him. "At last . . . Leslie's coming over at last."

Kendrake talked to himself more often these days, for the simple reason that the American cowboys were so loath to talk that he often longed for the sound of a human voice, even if it was his own. Kendrake liked the men who worked for him. They were hard-working, honest, loyal to the extreme, and they respected Kendrake and obeyed his orders while keeping about them a sense of self-worth projecting to the world their belief that no man was better than they. Some of Kendrake's fellow ranch-owners had a difficult time with that trait, Kendrake knew. They were very class-conscious, and couldn't accept the cowboy's view that the ranch hand was equal to the ranch owner, but Kendrake respected his men for that.

Kendrake got up from his chair and walked over to the calendar. The page showing was May 1892, so he turned it to July, made a circle around the 2nd, then let the pages drop back. He looked at it and chuckled again. There were only forty-one days remaining until Leslie would arrive.

From the cookhouse outside Kendrake caught the smell of frying chicken, and when he walked to the door he could hear someone softly strumming a guitar. He saw Quince standing on the front porch of the bunkhouse.

"Quince," he called.

Quince looked over at Kendrake, but, typically, didn't answer. Instead, he left the porch and walked to the bighouse to see what his boss wanted.

"Quince, I want to have a big celebration on July the second."

Quinced smiled. "You mean July the fourth, don't you, Mr. Kendrake?"

"July the fourth?"

"That's Independence Day."

"Heavens," Kendrake said with a chuckle. "Why would an Englishman celebrate the day we lost the Colonies? No, I mean July the second. That is the day Leslie arrives."

Kendrake looked closely at Quince's eyes to see how he would take the news of Leslie, for in fact Kendrake, borrowing a page from the cowboy's own book, had not mentioned the impending visit.

"I didn't know your son was coming, Mr. Kendrake," Quince said.

Kendrake smiled again, even more broadly than before. "You cowboys aren't the only ones who can keep a secret. I do quite well at it myself."

Quince's eyes flashed for a brief instant, then

in the bronzed cheeks of his face a bit of color appeared. "I know that, Mr. Kendrake, and don't think I'm not grateful."

The smile left Kendrake's face to be replaced by a more serious look. He put his hand affectionately on Quince's shoulder, though he knew that Quince was uncomfortable with such a display of warmth.

"Son, and I call you that because you are more like a son to me than a foreman, you need never worry about me keeping that secret, for it is one that I shall carry to my grave. And you've already shown your gratitude a thousand times over. I would never have made Three Crowns what it is today without you."

"Three Crowns is a fine ranch, Mr. Kendrake. Your son is a very lucky man to be coming to a spread like this. Why, he'll be as proud of you and of it as a peacock."

Kendrake laughed aloud. "Do you think so? Perhaps you should wait until you meet Leslie."

"Oh, I know he is likely to be a dude, Mr. Kendrake. Most Englishmen are, beggin' your pardon. But you've come through it well, and I reckon Leslie will be all right too, comin' from the same stock."

"Would you work with Leslie?"

"Sure, I'll teach him everything he needs to know. I'll teach him how to ride and rope, how to brand calves, everything about ranchin'."

"Quince, I'm a lucky man to have you as a foreman, and even luckier to have you as a friend."

"Well, now, Mr. Kendrake, I reckon that goes two ways," Quince said.

The cook stepped out of the cookhouse then, and began banging on an iron triangle which hung from a small crossbeam between the porch-roof supports. The clanging sound had an instantaneous effect on the cowboys in the bunkhouse, because the music stopped and the door burst open to pass a dozen or so running men to their meal.

"You'd better go before it's all gone," Kendrake said.

"Oh, they'll likely leave a bit for me," Quince said.

Kendrake laughed. "I may still be a dude, Quince, but I'm no tenderfoot. I've seen what a hungry mob of cowboys can do to enough food to feed an army. If you have it in mind to eat tonight, you'd best get over there."

"All right," Quince said, touching his hat. "I'll see you in the morning. Oh, and it's great news about your son coming."

"Yes," Kendrake said. And again he laughed, as if enjoying a private joke. "Yes, isn't it, though?"

As Quince walked to the cookhouse, he thought of the news he had just been given. It wasn't that much of a surprise. He had carried mail back and forth from town often enough to have seen the exchange of letters between Kendrake and Leslie. Leslie's last name was also Kendrake, so Quince figured him to be Stuart's son. But it would have been a violation of his code to ask about it. Besides, Stuart Kendrake obviously enjoyed springing his surprise on Quince, and if he wanted to enjoy his surprise, then Quince thought he had a right to.

In fact, Stuart had a right to do just about anything he wanted to do as far as Quince was concerned. For Stuart Kendrake had saved Quince's life, and Quince would never forget that. It had been five years since the train robbery, but Quince could still recall every moment of it with vivid detail.

The lonesome whistle of the approaching Union Pacific train brought to surface the realization of what he was about to do. Sitting in his saddle under the trees that dark night, with a cold, spitting rain blowing in his face, Quince tried one last time to talk the self-appointed but unchallenged chief out of the plan.

"Listen, Matt, I don't think we've thought this all the way through," Quince said. "We've had some fun, sure, but this, this'll mark us as outlaws for the rest of our lives."

"People like us are no better off than outlaws anyway," Matt replied. "We may as well have some money for it. Don't go running scared on me now."

"I can't help it, Matt, I'm tellin' you—"

"Aw, give the baby a sugartit to suck on," one of the other men said. "That'll keep him quiet for a while."

Quince pulled his poncho back to expose his gun, and he faced his taunter. "Pull your gun, Morris, or back down."

"Come on, he didn't mean anything by it," one of the other men said nervously.

"I said pull your gun," Quince said again, looking at the man with calm, unflinching eyes.

"Listen . . . I—he was right. I didn't mean

nothin' by it, I guess I'm just nervous, that's all. I don't want to pull agin' you. You're my friend."

"You and I are not friends," Quince said calmly.

"Well I don' want to pull a gun agin' you anyway. I'm sorry 'bout what I said. I din' have no right."

Quince looked at Morris for another tense moment. Then the sound of the whistle showed that the train was much closer now, and its closeness made one of the horses stamp his foot restlessly. Finally, Quince let the poncho fall back across his gun, and he turned in the saddle to look at Matt.

"All right," he said. "I don't like doing it, but I feel like I have no choice. You've pushed me into it."

Matt smiled broadly. "I knew you'd come around to our way of thinkin'."

"I haven't," Quince said calmly. "I'm as against it now as I ever was."

"You'll change your mind when you have that money in your hands." Matt pulled his handkerchief up so that it covered his nose and mouth, and he indicated to the others that they should do the same. He stood in the stirrups of his saddle and looked down toward the approaching train. The headlamp was in view now, a huge, wavering, disc, its gas flame and mirror reflector sending a long beam of light stabbing through the steadily falling rain. That sighting was closely followed by the hollow sounds of puffing steam, like the gasps of some fire-breathing, serpentine monster. As if to add to the illusion, glowing sparks whipped away in the black smoke cloud that billowed up into the wet, night, sky.

"Bates," Matt called. "Have you got that lantern lit?"

"Yeah," a voice said, floating up from a draw near the track.

"Git out there on the track 'n start wavin' it back 'n forth. When the train stops, you tell the engineer that the bridge has washed out up ahead. We'll take care o' the rest."

"Right," Bates called back.

"Is everyone set?" Matt asked.

There were four others with Matt, including Quince and Morris, and they all nodded in the affirmative.

"Git your guns out," Matt said. "Here it comes."

Bates began waving the lantern, and almost as soon as he started, Quince knew that their ruse would be successful, for the sound of vented steam and squeaking metal told him that the train was being braked. The train finally rumbled and rattled to a halt, stopping just below them, exactly as Matt had planned.

"Let's go," Matt said, and the five horsemen slapped their legs against the side of their animals and rode down to the track.

"I'll take the express car," Matt said. "Quince, you start at the back of the train 'n come forward, Morris, you start at the front 'n go back. Take ever'thin' any of the passengers have."

Quince started toward the rear of the train, but he couldn't go through with it. Robbing the express car was one thing—that money belonged to Wells Fargo, a big company could afford the loss. But the individual passengers couldn't, and he had no desire to steal from them. Instead of going to the

rear of the train as he was ordered, Quince stepped
from his saddle onto the platform at the rear of
the first car. He wasn't going to rob the passengers,
and he wasn't going to let Morris rob any of
them either.

When Quince stepped into the car he was surprised to see that it wasn't a regular passenger
car, but a private pullman. There were no rows
of chairs, just a large sofa, an overstuffed chair, a
table, and a bed. A man was sitting up in the bed,
peering through the window curtain, trying to see
what was going on outside.

"Well, well, well, what have we here?" Morris
said from the other end of the car. The man had
been reading, and there was a golden bubble of
light at his end of the car, coming from the gas
lantern by his bed. Morris, who was standing at
the foot of the man's bed, and pointing a gun at
the man, was illuminated by the light. Quince was
in the shadows, and as yet was unobserved by
either of the men.

"What is this?" the man asked. "Who are you,
and what are you doing in my car?"

Morris laughed.

"I'm robbin' you, mister."

"My word! Is this a robbery?"

Morris laughed. "Yeah, you might say that. You
might say it's a killin' too, 'cause after I take your
money, I don't intend to leave you as a witness."

Quince raised his pistol and cocked it. It made
a deadly, unmistakable, metallic sound, and Morris
jerked around in surprise.

"We're not killing anybody," Quince said.

"What? What are you doin' here?" Morris asked.

"You are supposed to start at the rear of the train. This is *my* territory."

"This is nobody's territory," Quince said. "We're not robbing any of the passengers."

"Who the hell said we're not?"

"I said we're not," Quince replied.

Morris looked at him for a long moment, as if trying to decide whether to attempt to take him. Finally, he smiled and slipped his pistol back into his holster. "Matt ain't gonna like this," he said. "Matt ain't gonna like it at all."

"I'll take it up with him," Quince said.

There was a sound of shooting outside and Morris smiled broadly. "Well, I guess we had to kill a few of the sons-of-bitches after all." He looked pointedly at Quince. "We might have to kill one more before this is all over."

"Out," Quince said, waving his pistol barrel toward the door.

Just as Morris started out there was the sound of another shot, this one much closer, and Morris came back into the car. He looked at Quince with a twisted smile of disbelief on his face.

"What is it?" Quince asked.

Morris was holding his hand over his chest, and at that moment, bright red blood began spilling through his fingers.

"I've been kilt," he said, almost ready to laugh over the incredulity of the event. He fell back against the wall, then turned and with a lunging motion toppled down the steps of the car, landing headfirst on the trackballast outside.

"Mr. Kendrake," a voice called from outside.

"Mr. Kendrake, it's all right, we got 'em all. Is there anyone else in there?"

The man in the bed looked toward Quince, and Quince started for the back door.

"No," the man warned Quince in a harsh whisper. "They'll shoot you the moment you set foot off this train."

"They'll damn sure shoot me if they come here," Quince said. He held his gun toward the door, ready to blast away at the first intruder.

"Wait, I have an idea," the man in the bed said. He got up and walked over to a large brass bathtub. "Get in here," he said.

Quince didn't question him, he just did as Kendrake asked. Once he was in the bathtub he lay on the botton while Kendrake dropped several towels over him.

"Be very quiet," Kendrake said, issuing a warning that wasn't really needed.

Quince heard several people coming into the car then, and they were laughing and buoyant.

"Those poor sons-of-bitches never knew what hit 'em," one voice said. "There were twelve of us ridin' guard for this shipment."

"One of 'em got away," another said.

"How do you know?"

"There were six horses, but there are only five bodies."

"Maybe one of the horses was to carry the loot."

"The sixth horse was saddled. No, my guess is he is somewhere on this train."

"Well, search every car. He won't get away

from us. We'll hang him, right here and now. You're sure no one else is in here, Mr. Kendrake?"

"Yes, I'm quite sure," Kendrake said. A while later Kendrake spoke again, but this time it was to Quince. "I think you can come out now," he said. "They appear to be satisfied that the sixth man either made good his escape, or never existed in the first place."

Quince sat up and let out a sigh of relief.

"Thanks," he said.

"Well, I suppose I should thank you, too, really, now shouldn't I? After all, that other rather disagreeable fellow may have shot me, had you not stopped him. I'm glad you were a part of this band of robbers."

"I'm not," Quince said. "In fact, I wish I had never fallen in with them at all."

"Was this your first time to attempt such a thing?"

"Don't get me wrong," Quince said. "My path hasn't always been straight and narrow, but I've never done anything like this before."

"What will you do now?"

"I don't know," Quince said. "Try and get away sometime during the night, I suppose."

"Have you ever worked on a ranch?" Kendrake asked.

"Mister, who out here my age hasn't? Of course I've punched cows."

"Would you like to do it again? For me?"

Quince looked at Kendrake and smiled. "You mean you'd trust me?"

"Without the slightest hesitation."

Quince extended his hand and took Kendrake's. "Then I reckon you've got yourself a cowboy."

"No," Kendrake said. "No, I don't."

"What do you mean?"

"I have myself a foreman," he said. "I'm counting on you to hire my cowboys."

That was five years ago, and in that five years, Three Crowns Ranch had become one of the most productive ranches in Wyoming. This was due in part to Kendrake's sound business management, but also to a large degree because Quince was an innovative, conscientious foreman, with loyalty to his employer and to his men. The cowboys worked well for Quince because they knew he never asked them to do anything he wouldn't do. The relationships of all the men at Three Crowns were very good, but there was none better than the relationship between Quince and Kendrake. Kendrake treated Quince as his own son, and Quince thought of Kendrake as the father he had never known.

And now, Quince instinctively knew that the relationship was about to be sorely tested, for Leslie was coming to America to live on the ranch. How would Leslie treat Quince? Like a brother? Or would Leslie be jealous, and consider Quince an interloper?

Quince had no idea how it would turn out, but he did know one thing. No matter what kind of person Leslie was, Quince would not let it affect his affection for, or loyalty to, Stuart Kendrake.

Even if it meant his leaving this place.

2

For Quince, there was something soothing about working with his hands, so when he saw that the wheels of one of the wagons needed to be packed with grease, he didn't ask anyone to do it. Instead he merely went about getting the blocks in place, and the wheels off, then he started packing the hubs by hand.

Quince had been working for about an hour when Rufus Butler came back with the supply wagon. Rufus was the cook, small of stature, but wiry and muscular. His clothes were old and worn, though Rufus kept himself and his kitchen spotlessly clean.

"Hello, Rufus," Quince called. "How did it go in town?"

"I got the supplies all right," Rufus said. Rufus climbed down from the wagon and sauntered over to where Quince was working. He removed his hat and wiped away the drops of sweat which dotted the high, broad forehead. "The town's ready for the Fourth of July celebration next week."

Rufus wore a drooping mustache beneath a nose which was rather large for his face. He had deep-set dark eyes under shaggy brows, and his cheeks were sunken and gaunt. His face was de-void of expression, but to the discerning observer, there were tell-tale signs of pain and sorrow from a past that no one dared to question.

"Boss, have you seen Indian Creek at the lower basin lately?" Rufus asked.

"Not for a couple of weeks," Quince said. "Why? What about it?"

"It ain't there."

Quince looked up in quick surprise. Rufus was a man of few words, but when he did speak he spoke plain enough, and true enough so that Quince knew he wasn't playing a game with him.

"Do you know why?" Quince asked. "Hell, there's been so much run-off it should be in a freshet stage now."

"That's what I figured," Rufus said. He took the makings out of his shirt pocket and started rolling himself a cigarette. "So I left the wagon 'n took one of the horses to ride back on the stream to see if I could figure out what happened."

"Did you find anything?"

Rufus licked on the paper and sealed the ciga-rette shut, then scratched a match on the sole of his boot and held the flame to the cigarette before he answered.

"Yep," he said. "Boss, there are some men there, damming off Indian Creek at the river. I don't know who they are or why they are doing it, but I thought you would like to know."

"You're mighty right I want to know," Quince said. "Mr. Kendrake is going to want to know, too. Thanks, Rufus."

Rufus nodded and put his hat back on, then

returned to the wagon to off-load his kitchen supplies. He had discovered the dried-up creek, determined the cause, and reported it. His involvement with that was finished now, and all he had on his mind was the running of his kitchen.

Quince walked quickly up to the front door of the Bighouse, then opened it and went on in. In the back of his mind he wondered if he would still have such freedom of the place when Leslie arrived. But he didn't wonder about it long, for his mind was now totally occupied with the concern of the water. Without the water the ranch would die.

"Quince," Kendrake said, looking up and smiling. He pointed to new curtains which hung at the dining room window. "What do you think? Will Leslie like them?"

The curtains were of muslin, and they filled with the soft afternoon breeze, and danced over the highly polished floor of the dining room.

"Yeah," Quince said, absent-mindedly. "They are nice. Mr. Kendrake, we've got a problem."

The smile left Kendrake's face, because he learned long ago that Quince didn't come to him with minor problems. It had to be a problem of some consequence, or Quince wouldn't mention it at all.

"What sort of a problem?"

"Rufus just told me that some men have dammed off Indian Creek at the river. The creek is drying up."

"My God, who would do such a thing?" Kendrake asked.

"I don't know," Quince said. "But I aim to find out. Would you like to go with me?"

"Indeed I would," Kendrake said. He took his hat from an antler rack on the wall and followed Quince outside. A moment later, they were mounted and riding toward the river from whence sprung Indian Creek, the main source of water for Three Crown Ranch. Without it, the supply of water was greatly limited.

It had been Quince's innovativeness which allowed Indian Creek to provide water in the first place. The creek was little more than a seasonal bayou when Kendrake first began ranching, but Quince connected the low spots and diverted the creek so that water followed what may have been an ancient riverbed. The result was a daily waterflow that rejoined the Platte River on the other side of the ranch. Thus, none of the water was wasted. It was an engineering feat of considerable skill, and Quince was justifiably proud of it.

"There they are," Kendrake said, as the two horsemen crested the last ridge and rode down toward the river. "My word, look at the size of that dam! They must have been working on it for some time now. Why didn't we know about this?"

"We haven't had any call to be up here since last fall," Quince said. "Like as not, they got the whole dam built, then closed the floodgates, and we never realized it until the waterflow stopped."

As Quince and Kendrake swung out of their saddles, a man, dressed in a business suit, walked over toward them. He was accompanied by two men carrying rifles, and wearing stars on their vests.

"You are trespassing on government property," the man said.

"This is public property!" Kendrake replied. "What do you mean we are trespassing?"

"This is the site of a government water improvement project," the man replied.

"Improvement! Why, you bloody rascal, you've squeezed dry every drop of water on my ranch!"

"Are you Stuart Kendrake?"

"You know bloody well I am," Kendrake sputtered. "Why wasn't I told of this?"

"Mr. Kendrake, my name is Lawrence Cauldwell. I am the District water commissioner for the United States Government. It is my duty, sir, to present you with this assessment for water improvement works, affecting your land."

Kendrake looked puzzled as he took the paper from Cauldwell. He read it, then began to cough and sputter so that Quince was afraid that he was suffering from some sort of an attack.

"Thirty-five hundred dollars!" Kendrake bellowed. "You steal my water, then you tell me that I must pay for the privilege? Why, that is an outrage! It's like paying one's own executioner!"

"I understand that's quite common in your country, Mr. Kendrake," Cauldwell said.

"This *is* my country!" Kendrake said. "And I have no intention of paying this assessment!"

"I'm afraid you have no choice, Kendrake. You will pay it, or we will confiscate your land and cattle and sell it for the monies due us. That is the law."

"You'll do no such thing," Kendrake said. "In fact, if you don't tear this dam down, I will!"

Kendrake shoved Cauldwell aside and started toward the dam, but before he had taken three steps, one of the armed deputies clubbed him with his rifle, not a skull-smashing blow, but a short, vicious chop, hard enough to drop Kendrake like a sack of potatoes.

"You son-of-a-bitch!" Quince swore, and he took a step toward the deputy who had hit Kendrake, but the other deputy cocked his rifle and leveled it at Quince.

"You take one more step, mister, and you are a dead man," the deputy said. His voice was flat and expressionless, and when Quince measured the look in his eyes, he knew that the law officer would do just as he threatened.

"Help your boss get to his feet," Cauldwell said.

Quince reached down to offer his hand to Kendrake, who, though he hadn't lost consciousness, had been dazed by the blow. Kendrake, with Quince's help, regained his feet, and began dusting his clothes.

"Are you all right, Mr. Kendrake?" Quince asked.

"Yes," Kendrake said. "Though I must confess to being a bit chagrined."

"Mr. Kendrake, you must accept my apology," Cauldwell said. "It is not the policy of the U.S. Government to assault its citizens, but it is the policy to protect its property. My deputies thought you intended to harm the dam."

"I did intend to harm it," Kendrake said. "And I will bring it down, whatever it takes."

"I'm sorry to hear you reacting that way, Mr. Kendrake," Cauldwell said. "Because of course, we can't allow that. And, I'm afraid we must insist upon your paying your just assessment."

"How can you call this assessment just?" Quince asked. "Don't you understand that your so-called water improvement project has taken nearly all of our water from us?"

"You are Mr. Parker, I believe?" Cauldwell said. "Yes."

"Mr. Parker, I understand you are the one who diverted Indian Creek in the first place?"

"Yes."

"Well, there you are, Mr. Parker. You stole water from the Platte River, thus denying the downriver ranchers and farmers their fair share. We just gave it back to them, and Three Crowns will have to foot the bill. You have thirty days, Mr. Kendrake." Cauldwell picked up the assessment and handed it to Quince, who slipped it into his vest pocket, then helped Kendrake mount his horse.

"I'll be back," Quince said.

"If you do come back, Parker," one of the deputies said. "I suggest you get a pass from the district office in Laramie. Otherwise, I might think you are trespassing, and you just might get shot."

Quince looked at them coldly, then he mounted his own animal. The laughter of the deputies rung hollowly in his ears as he rode off.

3

IT HAD BEEN Kendrake's idea to have a meeting of the other ranchers affected by the "water improvements." They gathered in the front room of the Bighouse at Three Crowns, and discussed how unfair the assessment was, and told how badly their rangeland was hurt by the move.

"I don't know about you other fellas," Ben Thompson said. "But I aim to take Mr. Goodpasture up on his offer."

"What offer is that, Ben?" Kendrake asked.

"He's offered me twenty-five cents an acre, 'n he'll pay the assessment charges himself."

"Twenty-five cents an acre?" Kendrake said. "Why, Ben, your land is worth twenty times that and you know it!"

"Not now, it ain't," Ben said. "It ain't doin' nothin' but holdin' the world together. If it weren't for the fact that Goodpasture let my cows onto his rangeland for water, they'd all be dyin'."

"Yeah," another put in. "He let my cows water too, but he's takin' every third cow."

"Better than letting them all die of thirst," a new voice suddenly said, and those who had gathered, looked up to see Charles W. Goodpasture standing just inside the door. He was a rather large man, broad-shouldered and square-chinned, with dark hair and snapping brown eyes. His ranch, Mountain Shadows, was larger than the combined holdings of everyone else gathered at the meeting. Three Crowns was large enough, at one-hundred-sixty-thousand acres, but even the Kendrake spread was small compared to the six-hundred-thousand acres controlled by Goodpasture.

Goodpasture ruled his land with the power and authority of a feudal lord, and no one could escape his influence.

"Gentlemen," he said, touching the brim of his hat and looking around the room. "I wasn't invited to this meeting, but I hope my company isn't unwelcome. If it is, I shall move on without delay."

"Of course you are welcome here, Charles," Kendrake said. "It's just that your ranch isn't affected by the new water project, so I didn't think you would have a vested interest in this gathering."

"Nonsense," Goodpasture said. "My good friends and neighbors are hurt by the water project, so I, too, am hurt by it. I want some way to resolve it, if we can."

"Do you have any suggestions, Mr. Goodpasture?" one of the other ranchers asked.

"Yeah," another put in. "Can you tell us how to get our water back?"

"No," Goodpasture said. "I discussed this matter with Mr. Cauldwell to some length, and it would appear that the government is quite resolved to the purpose of improving the water system for this part of the country."

"Improve!" Kendrake said. "I think that is the most disturbing aspect of this entire bizzare affair. How can they possibly call such interference an improvement?"

Goodpasture removed a pipe from his jacket pocket and began stuffing the bowl with tobacco.

"Well, Stuart," he said calmly, all the while tamping down the tobacco. "I can see why such a thing might get you riled. But we have to take a look at the long-range view of this operation. They tell me that if this water system isn't improved, then fifty to sixty years from now, this whole basin will be as dry as the great southwest desert. Now, we certainly don't want to see that, do we?"

Goodpasture took several puffs on his pipe.

"Sixty years from now?" Kendrake replied. "Nineteen fifty-two? Who among us will be here to see it anyway?"

"If not our children, then certainly our grandchildren," Goodpasture said. He lit his pipe and was now drawing large puffs from it. "We have to have something to leave for them."

"Mr. Goodpasture, if I can't get water back on my ranch, I won't have anything to leave my heirs *next* year, let alone sixty years from now," one of the ranchers said.

"No, nor me either," another put in, and his statement was seconded by several others.

"Well," Goodpasture said. "You could lease water rights from me."

"Lease? How lease?"

"Let your cattle run through my range, drink my water, and I'll take one-third of them."

"One-third? Isn't that a little steep?"

"Or," Goodpasture said, puffing quietly. "You could sell to me."

"At twenty-five cents an acre?" another asked.

"If you sell now," Goodpasture said. "But the longer you wait before selling, the higher my expenses will be, and the less I shall be able to pay. It might get to as low as a nickel an acre."

"You already know my answer, Mr. Goodpasture," Ben Thompson said. "I'm sellin' to you."

"Count me in too," another owner said.

"Yeah, and me," a third added. In all, seven of the ranchers agreed to either sell their land, or lease the water rights. But others, including Stuart Kendrake, held out.

"Stuart?" Goodpasture said. "You've no wish to take me up on my offer?"

"Goodpasture, you are asking that I turn over ten thousand head of cattle to you, at $25 a head," Kendrake said. "That is a quarter of a million dollars, just for water rights."

"Yes," Goodpasture said easily.

"I won't do it," Kendrake said. "I can't do it!"

"I'm sorry you feel that way," Goodpasture said. "For a thirst-maddened herd the size of yours could be dangerous. It could be very dangerous. Tuttle Creek will be dry by August, and you won't have enough water to satisfy them."

"I'll just have to take my chances," Kendrake said.

"Of course, my offer to buy up ranchland also extends to Three Crowns," Goodpasture said. "Not the house and outbuildings, of course. I would suspect you would want to live there."

"That's decent of you, Charles," Kendrake said in a serious tone of voice. "That's really very nice. But, all things considered, I don't think I'd be interested in that proposition either."

"Then what's left for us, Mr. Kendrake?" one of the other owners asked. "Most of us don't even have a source of water like Tuttle Creek."

"I don't know," Kendrake said. He pinched the bridge of his nose for a long moment, then drew a deep breath. "But I intend to do something," he added resolutely.

The meeting broke up shortly after that. Those who had decided to sell their land accepted Goodpasture's invitation to ride back to his ranch with him to close the deals, while the others exchanged words of mutual support and resolution, then, in twos and threes, began drifting away, back to their own spreads.

Kendrake stood at the front door for a long moment after the others left, sighed, ran his hand through his hair, then turned to go back inside and have a drink. He found a bottle and a nearly clean glass on his desk. He splashed about two fingers of whiskey into the glass, then held it out toward the calendar in salute to the circled date just two days away now which indicated Leslie's arrival.

"Leslie," he said, "I wouldn't have wanted all this going on for your arrival, but I guess it just couldn't be helped." He sighed and tossed the drink down, then started to pour another one as he thought about the meeting. But he didn't want to drink alone, so he started out to the bunkhouse to get Quince to have a drink with him. After all, Quince would want to know how the meeting went.

Kendrake was a little perturbed with Quince anyway. He had wanted Quince present for the meeting, but Quince begged out of it, saying that it was a meeting for the "owners" only, and that he, being a mere cowhand, would be out of place.

Kendrake told him that he was a mere cowhand as Shakespeare was a mere playwright, but Quince didn't react to the analogy, so it was a private joke. A private joke for now. That was another reason he was so looking forward to Leslie's arrival, for Leslie would be a link with his cultural past, as well as a link to his family.

Kendrake stepped up onto the front porch and knocked on the door. It was his building, and he knew that he had the right to open the door and go inside anytime he wanted, but he respected the cowboys' rights, and they respected his consideration.

The door was opened, and the cowboy who opened it stepped back to allow Kendrake to come inside. The bunkhouse consisted of one large room, thirty by thirty, with bunks around the wall, and a great common table in the center. The walls were papered with old newspapers and magazines, mostly for insulation, though here and there a picture that one or more of the cowboys found appealing would be cut out and given a position of prominence. The room was fairly well lighted, not only by a couple of kerosene lanterns on the great common table but by nearly a dozen flickering candles at the bunks, where cowboys were reading or working on their boots or engaged in some other task.

Some trunks had been pulled together by one bunk, and there a couple of cowboys were playing checkers while two or three others looked on.

"Good evening," Kendrake said. He looked around. "Is Quince here?"

"No, sir."

"Do you know where he went?"

"No, sir."

Kendrake breathed a sigh of exasperation. It was part of the cowboy code to say no more than was necessary, but on those occasions when he needed information, it certainly made for a frustrating experience.

"Did anyone see Quince leave?"

"I saw him," one of the others, a newer, younger hand, said. "He left with the cook." Though no one said anything to the young man, a few glanced at him with looks of clear disapproval. The young man, not understanding his *faux pas*, went on. "I think they are going to clear out some stumps."

"Clear some stumps? Tonight?" Kendrake asked.

"Yes, sir, they took the stump wagon."

"The stump wagon? *Nitro!* Oh my God, Quince is going to blow up the dam!"

"Let 'em do it, boss," one of the cowboys said. "You got a alibi, you was here with the others."

"No," Kendrake said. "Don't you realize the trouble that would cause? I've got to stop him!"

Kendrake ran quickly to the barn to saddle his

horse, and a moment later the boys stood out on the front porch of the bunkhouse to watch him ride off into the night.

"I hope Quince gets 'er blown before Mr. Kendrake gets there," one of them said quietly.

The echoing sound of a rifleshot reverberated through the canyon, and Quince pulled the team to a halt.

"Well, they seen us," Rufus said quietly.

"So far so good," Quince said.

"Yeah, if they'll let us put the rest of our plan through before they shoot us," Rufus said.

"Both of you, git your hands up!" a voice called.

The two men sat in the wagon and held their hands up as they were directed. Quince looked up toward the sound of the voice, but he could see nothing but rocks and shadows.

"Are you road agents?" Quince called. "Neither one of us have any money."

A rock came tumbling down the side of the hill, then another, and finally Quince could see a man coming through the shadows, holding a rifle on them.

"I ain't no road agent, Parker, and you damned well know it," the man said. "Now git out of that wagon and walk away from it."

"Remember to step out easy now," Quince whispered. "It won't take much to make this nitro go."

"What do you want?" Quince asked.

"What do *I* want?" the man with the rifle replied. "I want you both to stand away from this wagon with your hands up, and your mouths shut." He started toward the wagon. "I intend to have a look at what you're carrying."

"No!" Quince called, taking a step toward the wagon.

The rifleman cocked his weapon and pointed it menacingly at Quince. "What do you mean no?"

"I mean, there's nothing in it," Quince said. "Nothing you would be interested in."

The rifleman smiled. "Oh, I'm sure there ain't," he said. He walked over to it and turned back the canvas, then whistled under his breath. "Well now," he said. "Primer fuse, and kegs of black powder. Nothing that would interest me, huh?" The rifleman laughed. "Parker, you are a dumb son-of-a-bitch, did you know that? Do you really think a few kegs of gunpowder could take out this dam?"

"I figured it was worth a try," Quince said.

"I thought you was supposed to be so smart. Gunpowder wouldn't even make a dent in it. You'd have to have TNT, or dynamite, or something just as strong." The rifleman laughed. "I ought to let you go ahead and try, just to see the expression on your face when it doesn't work."

"All right," Quince said. "Let me try."

"You'd like that, wouldn't you? No, I'm not going to let you try. Now I tell you what I want you to do. I want you to unhitch the team, then you and that gimp-legged looking old man git on back to the bunkhouse."

"Come on, Rufus, we don't have any choice," Quince said.

Quince started back toward the wagon, but

before he did, he stopped on the edge of the road and looked down over the precipice, toward the dam below. The water behind the dam had built up, and the Plate was flowing at its highest stage, winking in the moonlight. What was normally Indian Creek was little more than a trail of mud now.

"Yeah, take a look down there," the rifleman said, chuckling. "Ain't that dam pretty? Too pretty for you to be trying to mess with."

"After the team is unhitched, I'm going to release the brake," Quince said in a quiet whisper. "If we both give it a shove, it'll go right over, and crash into the top of it. Do that, and the dam is finished."

"Right," Rufus answered. The two men unhitched the team, but before Quince could release the brake, Kendrake came riding in at a full gallop.

"Quince!" he called. "Quince, no!"

"Mr. Kendrake, get back!" Quince said. "Get away!"

The armed guard was confused by Kendrake's arrival, and he fired a warning shot at Quince and Rufus. The bullet crashed into the side of the wagon.

"My God!" Quince said. "Get out of here, Rufus, the crazy son-of-a-bitch is shooting at the wagon!"

"Come back!" the guard said, as Quince and Rufus started on the run. The rifleman fired a second time, and this time the bullet found a more volatile mark. There was a stomach-shaking boom as the nitro exploded and the wagon went into the air in hundreds of little pieces.

"Look out," Quince shouted, and he dived behind a pile of rocks, followed closely by Rufus. Mushrooming dust and smoke hung above them for several seconds, then began drifting away, leaving a hole where the wagon had been parked.

"Quince," a pained voice called.

"Mr. Kendrake!" Quince replied, getting up and looking around. "Mr. Kendrake, where are you?"

"I'm over here," Kendrake replied, and his words were thin and strained.

Quince saw him then, pinned beneath a large boulder. A small dark stream of blood trickled from his mouth, and as he breathed, the blood bubbled. Quince knew that his insides had to be badly smashed for that to happen, and he knew also that Kendrake was dying.

"Mr. Kendrake, my God, what were you doing out here?" Quince asked.

"I came to stop you," Kendrake said.

"But why?" Quince asked. "I was just going to blow that dam out of here."

Kendrake shook his head. "No," he said. "That isn't the way."

"It was the best way I could come up with."

"You've got to come up with another way," Kendrake said. He coughed once, and blood spilled again. He closed his eyes against the pain. "Leslie," he said.

"What about Leslie?"

"Don't let Leslie sell."

"I won't, Mr. Kendrake," Quince promised. "I won't let him sell."

Kendrake smiled through the pain. "Quince, there's something about Leslie you don't know.

Something you are going to be mighty surprised to find out."

"What?"

Kendrake shook his head. "No," he said. "Allow a dying man this one last pleasure. And hope."

"Hope? Hope for what, Mr. Kendrake?"

"What the hell happened here?" someone called, and Quince looked around to see Cauldwell arriving in a buckboard.

"Mr. Cauldwell, Mr. Kendrake has been hurt," Quince said. "I want to use your buckboard."

"Kendrake?" Cauldwell said, pulling his team to a halt. He climbed out of the buckboard and walked toward them. "What is he doing here in the first place?"

"Never mind that," Quince said. "Just help me move this rock off so I can get him in your buckboard. I'm taking him home."

"I don't know," Cauldwell said. "That buckboard belongs to the government, and—"

"Do as I say or so help me God I'll put a bullet in you where you stand!" Quince said angrily.

"Oh, all right," Cauldwell said. "Ernie, you get down here and help too," Cauldwell called to the rifleman who had fired the shot.

"Mr. Cauldwell, I don't know what happened," Ernie said, still somewhat stunned by the events. "I just fired a warning shot and all hell broke loose."

"You hit the gunpowder," Quince said. "I told you there was gunpowder in the wagon."

"I never knew gunpowder would go off like that," Ernie said.

"Well, now you know. Now, let's get Mr. Kendrake in this wagon. He's going to die at home, in his own bed. Not out here on the ground like some animal."

"He'll never make it back," Cauldwell said, looking at him. Kendrake's eyes were closed now, and his face looked deathly white in the light of the moon.

"I'll make it," Kendrake found the strength to say. "I'm determined to see the sun rise tomorrow. That's the day my Leslie arrives."

"Load him easy, now," Quince said, and the four men lifted Kendrake as gently as if he were a baby, and laid him in the back of the buckboard.

Kendrake spent a fitful night after they got him back to Three Crowns. The pain swept over his body in waves, carrying him almost to the threshold of his ability to endure it, then backing away to allow him some relief. When the pain was the sharpest he would squeeze Quince's hand as hard as he could, and Quince would return the squeeze, lending Kendrake some of his strength.

The clock tolled off another hour.

"I will live until morning," Kendrake said, but his words were so quiet that Quince had to put his ear right over his lips to hear them.

Kendrake stared at the window until the sky began to lighten, and finally the bright bars of early sunrise began streaming in.

"Open the window, please," Kendrake said. "I want to look at my ranch, and smell it, and hear it."

Quince pulled the curtains all the way to one side, then slid the window open. The silver light of early morning spilled in, and on the soft morning breeze there was the faint scent of wood smoke from the bunkhouse kitchen. Rufus was already at work.

"Prop up my pillows," Kendrake said, and Quince did as he asked.

Now Kendrake could see out, and he looked toward the corral and watched as two horses ran together, one of them biting the other playfully on the neck. The windmill answered the morning breeze and the blades started whirring. A rooster fluttered up to the corral fence, ruffled his feathers haughtily, then crowed proudly.

A couple of cowboys came riding down the trail from nighthawk duty. They didn't know about Kendrake, and they were whooping and hollering for Rufus to rustle them up some grub.

"I'll go quiet them down," Quince offered.

"No," Kendrake replied. He smiled. "It's like music to my ears."

"What the hell for?" one of the night-herders asked. His voice drifted in through the open window. "We've been working all night long while you guys lay around on your lazy ass, and now you say we're makin' too much noise?"

There were more whispers which Kendrake couldn't hear, then it grew quiet. Kendrake knew they had been told, and he was sorry.

Quince got up and walked over to the window to look out for a moment.

"It was a good life," Kendrake said, and for that one statement, his voice had all the vitality and strength it had ever possessed.

Quince turned when he heard that, and saw that

Kendrake's head had slipped down from the pillow, lying to one side.

"Mr. Kendrake?" he called. He walked to the bed, and saw that Kendrake's eyes were closed, as if he had drifted off to sleep. "Mr. Kendrake?" Quince picked up his hand and felt for a pulse, then slowly put the hand down, looked at the Englishman, and shook his head sadly.

Lord Stuart Northington Kendrake was dead.

4

THE PHAETON rolled down Front Street, the main street in Sweetgrass, and those who were riding by, walking along the board sidewalks, or just lounging against the front of the buildings, waved and called out to the passenger in the carriage.

The lone passenger was Charles W. Goodpasture, and the phaeton, which was being pulled by a matched team of snow-white horses, was being driven by a stately old black man, a former slave who had the distinction of being the only black man in Sweetgrass. He was a vain affectation acquired by Goodpasture, because he believed having a black coachman was the height of elegance.

Goodpasture returned the waves and greetings of the townspeople much as a sovereign would acknowledge his subjects. And indeed, there was little difference between Charles W. Goodpasture and a reigning monarch. For, just as a king's subjects are dependent upon his good graces and favors, so were the townspeople of Sweetgrass dependent upon Goodpasture. In fact, not only the townspeople of Sweetgrass, but everyone within a wide area of Wyoming was dependent upon him in one way or another.

In addition to his ranch, Mountain Shadows, Goodpasture owned the Cattleman's Supply Company, several feed and grain stores, a couple of hotels, and three of the four banks within a one-hundred-mile radius of Sweetgrass.

Goodpasture also owned the most prominent feature of Sweetgrass—the railroad. The railroad was actually a spur line which branched off from the Union Pacific Line at Laramie, looped around through Sweetgrass, then returned to the main line at Elk Mountain. There were two trains per day on the forty-mile loop, a morning train headed east, and an afternoon train, headed west. It was, of course, the same train, merely turned around at Laramie, and again at Elk Mountain, but everyone referred to it in such a way that many who had lived there since railroad service started thought there were two separate and distinct trains.

Front Street ran parallel to the railroad, and was lined on one side with the business establishments of the town, many of which Goodpasture owned, and on the other side with the railroad itself. The Front Door, a large, purple, majestic mountain, loomed over the north end of the town. It received its rather peculiar name from the fact that it shielded the town from the icy blasts of blizzards, like closing a front door. Its presence allowed Sweetgrass to survive, while other settlements had succumbed to the brutal winters which had driven so many away.

Goodpasture leaned forward to speak to the black driver.

"Stop in front of Rosita's, would you, Andrew?"

"Yes, sir," Andrew replied, pulling the horses to a stop. Andrew hopped down, rather gracefully for a man of his age and heavy build, and folded the step down so that Goodpasture could debark. "Shall I wait here, sir?" he asked.

Goodpasture looked at the saloon. The name "Rosita" was painted in red on the big glass window, and the red letters were outlined in gold filigree.

"Yes," Goodpasture said. "I don't know how long I'll be, but I want you here when I come out."

"I'll be here, sir," Andrew promised him.

Inside Rosita's, its manager and namesake Rosita Mendoza saw Goodpasture stepping out of his carriage. Rosita was a striking woman, tall and willowy, with a golden complexion, blue-black hair, large brown eyes framed by lashes as delicate as a lace fan, and high cheekbones which accented her beauty. She had come to Sweetgrass two years ago, and from somewhere produced the money to buy the establishment she now called Rosita's. Several men had attempted to buy more than drinks from her, but she had turned them all down, though doing so in such a way as to sustain their interest and their loyalty as customers.

She had not turned *all* the men down. It was no secret that Goodpasture had succeeded where others had failed, and she smiled broadly as she saw him approaching her establishment.

"Manuel," she said quickly. "Where is the special stock?"

"It is finished, *señorita*," Manuel replied. He, like Rosita, spoke with an accent, but while his accent was harsh and jangled the nerves, hers was soft, and cultured, with a lilt to it which was almost musical.

"What do you mean, finished? The last time he was in here I served him myself, and I know that the bottle was nearly full."

"*Si*, it was, *señorita*," Manuel said. "But I sold it."

"You sold the private stock?" Rosita asked, as if unable to believe what she was hearing.

"*Si*," Manuel said. "But it was for a good price. And I put the money in the cash drawer. You can look and see for yourself."

"I don't care if you received a king's ransom for it," Rosita said sharply. "That is not to be sold, do you understand?"

"*Si, señorita*."

"Now, go quickly and get another bottle," Rosita ordered.

"*Si, señorita*," Manuel said. "I will go quickly." Manuel pulled the bar towel from his belt, wiped his hands, then tossed the towel on the bar. He disappeared through the door at the rear of the bar, but as far as Rosita could determine, he was not hurrying.

Rosita turned to look in the mirror behind the bar, and she touched her hair to ensure that it was properly done. She saw the other customers in the bar, nearly a dozen, all of whom were relatively affluent. Her clientele reflected the quality of her establishment, and she felt a sense of pride.

"You needn't arrange your hair, Rosita. I find it perfect, just as it is," Goodpasture said, stepping up to the bar at that moment.

Rosita flushed, for she had not intended to be caught primping.

"Charles," she said, only the *Ch* came out much softer, almost like the letter *Sh*. "It's good to see you."

Rosita looked at Charles. His wealth and power were already legend, but she also thought him a very handsome man. His hair was dark, though now brindled with gray at the temples, and his moustache was neatly trimmed and elegant. He had eyes which could only be described as arrogant, and they accented his appearance in a way which made his power all the more evident.

"Won't you join me?" Charles asked.

"Of course," Rosita replied. "I sent Manuel after your private stock," she explained.

Charles looked at her as she sat across from him. Her dress was bright red, trimmed in black, and cut low enough to show off the skin of her shoulders, and the rise at the top of her breasts.

"You heard about Kendrake?" he asked.

A hint of sadness came across Rosita's face. "Yes," she said. "It is the talk on everyone's lips. It is very sad for such a thing to happen. But surely he knew the danger of such a move?"

"It was not his fault," Charles said. "It was the fault of that fool foreman of his."

"Quince Parker?"

"Yes. He had it in his mind to blow up the dam,

and he took a wagonload of nitro there. Kendrake was trying to stop him from doing it."

"I saw Quince Parker a short time ago," Rosita said. "He was riding toward the depot and he was leading a second horse. I thought it a rather odd thing for him to be leading a second horse, and wondered why he was doing it."

"He was leading a second horse you say?" Charles said. He looked puzzled. "I don't know why he would be doing that, unless—" suddenly Charles smiled. "Yes, of course, that's it."

"What?"

"This is the day young Kendrake comes to town," Charles said. "Parker has come in to meet him. There was to be a celebration today. I had nearly forgotten that in light of all that has happened."

"You mean the young Kendrake doesn't know of his father's death?" Rosita asked.

"No, of course not. How could he know? He's had to come nearly five thousand miles by land and sea over the last month. There was no way to get a message to him."

"Oh, how awful!" Rosita said. "How tragic it must be to come all this way, only to find out that your father is dead!"

"Yeah," Charles said. "It can't be a very good position for Parker to be in either, can it? After all, it is his fault that Kendrake is dead, and he's going to have to tell Leslie."

"You don't like Quince Parker, do you?" Rosita asked.

"No," Charles said.

"Why not?"

"If it had not been for Parker, Kendrake would have failed long ago, and Three Crowns would now belong to me."

"It's going to belong to you anyway, isn't it?" Rosita asked.

"Yes," Charles said. "But it would have been much simpler, had Kendrake just listened to me long ago, when I made the first offer."

"Must you always win?" Rosita asked.

"Yes," Charles said. He looked at Rosita with a half smile on his face. "Do you disapprove?"

"Maybe," Rosita replied, and she separated the word so that it became two words. "I think it is not good that you get everything you want all the time."

"I don't agree with you," he said. "I think I should get everything I want, anytime I want it. Like right now, for instance." Charles looked at Rosita in a possessive way that she recognized, and she smiled a small, self-assured smile.

"Suppose I denied you?" she teased.

"It is not in your power to do so," Charles said. He looked around the well-appointed saloon. "Not if you wish to keep what you have."

For just an instant, so quickly that no one, not even Charles noticed it, a screen of fear dropped across Rosita's eyes. But it passed quickly, and the screen was lifted to be replaced by a look of seductive anticipation.

"I am sorry I was so long, *señorita*," Manuel apologized, arriving at that moment with a bottle and two glasses on a tray. "But I had to go to the cellar for the bottle."

"We won't need it just yet," Rosita said, standing and looking across the table at Charles in open invitation.

"We'll take it with us," Charles suggested, reaching for the bottle.

"Si, señor," Manuel said, unperturbed by the inference.

Rosita led the way up the back stairs, down the narrow, carpeted hall, and into her room. Slatted shutters were pulled closed over the windows, blocking out the afternoon sun, and the room was lighted with alternate bars of sun and shadow.

Charles reached for the whiskey, and when he saw that there were no glasses, he pulled the cork and drank right from the bottle, never taking his eyes off Rosita.

Rosita undid the red ribbon which held her hair and shook her head to let it tumble down. It fell softly across the golden skin of her shoulders.

"Get undressed now," Charles said thickly, and Rosita, with the same, self-assured smile, began removing her clothes, pushing her dress down her body until it fell to the floor in a shimmering pool of silk.

Charles watched in fascination, treated to the expanse of smooth skin, breasts, firm, well-rounded, and tipped by red nipples drawn suddenly tight by their exposure to the air, and a small triangle of hair at the junction of her legs.

"Do you like?" Rosita asked.

"Yeah," Charles said. "I like."

Charles slipped quickly out of his own clothes, and watched as Rosita folded her dress neatly, and placed it on the chest near a water basin.

Finally, she turned to face him once more. Her body was subtly lighted by the shaded light, and she licked her lips invitingly, and raised her arms toward him.

Charles moved quickly to her, pulling her to him, kissing her open mouth with his own, feeling her tongues dart against his. He moved her toward the bed, then climbed in after her and crawled on top of her.

Rosita warmed as quickly as Charles, and she received him happily, wrapping her legs around him, meeting his lunges by pushing against him, She lost herself in the pleasure of the moment, until a few minutes later she could feel him jerking and thrusting in a savage fury, spraying his seed into her and finally collapsing across her.

Later, after they had made love, Charles left the bed and padded barefoot over to the window. He pushed one of the shutters open, allowing a square of light to splash into the room, and he stood there looking through the window across the town, toward the crowd which was beginning to gather at the depot.

The bedsprings squeaked as Rosita sat up.

"Charles," she said, again with the soft sounding *Ch*. Her voice was soft and pleasant sounding, and reminded Charles of windchimes he had heard hanging in the breeze.

"Yes?"

"Why do you not marry me?"

"I told you," Charles said. "I have no time for marriage right now. I have too much to do."

"Yes, I know," Rosita said. "You must build your

empire. But already your empire is one of the largest in the west."

"I cannot expect you to understand," Charles said, looking back toward her. Rosita had not yet dressed, and was now sitting with her knees pulled up and her arms wrapped around them. In such a way she was showing the smooth lines of her nude form, while her modesty was momentarily preserved. "And it is precisely because you don't understand that I cannot marry you."

"I think you do not marry me because of what I am," Rosita said.

"Don't be silly," Charles said. "Has that ever stopped me from seeing you?"

"Why do you not invite me to Mountain Shadows?" Rosita asked. "I have heard of the huge parties you have there, and I am hurt because I have not been invited."

"Ah, you wouldn't enjoy them," Charles said. "Hell, I don't enjoy them myself. I just have them because they are necessary for my business."

The sound of a train whistle drifted into the room, and Charles looked back toward the depot. "Well," he said. "Leslie Kendrake will be on that train. I wouldn't want to be in Quince Parker's shoes right now."

"Oh, I had nearly forgotten," Rosita said. She got up and reached for her dress. "I would not have done this had I remembered."

"Why not?" Charles asked, surprised by her comment.

"Because," Rosita said. "It isn't right. We thought only of our own, sinful pleasure, while poor Leslie Kendrake must bear the tragedy of

Señor Kendrake's death." Rosita crossed herself quickly.

"Don't be silly," Charles said with a little laugh. "Kendrake isn't dead because of what we did here." The train whistle blew again, and Charles looked back through the window. Now he could see the train in the distance. "You know, I think I'll just get dressed and run down to the depot. I want to see how Parker handles this."

Charles chuckled in eager anticipation as he dressed, while Rosita, unable to understand why he would find joy in such a sad event, left the room to return to her own duties.

5

QUINCE LEANED against the weathered boards which made up the wall of the depot, and watched the train approach. He was sick at heart over what he must do now, for he had to meet Leslie Kendrake, and tell him what had happened. Instead of riding out to Three Crowns, to a gala celebration, Leslie Kendrake would be riding out to see the elder Kendrake stretched out in a pine box in the living room of the bighouse.

Though Quince's task was melancholy, the mood of the crowd awaiting the train was anything but. The coming of a train, any train, was a public event in Sweetgrass. Trains brought visitors, friends, relatives. They brought letters, mail-order goods, newspapers and treasures. Trains were visible proof that Sweetgrass, so far from everything, was not totally isolated from the world.

The crowd waiting for the train was made up of families waiting for their relatives, merchants waiting for their wares, and businessmen waiting for appointments. And, as at any crowded event, there were vendors, plying their trade.

There was a crowd gathered around one of the vendors, a patent medicine man. He was tall and thin, wearing a black suit which was badly in need of cleaning. His long, bony index finger jabbed at the air as he spoke.

"Yes, ladies and gentlemen, I have come bearing a new miracle drug that will work wonders for all illnesses. If you suffer from ulceration of the kidneys, loss of memory, weak nerves, hot hands, flushing in the body, consumption, torpidity of the liver, costiveness, hot spells, bearing-down feelings, or cancer, this marvelous Extract Buchu will be your salvation. And here is something else this drug will do that no other drug can. It will cheer you up when you are blue, calm you down when you are agitated. It works in all ways of mind, spirit and body, and this marvelous elixir can be yours for ten cents. Yes, sir, ladies and gentlemen, one-tenth of one dollar, and the miracles of modern medicine can go to work for you right now."

Quince thought of the medicine man's absurd claims. It would be wonderful, he thought, if there were some miracle drug which would make the job he was about to do easier.

The train rumbled into the station, then came to a screeching halt. A hiss of white gushed from the escape valve just forward of the huge driver wheels, and tendrils of steam purpled as they drifted away in the late afternoon sun.

"Sweetgrass!" a booming voice said, and the voice was followed by a rather rotund man, looking importantly at his watch as he stepped down onto the station platform from one of the cars. "This station is Sweetgrass!"

A tall, well-dressed man stepped down and looked around in confusion. He was wearing a small-brimmed, low-crowned hat, and Quince stepped away from the side of the station and started toward him. He knew without being told that this was Leslie.

"Mr. Templeton?" a voice called.

"Yes, I'm Curtis Templeton," the man answered, smiling, and extending his hand to the one who called to him.

"Did you bring your samples?"

"Yes, they are in the baggage car," the man said, and Templeton and the man who greeted him started forward along the train.

So, that wasn't Leslie Kendrake. But who else could be Leslie Kendrake? Only three others stepped off the train, an older couple—obviously man and wife—and a young woman.

"Board!" the conductor shouted, looking at his watch, and the few people who were waiting to leave, started toward the train then.

"Say, wait!" Quince called, starting toward the train. "This isn't everybody."

"We can't wait, mister," the conductor called. "We've got a schedule to keep. They should'a been here by now if they were going to ride."

"No, not somebody getting *on* the train, somebody getting *off*," Quince said. "I'm supposed to meet a Leslie Kendrake here. Are you sure everyone on board knows where they are?"

"There were only four passengers ticketed for Sweetgrass, and all four of them got off," the conductor said. Then, as if by that statement he had fulfilled whatever obligation he had to answering the inquiry, he yelled, "Board!" one last time, waved at the engineer, and climbed back on.

The whistle blew, the steam valve was closed, and the train jerked hard, along the whole line of cars. There was a second jerk, not quite as severe as the first, and then the train started to roll forward, slowly at first, then more quickly, until, one by one, the cars rolled in ever increasing speed as the train pulled out of the station.

Quince watched the train leave, then he stepped out on the track and stared after the last car as it pulled away, watching it diminish in size until it was quite small in the distance. Finally, he sighed, and stepped back onto the platform.

"Mr. Parker?" a voice said.

"Yes," Quince replied off-handedly. He wondered what he was going to do now.

"I am Leslie Kendrake."

Quince looked up in quick surprise, for there, standing on the platform, was a young, blonde, and beautiful woman!

"*You* are Leslie Kendrake?" Quince asked in disbelief. "But you can't be!"

The young woman laughed, a light, lilting laugh, and she tossed her head so that her long blonde locks fell away from her face. She had wide, innocent blue eyes, a small upturned nose, and full sensuous lips, now curved upward in a smile. She was well aware of his confusion, and she relished in it.

"I assure you, Mr. Parker, I am Leslie Kendrake. My father said you might be surprised when you met me."

The girl's words were spoken with a decided English accent, and Quince realized then that she was telling the truth.

"But why?" he stammered. "I mean, why didn't Mr. Kendrake tell me that you are a woman?"

"Why indeed?" Leslie replied. "Perhaps he has acquired a droll sense of humor since coming to your American West." She laughed. "I knew of his little joke—he told me in his last letter. He'll be pleased to know that it worked just as he thought it would." Leslie looked around. "But where is he? Why isn't he here to meet me?"

Quince looked at the ground and found something to do with the toe of his boot for a moment. He took a deep breath before he spoke, because it was even harder to say what he had to say now, than he thought it would be.

"Miss Kendrake," he said. "I've got some awful news for you."

"Awful news? What kind of news? Mr. Parker, is it father? Has something happened to father?"

"Yes'm," Quince said.

Leslie Kendrake felt a sudden cold chill pass over her body. She knew then, without Quince Parker saying another word, that her father was dead. She felt a numbness descend over her, and her arms grew terribly heavy. She wanted to shout out against the injustice, to scream in grief, but she could do nothing but stand there and hold on, to keep herself together.

"My father is dead, isn't he?" she finally said.

"Yes'm, I'm afraid he is," Quince said. "It happened last night. That is to say, the accident happened last night. But he didn't die until this morning."

"Would you take me to him, please?"

"Yes I will," Quince said. "But now I've got a little problem."

"What type of problem? Is there some reason I can't see my father?"

"No, it's not that, Miss Kendrake," Quince said. "It's just that, well, I thought you were going to be a man, so I brought a horse for you to ride. It's quicker by horseback, than by following the wagon trail, and I thought you would rather do that."

"I appreciate your thoughtfulness," Leslie said. "But I can't very well ride in this dress."

"Perhaps I may be of some assistance," another voice said, and Leslie looked over to see a well-dressed man approaching htem. He tipped his hat courteously. "My name is Charles W. Goodpasture. I must say I, too, am surprised to see a lovely lady rather than a man. But the surprise is a charming one."

"Mr. Goodpasture, yes," Leslie said. "My father has mentioned you in his letters to me."

"Lady Leslie, may I express my condolences over your father's death? Everyone in Wyoming will feel his loss, I assure you."

"Thank you," Leslie said. "Mr. Goodpasture, have you a carriage?"

"Indeed I have," Charles said.

"Then might I prevail upon you to take me to my father's ranch? Mr. Parker brought a horse, but I'm afraid I am not dressed to ride it."

"Of course I will take you there," Charles said graciously. "My only regret is that there will be such a sad conclusion to our journey."

Charles offered his arm and Leslie accepted it, then started toward the carriage. After a few steps she stopped and looked back toward Quince, who was still standing there in melancholy contemplation.

"Mr. Parker, I will see you there?"

"Yes," Quince replied. "I'll take the shortcut and arrive before you. Lady Leslie, let me say again how sorry I am."

"Thank you," Leslie said.

They reached Goodpasture's phaeton a moment later, and Charles helped Leslie in, then climbed in beside her. "Andrew," he called. "Take us to Three Crowns."

"Yes, sir," Andrew said, clucking at the team.

"Poor Mr. Parker," Leslie said. "What a difficult thing this must have been for him to do."

"I'm sure it was," Charles said. "But you made it easy for him. You took it so bravely."

"I don't know whether I took it bravely, or whether I am numbed from the suddenness of the news. You know I haven't seen my father in five years. Who died? The English lord I said goodbye to so long ago, or the American cattle rancher I never knew?"

Charles reached over and patted her hand affectionately. "Whichever it was, Lady Leslie, I want you to know that you may depend upon me for anything you need. I shall be glad to help in every way."

"Thank you, Mr. Goodpasture," Leslie said.

"He is in there," Quince said later when the carriage finally arrived at Three Crowns. Quince, as he had said he would, beat them back to the ranch, and was waiting out front when the carriage arrived. Leslie went into the house with him, without even taking the time to look around, though in the rapidly failing light all the ranch wasn't visible to her now, anyway.

Leslie looked into the living room, and spied a coffin resting on saw horses. The coffin was draped with a wine-colored cloth, and tall, slender candles burned at the head and foot.

"I've arranged for his funeral to be held as soon as you give the word," Quince said.

"Thank you," Leslie replied.

Leslie walked on into the room and looked at the still form of her father. As she looked at him, she began remembering things about this man she hadn't seen in so many years. Little things tumbled back into her mind as sharply now as if they had just happened. She could hear the last conversation she had with him.

"Leslie, I'll be going on to America now, and when I've made the ranch productive and when you've finished your school, you'll join me there."

"But, father, America is so far away. And mother's grave is here. Are you going to leave her behind?"

"Child, your mother isn't in that grave. She's here in our hearts, and that's where she'll always be. Just as I will be in your heart when I die."

"Father, don't talk about dying. I don't want you to ever die."

"Darling, we all must die. We can't go to heaven until we do."

"I, uh, had the undertaker come in today and fix him up some," Quince said.

"Thank you," Leslie replied. She stood quietly for a moment, then looked at Quince. "Is there an Anglican Vicar near by?"

"There is an Episcopal Priest in Laramie," Charles said, and Leslie turned to see him standing in the door. "Your father seemed satisfied with that."

"Yes, he will do nicely," Leslie said. "Do you suppose we can get him out here by day after tomorrow?"

"That might be a problem," Quince said. "That's July Fourth."

"July Fourth? Is there some significance to that date?"

"That's Independence day," Quince said. "Everyone will be celebrating."

"Oh, yes, I had forgotten," Leslie said. She sighed. "Well then, if it is possible, we should get him here by tomorrow."

"We can make a telephone call from Sweetgrass," Charles said. "I have one of the instruments in my bank there."

"Thank you," Leslie said. "Now if you don't mind, Mr. Parker, would you please show me where I am to sleep tonight? I am very tired, and I want to be alone with my thoughts for a while."

Leslie followed Quince down the hall of the house until he stopped by a door. He opened it, and motioned toward it with his arm. "Mr. Kendrake meant for you to sleep in here," he said. "I think you'll find everything you need to make yourself comfortable."

"Is there anyone else in the house?" Leslie asked.

"No, ma'am. All the others are out in the bunk-house."

"You also?"

"Yes, ma'am."

"Mr. Parker," Leslie said. "Would it be too much to ask you to stay in the house tonight? I'd rather not stay here all alone."

"I'll sit up in the living room," Quince offered.

"Nonsense. Surely there is another bedroom somewhere?"

"Yes, of course, but—"

"Then I want you to go to bed. I will be comforted by the mere fact that you are here."

"All right," Quince said. "If you want."

"Thank you," Leslie said. She smiled warmly at him. "Good night now."

"Goodnight," Quince said.

Quince watched Leslie close the door, then he turned and went back into the living room. He felt a rush of shame, for despite the solemnity of the occasion, he wanted to shout from the rafters! The reason? Because he had never seen a woman more beautiful, or who had moved him more, than Leslie Kendrake!

"Are you going to tell her that you were responsible for her father's death?" Charles asked.

"What?" Charles's question had snapped Quince back to reality.

"I think you should," Charles went on. "She may be more likely to forgive you if she hears it from you."

"But I'm not responsible for her father's death," Quince protested.

"That's not what everyone else thinks," Charles said. "And that's not what she is going to think either when someone finally tells her what really did happen."

"I see," Quince said. "Then I take it *you* didn't tell her on the way out here?"

"No," Charles answered. "She asked me, and I said only that he was killed in an explosion at the dam."

"Well, I must confess that I wouldn't have expected that courtesy from you, Goodpasture," Quince said. "I never fancied us friends."

"My dear boy," Charles said. "I have nothing against you, mind, but neither do I feel it necessary to do anything for you."

"Then why did you do this?"

"I want to make things as easy for Leslie Kendrake as I can. The more quickly she acclimates herself to the situation, the more quickly she will be ready to sell Three Crowns to me."

"Three Crowns isn't for sale," Quince put in quickly.

"Oh, I think it will be," Charles said. "In fact, we discussed just such a thing on the drive out here, and I am happy to say that, at the moment, Leslie Kendrake seems more than willing to sell."

"Surely you didn't ask such a thing of her now, with her father not yet buried?" Quince asked.

"Please, Mr. Parker, allow me some credit for decency. Of course I didn't ask her now. But, we did discuss the fact that it was something which needed to be considered, and she replied that she wanted only to leave as quickly as she could and return home to England. Naturally, I told her that I would buy the ranch from her to help her out, if that was what she truly wanted to do."

"I'm sure you were just being helpful," Quince said sarcastically.

6

STUART KENDRAKE had been a well-liked man. His ranch was large enough for him to be considered a Wyoming cattle baron, and, in fact, he was a charter member of the Cheyenne Cattleman's Club. The fact that he held an English title made him a popular figure with the other cattle barons, for in a land where such titles were forbidden they all shared his title by association. But Kendrake was also a friend to the small ranchers, for he had never, in the words of the cowboy, "jerked a cinch into anyone." He was exceptionally fair in his dealings with all men, and he was honored and respected for that. No cowboy who had ever ridden for Three Crowns ranch had anything but good to say of the gentle Englishman who owned it.

Because of that, and because a funeral was a social event as surely as a wedding or a spring dance, there was a great crowd at the Sweetgrass graveyard. The scene created a small degree of incongruity, however, for Sweetgrass was decked out for the Fourth of July celebration which would be held the next day, and American flags were everywhere in abundance, while upon the freshly covered grave of Stuart Kendrake there was, fluttering in the breeze, a Union Jack.

Leslie stood at the graveside for a long time, even after the others had gone, and she looked at the pile of dirt that covered her father. She had wept bitter tears over the last twelve hours, not so much for the father she had lost, but for the father she had scarcely known. She had been ten when her father left for India, and fifteen when he returned, broken-hearted over the death of his wife, who had remained in England with Leslie. He was home but two short weeks, then he left for America to administer some land he had inherited from his father, while Leslie remained in England to finish school.

Leslie's mother was dead, but her father had insisted that she stay in England until her education was complete, and Leslie reluctantly agreed. Now, after having seen him only two weeks in ten years, Leslie had come all the way to America, only to find him dead.

It wasn't fair, and the tears Leslie had shed were as much in protest over the injustice of the situation as they were for grief.

After a long moment, Leslie sensed someone close by.

"I never knew my own father," Quince said. "But if I had known him, I couldn't have cared more for him."

Their walk carried them back to the buckboard, and he helped Leslie in, then he walked around and took up the reins himself.

"The whole town seems ready to celebrate the

Fourth of July," Leslie said, looking at the flags and bunting. "It must be like Christmas for you Americans."

"In a way, I suppose it is," Quince said. "Or like everyone's birthday rolled into one day. They are going to have a picnic and dance tomorrow. Mr. Kendrake was looking forward to it, because he wanted to show off his new country to you."

"Do you think everyone would be too shocked if I came?" Leslie asked.

"What?" Quince asked, who, though not shocked, was surprised by her statement. "Why, no, no, I don't think *everyone* would be shocked. I think it would be wonderful if you went to the celebration."

"Good," Leslie said. "Then I shall go, and you will take me if you don't mind."

"Mind?" Quince said with a huge grin. "I'd *love* it!"

"I shouldn't like to go back to England with only the melancholy memory of burying my father to mark the trip," Leslie said.

"Go back to England?"

"Yes. Mr. Goodpasture has offered to buy the farm—"

"It's a ranch," Quince put in.

"The ranch," Leslie went on placidly. "Mr. Goodpasture has offered to buy the ranch from me, and I intend to sell and return to England as quickly as I can."

"I see," Quince said. "What kind of offer has he made?"

"He hasn't exactly made an offer yet," Leslie

said. "But he assured me that the offer would be fair. We spoke of it yesterday as he drove me out to the ranch."

"Excuse me, Miss Kendrake, if I sound like I'm butting in, but how would you know whether the offer is fair or not?"

"Mr. Goodpasture has offered to find a barrister for me. I'm certain that a barrister representing my interests would be able to ascertain whether or not the offer was, indeed, fair."

"I wouldn't trust any shyster-lawyer Goodpasture came up with any further than I can throw a steer, and that's not very far," Quince said hotly.

They had left the town now, and were going along at a fairly good clip on the winding road which led to Three Crowns. Leslie, surprised by Quince's evaluation of Goodpasture, turned toward him, and brushed an errant strand of blonde hair from her eyes.

"Mr. Parker, are you telling me that Mr. Goodpasture would intentionally *cheat* me?"

"Yes," Quince said. "He's been wanting Three Crowns ever since your father started it."

"But of what value is Three Crowns? Mr. Goodpasture told me there is no water on the rangeland."

"There is a little," Quince said. "But we do have a problem, since they dammed up Indian Creek."

"Indian Creek? Isn't that where father was killed?"

"Yes," Quince said.

"How did it happen? Mr. Goodpasture said it was an explosion of some kind."

Quince took a deep breath. He knew it would

have to come out sooner or later, but he had hoped it would be later. Much, much later, after she had had time to know enough about what is going on to understand his action. Now, she would have to accept it for what it was.

"I guess you might say it was my fault," he said, his voice showing plainly that he had no wish to say this. "I took a load of nitro down to blow the dam. There was an accident, the nitro exploded, and your father was killed."

Leslie put her hand on Quince's hand, and he felt the cool touch of her fingers. "I know how awful you must feel," she said. "And you mustn't blame yourself. Really you mustn't."

Quince smiled wanly. "You mean . . . you mean you don't hold it against me that I was responsible?"

"Of course not," Leslie said. "I suspect I know how deeply you cared for my father. I know how badly you feel about what has happened. I could never find fault with you for what was obviously an accident."

"Oh," Quince said, letting out a long sigh of relief. "Leslie, you don't know what a burden you've lifted from me," he said.

"Oh, stop the carriage," Leslie said, pointing to the side of the road. "Those flowers, they are lovely! They are like tiny flames at the tips of the stems. What are they?"

"They are called indian paint brush," Quince said. "They are pretty." He noticed with pleasure that she had not corrected him when he called her Leslie.

"Pretty? They are beautiful. I've never seen

such a vivid red. Oh, do let me gather a bouquet."

Quince stopped the buckboard, then hopped out, and went around to help Leslie down. The field before them waved with flowers, not only the bright red indian paint brushes, but other flowers as well, white and yellow oxeye daisies, and the slender, white-and-blue columbines which winked from the broad field like pale stars.

Across the field, a great range of mountains rose to snowcapped peaks.

"Oh," Leslie said. "This is so breathtakingly beautiful!"

"I reckon it is," Quince said. "I reckon you can see why your dad loved it so." He turned to look at Leslie. "And why he asked me on his death bed not to let you sell Three Crowns."

Leslie blinked, then dropped her eyes to the ground. "That's not fair," she said quietly.

"Maybe it's not," Quince said. "But I can't just let you sell it without at least tellin' you what your dad wanted."

As Quince spoke to her, he put a hand on each shoulder . . . then, though he hadn't planned it, and was as surprised by his action as was Leslie, he pulled her to him and brought his mouth down on hers for a kiss.

Leslie was shocked by Quince's action, and she struggled against him, both from shock and fear, for she had no idea where such an impetuous move would lead. But the harder she struggled, the more determined he became to hold her, until finally she abandoned the struggle and let herself go limp in his arms.

Then a strange thing began to happen. The surprise changed to surrender, the fear to curiosity, and then to sweetness. It was shocking and thrilling at the same time, and involuntarily a moan of passion began in her throat. Her blood felt as if it had changed to hot tea, and her body was warmed with a heat she had never before experienced. The kiss went on, longer than she had ever imagined such a thing could last, and her head grew so light that she abandoned all thought save this pleasure. Finally, Quince broke off the kiss, and Leslie was left standing there as limp as a rag doll.

"I . . . I'm sorry," Quince said, turning away from her, unable to meet her eyes.

"Another one of your tricks to prevent me from selling the ranch?" Leslie asked with a biting edge to her voice.

"No," Quince said. "No, it's not, I swear it. Lady Leslie, please, you must forgive me."

The remainder of the ride could have been tense, but the sheer beauty of the land evoked more observations and comments from Leslie, so that by the time they reached the ranch, the tension had dissolved.

Rufus met them as they drove through the gate. Rufus was short and bandy-legged, almost comical looking, despite the deep, brooding eyes which seemed to hold some terrible secret.

"Was they many at the fun'rul?" Rufus asked.

"Yes," Quince said.

"Well, I said my goodbye's to the gent before he left here," Rufus said. "I don't hold no truck with fun'ruls, 'n Mr. Kendrake, he knowed that, so I don' reckon he's a'gonna hold it agin' me none. Miss Kendrake, I know this here ain' the best time to ask you, but how are you a'likin' the West?"

"It's beautiful country, Mr. Rufus," Leslie said.

"You can jus' call me Rufus," Rufus said. "Yes'm, I reckon it is beautiful country. Though they's been many who got tuk in by it, 'n wound up gettin' themselves kilt, 'cause they wasn't alert."

"Yes, I can see how that might happen," Leslie said. "The mountains could be dangerous, the desert could be dangerous. And of course there are all sorts of wild animals, I imagine. And Indians, too."

"Yes'm, there's them things, I reckon," Rufus said. "But all them things put together ain't kilt as many as bad men."

"Bad men?"

"Gunmen, mostly," Rufus said. "Outlaws 'n the such. Are you hungry? I know it isn't dinner time, but I thought you might like some tea and biscuits."

Leslie smiled. "How sweet of you," she said. "Yes, I think the tea would be nice, though I shall pass on the biscuits, if you don't mind."

"At least try one," Rufus said.

"Yes," Quince sput in. "Rufus makes the best biscuits you've ever tasted."

"And you'd be hurtin' my feelin's if you didn't try."

Leslie softened. "Then of course I shall try one of them."

Rufus grinned broadly and left to get the biscuits.

"You've made him a happy man," Quince said.

"He's a funny little man, isn't he?" Leslie said. "He's very nice, but he reminds me of a pixie. And all his talk of gunmen and outlaws. What would he know of such people?"

"You would be surprised what he knows," Quince replied darkly.

Leslie's first surprise came just a moment later, when Rufus set a plate of cookies on the table before her.

"Biscuits!" Leslie exclaimed happily, picking up one of the cookies. "I mean real *English* biscuits!"

"Those just look like cookies to me," Quince said, obviously puzzled by the whole thing.

"Yes, they are," Leslie said. "You see, what we call biscuits, you call cookies. What you call biscuits, we call rolls. Imagine my disappointment the first time I tried to order biscuits in America. But here, I have the *real* thing!" She tasted one of them. "Uhmm, and they are *delicious!*"

"Thank you," Rufus said.

"Rufus, how did *you* know this?" Quince asked.

"I just picked it up somewhere I guess," Rufus said. "Anyway, Miss Kendrake hasn't had all that good a welcome to the West, so I just wanted to do something nice for her."

"Thank you," Leslie said, and tears leaped to her eyes as she thought of what Rufus had done for her. "You'll never know how much I appreciate this."

"If you can think of anything else I can do, just let me know, and I'll do it," Rufus offered.

"You are very kind," Leslie said. She laughed. "If it shouldn't embarrass you, I would tell you that you would make an excellent nanny."

"If you want me to be a nanny, then that's what I'll be," Rufus said.

"You wouldn't be embarrassed?" Leslie teased.

"Ma'am, it's been my experience that the only folks what gets embarrassed is them what ain't sure of themselves."

"That's a most astute observation," Leslie said, surprised by his answer. "Yes, most astute. What about you, Quince Parker? Are you ever embarrassed?" she asked, looking at him with a quizzical smile.

"I guess I've made a fool out of myself a few times," Quince mumbled.

"I dare say you have," Leslie said, and the expression on her face told him she was thinking of his action this afternoon, though more with a sense of humor than anger. "Nevertheless, I am willing to go to the celebration with you tomorrow, if you still want to take me."

Quince rewarded her with a wide grin. "You mean, it's all right? You aren't mad at me?"

"I shall put it down to youthful enthusiasm and foolish bravado," Leslie said. "And I shall hold you to your promise to guard against such indiscretions in the future. Now, under those circumstances, do you still wish to take me?"

"Leslie, I'd take you under *any* circumstances," Quince said.

"Then I shall look forward to it," Leslie said.

Quince smiled happily, then he stood up and asked to be excused. "I want you to forgive me for running out on you," he said. "But I have some things which need attending to. I'd better get on them while it's still light enough to see."

"Yes, of course, do what you must do," Leslie replied. "I'll just enjoy my tea," she picked up a cookie and smiled at Rufus. "And biscuits."

Quince left the bighouse and saddled a horse, then started riding the fence line leading to the North range. This was a job which could have been done by the greenest of the hands, but it was a job Quince enjoyed. He found the riding very pleasureable.

Quince was nearly one mile from the Bighouse when he stood in the stirrups, removed his hat, slapped it against his side, and shouted, "*Yahoo!*"

7

FOR ONE FULL DAY, Sweetgrass gave itself over to having fun. There were horse and foot races during the day, as well as a large picnic, complete with watermelons and pie-eating contests. There were fireworks galore, and then, when the sun went down, lanterns were hung around a wooden platform in the park, music was provided by the volunteer fire-department band, and a dance was held.

It seemed that nearly everyone went out of their way to welcome Leslie Kendrake to Sweetgrass, and though a few mentioned her father, the overall theme of the evening was uplifting, and Leslie enjoyed herself very much.

Leslie was much in demand as a dancing partner, and she danced nearly every dance with someone new. Quince had his share of dances with her, though, and he stood on the edge of the wooden floor near a stack of hay-bales watching as first one and then another cowboy guided Leslie around, waiting patiently for his next opportunity.

The music played, and the dancers swirled, and during one of the turns Leslie looked over toward Quince and smiled such a dazzling smile that

Quince thought he would shout out loud. Never had any woman caused him to feel as she did, and he wanted to jump up and shout, and kick his heels together in joy. But that joy was tempered with the realization that she would soon be returning to England, and in all likelihood, he would never see her again.

"She is lovely, isn't she?" a voice said, and Quince turned to see Charles Goodpasture.

"Yes," Quince said. "I think she is the most beautiful woman I have ever seen."

"It almost makes me wish I hadn't offered to buy the ranch," Charles said. "For in so doing, I am surely driving her back to England."

"Then don't buy it," Quince said. "Let her keep it."

"What would she do with a dead ranch?" Charles asked.

"I'll find a way to keep it going," Quince said.

Charles looked at Quince for a moment, and pursed his lips. "Yes," he said. "I daresay you just might at that. Unfortunately, you won't get the opportunity. I intend to buy it as soon as the will is probated, and she can legally sell."

"Goodpasture, you are a vulture, do you know that?"

Charles didn't get the opportunity to respond, because at that moment the music ended, and Leslie left the floor, heading for Quince and Charles.

"My," she said. "Such dancing leaves me breathless. But I don't know when I've enjoyed myself so."

"I thought you might enjoy a cool glass of

lemonade," Charles said, offering her a glass, and
Quince felt a pang of jealousy and a twinge of
disgust with himself for not thinking of the same
thing.

"Oh, thank you," Leslie said, taking the lemonade and putting it to her lips. "Uhmm, delicious,
and welcome, I assure you."

"I'm sorry I didn't get here in time to get my
name on your dance-card. I was detained by
business."

"Perhaps Quince will allow you to take his turn
next," Leslie suggested. She looked at Quince
questioningly.

Quince didn't want to give up his turn to anyone, and he particularly didn't want to give up his
turn to Charles Goodpasture. But he smiled nevertheless, and with a slight nod of his head ac-
quiesced.

"Thank you, Parker," Charles said. "I truly appreciate that."

"Ladies and gentlemen, the band is going to
take a fifteen minute rest," the bandleader said
and some of the more disappointed young men
shouted their disapproval at the band's action, but
most of the women, who, like Leslie, had danced
every dance, were as ready for a break as the
band, and they approved.

"Would you care to sit on this haybale?" Quince
offered.

"Yes, thank you, I would appreciate that," Leslie
said, sitting at his invitation.

"Tell me, my dear, are you enjoying America?"
Charles asked.

"Yes," Leslie said. "I'm enjoying it ever so much more than I thought, despite the loss of my poor father. In fact, I've only tonight come to a conclusion."

"What conclusion is that?" Quince asked.

"One that I think you may approve," Leslie said. "I've decided not to sell Three Crowns."

"You've decided not to sell?" Quince said, fairly shouting it in his excitement. "Oh, but . . . how wonderful!"

"Lady Leslie, you can't be serious!" Charles said.

"I am serious," Leslie said. "I've been thinking about it all day. After all, I have no close relatives in England, and nothing in England to go back to. I had always planned to make my life in America, and now I shall go through with it."

Any hint of displeasure which may have been present in Charles's face disappeared immediately, and he smiled easily at her. "Then may I extend a welcome to my most beautiful neighbor?" he said. "And offer my help in anything that is within my power."

"If you are serious about that, you might take down the dam at Indian Creek," Quince suggested.

Charles sighed. "Mr. Parker, you don't seem to understand that I have nothing to do with that dam. That dam was put there by the Government."

"If they put it there, you influenced it," Quince charged. "For Mountain Shadows was the only ranch in the entire valley which profited from the so-called water improvement."

"That was my good fortune," Charles said. "But it could have as easily been the other way. In any case, I doubt that I would have been so foolish as to try and destroy a government project by using nitroglycerine."

"You mean it was a government project?" Leslie said. "I didn't know that. That seems so unlike father to try something which would have been against the law, even if it had succeeded."

"Your father didn't try it," Charles said.

"What do you mean?" Leslie asked.

"I see you haven't told her yet," Charles said.

Quince looked at the ground for a long moment before he spoke again. "He was killed in that explosion, but he wasn't helping me set it, he was trying to stop it."

"I see," Leslie said quietly. "You were acting on your own, then?"

"I was," Quince said. "I . . . the dam . . . it had us completely choked off. I was just trying to help your father, but I wound up killing him instead. You'll never know how sorry I am, Leslie."

Leslie reached out and put her hand on Quince's hand and sighed. "Quince, I know you are sorry. And I know you had no intention of hurting father, so I don't blame you for that."

"Thanks," Quince said, giving a sigh of relief.

"But on the other hand, it does show a degree of immaturity on your part, doesn't it?"

"What do you mean?" Quince asked.

"Obviously my father didn't approve of what you were trying to do, or he wouldn't have tried to stop you."

"Well, I suppose he was against it," Quince said.

"But you tried it anyway."

Quince frowned at Leslie. "I thought you weren't going to hold that against me," he said.

"Oh, Quince, don't you see?" Leslie asked. "I'm not holding my father's death against you. I know you didn't want any harm to come to him. But what I am holding against you is your immaturity."

"Oh, so I am immature, am I?" Quince replied.

"I'm afraid so."

"Well, now, just how immature can I be?" Quince challenged angrily. "Mr. Kendrake had enough confidence in me to make me the ramrod of Three Crowns. He told me many times that he couldn't run it by himself, and I don't think you can, either."

"I can't run it by myself," Leslie said.

Quince smiled a small smile of victory. "Then I guess you'll have to rely on some one who is immature."

"No," Leslie said. She sighed again. "I'm sorry, Quince, but I'm afraid this quite changes things now."

"Changes things? What do you mean?" Quince asked.

"Simply this. If I stayed in America, I would be dependent upon you for help. But by your action, you have shown a measure of immaturity, a dangerous immaturity, and I fear I wouldn't have full faith and confidence in your judgment. I was foolish to think I could stay here anyway. I was swayed by the beauty of the land, and the excitement of the situation. Reluctantly, I must return to my earlier decision." She turned to look at Charles who had been taking in the entire conversation, though not participating. "Mr. Goodpasture, I will sell Three Crowns to you."

This time it was Charles who smiled broadly. "Well, now, Miss Kendrake, you won't be regretting your decision, I assure you. I'll give you the top price, not only for your land, but for all your cattle as well. Yes, ma'am, you've made a very wise decision."

"Well, Goodpasture, you seem to have won another one," Quince said angrily. He turned and started to walk away.

"You needn't take it that way, Parker," Charles said. "After all, it is clearly her decision to make, and it shouldn't affect you one way or the other."

"Quince," Leslie called after him. "Quince, where are you going?"

"I'm going someplace where the company is more to my liking," Quince replied.

"But your dances?" Leslie said. "What about the remaining dances?"

"Give them to Goodpasture," Quince called back angrily. "He is obviously a man more suited to your ideals than I."

"He just may be at that!" Leslie replied, showing that she could be as angry as Quince.

Even as Quince was leaving the dance, hearing himself shout angrily at Leslie, he knew how foolishly he was acting. He heard his words with a sense of detachment, as if someone else was saying them, and he was no more able to control them than he would have been if it had actually been someone else.

Behind him the band played a fanfare, preparatory to beginning again, and the men cheered, but the music and the cheering was fading in the distance as Quince walked quickly and angrily away from the park.

Square patches of yellow light lay in the streets, projected from the windows of the buildings. Ahead, and the most brightly lighted of all the buildings, was Rosita's saloon.

Quince stepped in through the swinging gates, worked his way through the milling crowd, and finally reached the bar.

Though Rosita didn't normally work the bar, this was a special night, and the crowd was very large, so she was working as hard as Manuel.

"Señor Parker," Rosita said, smiling as Quince stepped up to the bar. "It has been a long time since I have seen you in here. I thought you would be showing the English lady a good time today."

"Let Goodpasture show her a good time," Quince said angrily. He pulled the cork from a bottle of whiskey and poured himself a glass."

"Goodpasture?" Rosita said. "Señor Goodpasture is with the English girl?"

Quince tossed the whiskey down, feeling it burn its way through his throat, then lie in his stomach, spreading its warmth through him.

"Yeah," Quince said, pouring himself another glass. "It seems she prefers his company to mine. I am too immature for her."

"He said he would be here by ten o'clock," Rosita said.

"Oh, Rosita, my girl, I am certain he won't

make it," Quince said. He started to pour himself a third glass.

"No," Rosita said, reaching her hand out to stop him.

"Don't tell me *you* don't want my company either," Quince said.

"Oh, I think your company is just fine," Rosita said. "It's just that I believe you will enjoy this whiskey more." She pulled a bottle of Goodpasture's special stock from under the bar and poured a glass for him. He tossed it down as quickly as he had the other two.

Quince smiled. "Rosita, girl, I have to confess that at the moment I'm not drinking whiskey for the taste, so it really doesn't matter what kind I have."

"Good," Rosita said. "Then as a special favor to me, you will drink from *this* bottle." She poured him another glass.

Quince was beginning to feel the effects of the whiskey he had drunk, and he looked at Rosita with a quizzical expression on his face.

"Rosita, it seems you are plying me with drink."

"Am I?" Rosita asked, pouring another glass as soon as he finished that one. She smiled at him, and by now Quince was so drunk that her smile seemed to leave her face and float before him. "It's just that I thought you might appreciate drinking *Señor* Goodpasture's whiskey."

"Goodpasture's whiskey?" Quince said. "You mean this is his special whiskey?"

"*Si*," Rosita said with a conspiratorial smile.

"Yeah," Quince said. He drank it, then held his

glass out for another. "Yeah, I guess I do appreciate it at that."

At that moment, Andrew, Charles's black carriage driver, came into the bar.

"Hey," someone said. "There's a nigger in here."

Andrew, unperturbed by the comment, stood quietly until Rosita saw him. "Did you come to see me, Andrew? What is it?" she asked.

"Beg pardon, ma'am," Andrew said with a slight bow. "But Mr. Goodpasture, he won' be heah tonight. The English lady, she comin' out to Mountain Shadows as a house guest."

"I see," Rosita said. "Did he send you to tell me that?"

"No, ma'am," Andrew said. "I done took it on myself to tell you that, 'cause I knew he was plannin' on comin' here later 'n I thought you might wonder where we was at."

Rosita put the cork back on the bottle of whiskey she had been pouring for Quince, and handed the bottle to Andrew.

"*Gracias*, Andrew," she said. "Here, a little something to help you celebrate the *fiesta*."

Andrew smiled broadly. "Thank you, ma'am," he said, sliding the bottle into his inside jacket pocket. "Thank you, kindly." He turned and left quickly, lest she change her mind and take his prize away from him.

"So," Quince said. "I don't get to drink any more of Goodpasture's whiskey, huh?"

"No," Rosita said. She smiled seductively. "But I might offer you something else belonging to *Señor* Goodpasture, if you are in the mood."

"Oh?" Quince replied. "What?"

"Me," Rosita said.

"You?"

"You could come up to my room if you like."

The thought had not previously occurred to Quince. He had come to Rosita's not to see Rosita, but to drink away his anger and frustration over the unexpected turn of events. But now that the offer was made, why not take her up on it? After all, Quince, like many of the other cowboys, had made more than one half-hearted attempt to accompany Rosita to her room. And now she was offering him just that opportunity.

And yet it was a relatively hollow victory, for since he had met Leslie, Rosita and all other girls seemed a dull and distant second. Still . . . Andrew had said that Leslie would be staying at Mountain Shadows tonight, so why not?

"Yeah," he said. "Yeah, I'd like."

"You go on up now," Rosita said. "I'll be up in a few minutes."

Quince pushed himself away from the bar and looked around the room. Time had seemed compressed by the number of drinks he had consumed, because he had obviously been there for much longer than he had realized, because the pushing, bustling crowd which had been there when he arrived was reduced to no more than half a dozen men, most of them gathered around one table in the back of the room, engaged in a game of cards. None of them even glanced at him as he climbed the stairs to Rosita's room.

Quince unbuttoned his shirt and slipped it off, and was just starting on his breeches when Rosita came into the room. She walked over to him and put her hand on his shoulder and ran it along the smooth skin and hard muscles, then down across his chest.

"Ohhh," she said. "What a nice way to get even with *Señor* Goodpasture, don't you think? Let him have his English girl."

"Let's not talk about them," Quince said, pulling Rosita against him for a kiss.

"Let's not talk about who?" Rosita answered, returning Quince's kisses eagerly and exploring more of his body with her hands.

Though Rosita had confined herself to Charles alone for the last year, the truth was that before coming to Sweetgrass, she had worked in the Cheyenne Social Club, unabashedly billed as "the best whorehouse in the west". It was there that Charles discovered her, and it was he who helped her get established in Sweetgrass. But in her colorful past Rosita had been with many men, and with many who were drunk. She knew from experience that alcohol, when used to the point of drunkenness, usually inhibited a man's sexual capacity. But she was not to be disappointed by Quince. Drunk though he was, he was strong and virile, and as he took her, she rose eagerly to meet him. And such was the pleasure of the lovemaking that she closed her ears to the cry he uttered just as he finished, and right before he passed out.

"Leslie," he gasped.

8

Leslie had been surprised and hurt by Quince's odd behavior. She had expected him to return to apologize later, and she had made up her mind that she would accept his apology, though she intended to let him know how hurt she had been.

But Quince never returned. Charles remained to avail himself of every opportunity to dance with her, and when, just before midnight, the bandmaster announced the last song, Charles was there to claim the dance which had been carded for Quince.

Even as they were dancing, Leslie looked over the thinning crowd, hoping to see him.

"He's in Rosita's saloon," Charles said. "By now he is quite drunk."

"What?"

"You are looking for your foreman, aren't you? Parker?"

"Well, I suppose I was," Leslie said. "To be honest, I'm a little concerned as to how I shall get home tonight. I certainly can't make the trip by myself."

"No," Charles said. "Nor would I expect you to travel with Parker in his present state."

"How do you know he is drunk?"

"I sent one of my men to check on him," Charles said. "I knew you would be worried."

"Oh, how kind of you," Leslie replied dully.

The band played the last bar of music, then the bandsmen started returning their instruments to the cases. The dancers, a few voicing their disappointment with the conclusion of the evening, began leaving the floor.

"Now my problem becomes most acute," Leslie said. "I really don't know what I shall do. Oh, how dare he abandon me this way!"

"You shouldn't be surprised," Charles said. "You pegged him right when you said he was immature. And as for what you shall do, you shall come home with me."

"Mr. Goodpasture, I couldn't do that," Leslie said.

"Why not?" Goodpasture asked. "I have four lady housekeepers and cooks who live at Mountain Shadows. Your reputation would be quite secure, I assure you."

"Oh, it's not that," Leslie said. "It's just that I couldn't put you out so."

"Nonsense," Charles replied. "I can think of nothing which would give me more pleasure than to put up the daughter of my very best friend."

"Well," Leslie said, clearly giving in to his argument. "I have to go somewhere, I suppose, and it is obvious that Quince isn't going to return for me." She looked at him and smiled. "I accept your kind offer, sir."

"Good, good," Charles said. He looked around. "Now where *is* Andrew? He was here but a moment ago. I saw him standing near the carriage."

"Isn't that your carriage?" Leslie asked.

"Yes, it is. Well, he can't have wandered far."

"Oh, look," Leslie said, pointing into the sky. There, above the roofs of the town, rockets were bursting in air, sending out golden showers of glowing sparks. "Isn't it beautiful?"

Two more rockets swooshed into the air, and so fascinated were they with the fireworks display that they didn't even see Andrew return from Rosita's Saloon and hide a bottle in the boot of the carriage.

When Quince Parker awoke the next morning, he felt as if a herd of cows had been driven through his head. He was nauseous and thick-tongued, and his head was spinning like a top. He smelled coffee and was puzzled until Rosita stuck her head through the door.

"Good morning," she said. "I have coffee ready. Will you want breakfast?"

"No," Quince said quickly. "No food, please."

Rosita laughed and handed a cup of black coffee to him. "I told Manuel that you would not wish to eat this morning."

Quince sucked some coffee through lips, extended to keep them from being burned by the hot liquid, and he looked around the room with a puzzled expression on his face.

"Don't you know where you are?" Rosita asked.

"Am I . . . is this your room?"

"*Si.*"

Quince took another drink of the coffee, and

tried to quiet the pounding drum in his head. "Did we spend the night together, Rosita?"

"*Caramba*," Rosita said in mock anger. "Am I such a woman that you could spend the night with me and forget?"

It came back to Quince then . . . the perfumed sheets, the yielding flesh, the hot moments of pleasure.

He smiled at Rosita. "No," he said. "No, I didn't forget."

"I do not believe you," Rosita said, pouting.

Quince reached up to her, and touched her earlobe gently. "Do you believe me now?" he asked. For during the night he had discovered that Rosita was particularly sensitive to a kiss on the earlobes, and she had writhed in exquisite pleasure at his inventiveness.

Rosita smiled, and the hint of a blush came to her cheeks. "You are quite a man," she said. "You were so drunk, I don't know how you could remember."

"And I don't know how I could forget," Quince said.

The smile left Rosita's face, and a hint of sadness moved across her eyes. "And do you remember also the name you called out in the darkness?"

Suddenly Quince remembered that as well, for though he had assured himself that he was showing that he cared nothing for what Leslie might decide to do, he had in fact thought only of her at that extreme moment. He looked down in shame and embarrassment.

"I'm sorry," he said.

Rosita smiled again. "Don't worry," she said.
"We were both using each other last night. It is
good, is it not, that we had each other to use?"

"Yes," Quince said. "It is good."

A knock on Leslie's bedroom door awakened her
the next morning. She pulled the pillow over her
head, but the door opened and a maid walked in
and started raising the shades. Sunlight streamed
into her room.

"Oh," Leslie moaned. "Oh, what is it? Why are
you in here?"

"*Señor* Goodpasture is waiting breakfast for
you, *Señorita*," the maid said.

"What time is it?"

"It's six-thirty, ma'am," the maid said.

"*Six-thirty?*"

"*Si.*"

Leslie yawned. "Tell Mr. Goodpasture I thank
him very much, but it's just too early for breakfast
now."

"Please, *Señorita*," the maid said with a sense of
desperation in her voice. "Please get up. *Señor*
Goodpasture is not a man one says no to."

"Oh, is that so?" she said. She sat up in bed
then, and ran her hand through her hair. "Well,
we'll just see about—" She saw her trunks and
baggage then, and through the open door of the
closet all of her clothes. "How did that happen?"
she asked, pointing to her clothes. "I left those
clothes at Three Crowns. How did they get over
here?"

"I don't know, *Señorita*," the maid replied. "I
hung them up for you at five this morning. They

were in the hallway outside the door to your bedroom."

"But I don't understand," Leslie said. She got
out of bed and walked over to the closet and
looked through the clothes hanging there, as if to
reassure herself that they were, indeed, her own
clothes.

"What may I tell *Señor* Goodpasture?" the maid
asked anxiously.

Leslie sighed. "Never mind," she said. "I'm wide
awake now. I might as well get dressed and join
him."

The maid smiled at the welcome news and
withdrew, and Leslie began to select her dress.
She found a pink dress with deceptively simple
lines, and with lacework on the bodice which was
incredibly delicate and beautiful. Then she took
pains getting dressed, purposely taking as long as
possible, to show Charles that though he might
not be a man one said no to, she was a woman who
could tell anyone to wait until her own good time.

Charles stood as soon as Leslie stepped into
the dining room, and the look of pleasure on his
face was ample reward for the pains Leslie had
taken in getting dressed.

"Good morning," Charles said. "I'm glad you
could join me for breakfast."

Charles was wearing an open-necked shirt and
no jacket. It was the first time she had ever seen
him without a jacket and tie, and this way he
looked younger than she had imagined. He was
sun-tanned and slim, and though the grey at his
temples was still prominent, his hair and moustache seemed even darker. He came around to

hold her chair while one of the maids began spooning scrambled eggs from a silver chafing dish onto a plate.

"That's plenty," Leslie said, holding up her hand. "I've never discovered what attraction large breakfasts hold for Americans."

"I want to apologize for my mode of dress today," Goodpasture said. "But I have to look over some of the ranch. Perhaps you would like to join me?"

"All right," Leslie said, noticing that a small silver pot of tea sat before her place. "I suppose I would be interested at that."

"In case you may wish to change, your things are here."

"Yes, so I discovered," Leslie said, and though she had forgotten that for a moment, when he mentioned it to her she felt a tremor of agitation once more. "Why did you do that?"

"You are planning to sell Three Crowns, are you not?"

"Yes."

"Then I must confess to a personal reason," Charles said. "I didn't want you to stay over there and become sentimentally attached to the ranch, so that you might change your mind again. I know it was presumptuous of me, but, well, that's the reason and I shall be honest about it. I hope you will forgive me."

Charles's candidness caught Leslie off-guard, and the anger fell away. She smiled despite herself. "It was presumptuous of you," she said. "But, if you insist upon offering me the hospitality of your home, then I shall accept it."

"Good for you," Charles said.

They talked through breakfast, and Leslie began telling him stories of her school days, and the friends she had left behind in England. Charles had travelled to England a few years before, and finding someone who knew some of the same places she knew was almost like finding someone from home. He was an interesting conversationalist, and a very charming man, and Leslie discovered that she was enjoying her breakfast a great deal.

And she was also eating a great deal. She finished her third piece of toast before she realized what she was doing.

"My goodness," she said. "I have *never* eaten so much."

"It's the clear, Western air," Charles said. "It gives one a quite substantial appetite."

"Did my father develop such an appetite?" Leslie asked.

"Your father? Well, I . . . I really don't know."

"I thought you said he was your best friend."

"Well, he was," Charles said. "And my neighbor, but you must realize that his ranch is fifteen miles away. It isn't uncommon out here to go for months at a time and never see your nearest neighbor—especially if you are a good rancher, because then you've no time for socializing."

"Was my father a good rancher?"

Charles took a pipe from its holder, filled it with tobacco, then took a match. He held it up, meeting her eyes and silently questioning whether he could smoke, and when she nodded yes, he lit the pipe before he answered her question.

"Your father was a very good man," Goodpasture said. "I don't think anyone who ever met him ever had anything but good to say of him. He was hard-working, honest, and generous to a fault."

"But, was he a good rancher?" Leslie asked, again.

"Alas, my dear, I'm afraid not," Charles said. "And one of the reasons he was not, was that selfsame streak of generosity. He did not choose his employees with his brain, he chose them with his feelings. If he liked someone, or if he felt sorry for someone, he would hire them. The most incompetent and lazy cowboys always knew he had a job on Three Crowns Ranch."

"Are you referring to Quince?" Leslie asked.

"It isn't my place to say," Sharles said. "But I know that your father was genuinely fond of Parker, and I've no doubt but that Parker was genuinely fond of your father. But, through your own observation, you have noticed a lack of dependibility in Parker. And this fellow, Rufus, who works as a cook and all-around handy man, he is as strange a duck as one is ever likely to encounter."

"Rufus is a nice man," Leslie said defensively. She remembered the tea and biscuits Rufus had gone to the trouble to prepare for her.

"He's a fiercely loyal man, I know that," Charles said. "But there is something about him, something I can't quite put my finger on. I am always uneasy around him."

"What will happen to all of my father's men when you buy Three Crowns?"

"Any man that wants to keep his job will be able to," Charles said. "I can always use good men. But I won't keep on a sluggard, so he'll have to prove himself to me. As for Parker and Rufus, why, I'd just as soon not have them around the place, and I imagine they'd just as soon not work for me anyway."

"Oh, Charles, I would hate to think that I am the cause of them losing their jobs," Leslie said.

"Lady Leslie, the truth is, even if you kept Three Crowns, you would wind up having to fire Parker anyway. He couldn't handle it before the water supply was cut off. Without a source of water, he would run you into bankruptcy so fast that you would wind up with nothing."

"Why was the water supply cut off?" Leslie asked. "You must know that Quince thinks you are to blame."

"Yes," Charles said. "I know he feels that, and I can't say that I blame him. After all, I stand to gain everything by it, while Three Crowns, and most of the other ranchers around here, are losing in the deal. But the truth is, Mr. Cauldwell has made surveys all through here, and he determined that too much water was being diverted away from the main river channels. He decided that if the water didn't flow through the channels they were supposed to flow through, all this land here would eventually become desert land. I just happen to be the lucky one. The main channel flows right through my land."

"If Three Crowns has no source of water, why would you want it?"

"Because it has excellent grasslands," Charles said. "And I have a source of water, I could let my stock wander onto Three Crowns for grass, and back to the river for water. I have offered, by the way, a water-lease arrangement to all the ranchers who were effected by this project. Some have accepted me, some have rejected it, and others have sold out to me."

"Was my father going to accept the water lease arrangement?"

"Oh, I'm certain he would have," Charles said easily, "though Parker was very loud in his opposition to it."

"As far as I'm concerned, that's all the more reason for me to sell," Leslie said. "Without water, I don't see how we could raise cows, and if Quince won't agree to your water-lease arrangement, then there is nothing else we can do."

"Precisely my point," Charles said. He stood then, and walked over to pull her chair back for her. "Now, Lady Leslie, how would you like to ride around and view the ranch?"

"I would love to," Leslie agreed. "But I insist that you not call me *Lady* Leslie. Leslie will do."

When they walked through the front door, Leslie noticed that a small, spring buckboard had been drawn up, and Charles started toward it.

"Charles, couldn't we see better if we rode horses?" Leslie asked.

Charles stopped with his hand resting on the side of the buckboard, and looked back toward Leslie. "Can you ride a horse?" he asked.

"If you'll give me a moment to change clothes, I'll show you," Leslie said.

"I'm not certain we have a lady's sidesaddle," Charles protested.

"A side-saddle?" Leslie said. "No, thank you. That is the most foolish invention ever contrived. I will ride in a conventional saddle, if you don't mind. And, Charles, do get me a spirited animal."

Moments later, Leslie returned, this time wearing a riding habit. Charles, who had been to England, recognized the attire, and he smiled. "Leslie, I hope you don't expect a leisurely ride though the English countryside. We'll be encountering fences, bushes, gulleys, all sorts of obstacles. One doesn't take an easy ride around a ranch."

"I'll do my best," Leslie said, and she swung up onto her mount. Then, before Charles could react, she slapped her feet against the horse's sides, urging him forward. The horse burst away as if shot from a cannon, and Leslie, leaning low over his neck, headed for the white picket fence which surrounded the lawn. With a gentle urge, the horse was up and over, as gracefully as a flying bird, then she took him down the banks of a creek and across. His hooves sent out a shower of silver as he went through the water, then, with hardly a break in stride, the horse was up the opposite bank. Once there, Leslie turned the animal and brought him back over the same route, again a fan of water, a soaring negotiation of the fence, then she reined up smartly in front of Charles, and leaned over to pat the animal's neck. She smiled at Charles.

"Will that do?" she asked.

"Where did you learn to ride like that?" Charles

asked, staring at her in open-mouthed amazement.

"In England, we do it for sport," Leslie said. "We select a church steeple off in the distance, then ride straight for it, negotiating all obstacles in the path. That's given the sport its name."

"Steeplechase," Charles said. "Yes, I've seen it done. But I had no idea you were so adept."

"Then we can see your ranch?"

"Yes, of course," Charles said. He hung a basket on the saddle pommel. "We'll even find a spot for a picnic," he said, patting the basket.

Despite Leslie's proven equestrian ability, no such skill was necessary as they rode about the ranch. The ride, as Charles had suggested, was considerably more strenuous than a leisurely stroll along a smooth road, but it did not come close to taxing Leslie's horsemanship.

The more Leslie saw of the ranch, the more inspiring this vast country became to her. There were mountains all around, some so close she could see every tree, rock, and draw, and others so far away that they formed only an indistinct purple line on the distant horizon. Soon it became obvious that their path was taking them up one of the mountains, for as she turned to look behind her, she saw the valley dropping away.

They had climbed for nearly an hour, with the last ten minutes taxing the animals and their riders, when Charles spoke.

"We'd better get off and lead them the rest of the way."

"The rest of the way where?" Leslie said, and now she was breathing quite heavily from the exertion. "If we go any higher, I fear we shall bump into the moon."

Charles laughed. "It's just a little way further," he said. "And I do want you to see it. It is a perfect place for our picnic."

"All right," Leslie said, and bending forward at the waist to maintain her balance, she led her horse on up the trail behind Charles.

They didn't speak for the next several moments, because speaking would have required too much breath. Finally they reached the very top, and Charles pointed to a rock overhang.

"That's where we're going," he said. "I want you to take a look."

Leslie followed him to the lookout point, then drew her breath in sharply. The whole valley floor was displayed before her eyes, and it looked like a miniature table-model of a landscape. She could see all the buildings of Mountain Shadow, and she could even see Three Crowns, though from this distance she saw little more than the distinct mountain with the three tops. She could see Sweet-grass, too, and the railroad, now a long, thin, pencil line across the valley floor. It was an incredible sight.

"It's beautiful," she said.

"I hoped you would like it," Charles said. He had carried the basket with him, and he opened it, and pulled out a bottle of champagne.

"Ah, it is still cool," he said. "It was well cooled when we left, and I had it packed in a bag of sawdust."

"Champagne?" Leslie said, smiling a quizzical

smile. "I can't believe all this. Why have you gone to so much trouble?"

"Because I find you a fascinating woman," Charles said, popping the cork from the bottle. He poured a glass and handed it to her. "Prosit."

9

THE LAW OFFICES of Poindexter, Heckemeyer and Norton were across the street from the Bank of Sweetgrass. The building was no more nor less elaborate than any of the other buildings along Front Street in Sweetgrass, but it enjoyed a certain degree of uniqueness in that it was owned by the three lawyers and not rented from Charles Goodpasture, as were most of the other business establishments in town.

Leslie, who had spent the last three days as Charles's houseguest, rode into town with him in the carriage in order to hear the reading of the will. Afterwards, she planned to conclude the sale of Three Crowns to Charles.

"I have the bill of sale already drawn up," Charles said. "And, I have a bank draft for the money." He patted his inside jacket pocket, and smiled. "By lunchtime, you will be a wealthy woman, Leslie."

"There's Quince," Leslie said, pointing to the foreman who was just getting off his horse in front of the office.

"What is *he* doing here?" Charles asked in a disapproving tone.

"I would expect him to be here," Leslie said. "In fact, I'm certain that father remembered Quince in his will. After all, Quince was almost like a son to him."

"Yes, of course, you are right," Charles said. "It is just that he treated you so rudely the other night that I wouldn't think he would have the nerve to show his face around here."

Quince looked back toward the approaching carriage only briefly, then, without a wave or the slightest acknowledgment, he walked across the porch and on into the offices.

"I see he is still being rude," Charles noted.

"Perhaps he is just embarrassed by the other night," Leslie suggested.

"You are too kind to him," Charles replied.

Andrew pulled the team to a halt in front of the offices, then stepped down to lower the assist step so that Leslie and Charles could get out.

"Remain with the carriage, Andrew," Charles said.

"Yes, sir."

Charles held the door open for Leslie, then followed her inside. A law clerk was waiting just inside the door, and he pointed to another door.

"Mr. Poindexter will be reading the will in there," he said. "Just go right on in."

"Thank you," Leslie said.

A clock ticked loudly on the wall of Poindexter's office, and the hands on the Roman numeral face pointed to three minutes after ten. Quince was standing across the room finding something of great interest to look at through the window, while Poindexter, a small, bald-headed man, was sitting behind his desk, industriously polishing his wire-frame glasses.

"Good morning, Quince," Leslie said.

Quince looked around, and the expression on his face was one of shame. "I . . . I'm sorry about the other night," he mumbled.

"Oh, don't give it a second thought," Leslie said graciously.

"Abner, let's get on with this, shall we?" Charles said. "I want to get everything taken care of so I can transfer the property."

"Yes," Abner said, fixing the glasses upon his nose, and looping the hooks over his ears, one at a time. "Yes, I have it right here." He reached for a heavy brown envelope, and held it up. "Won't you all please be seated?"

There were two chairs drawn up in front of Abner's desk, and Leslie sat in one while Charles sat in the other. Quince settled into a large, leather couch over near the wall. He laid his ankle across his knee, and hung his hat from the toe of his boot.

"I must have two additional witnesses," Abner said. "If you'll excuse me for a moment, I will get my law partners."

Abner stepped out of the office, leaving Charles, Leslie and Quince alone.

"Are you enjoying your stay at Mountain Shadow?" Quince asked.

"Yes, very much. It's really quite a lovely place," Leslie said.

"You must come out this evening," Goodpasture put in. "We are having a going away dinner for Leslie."

"Thank you for the invite," Quince said. "But I have chores to do at the ranch."

Charles laughed. "Why waste your time?" he asked. "In less than an hour, Three Crowns will belong to me."

"Leslie, don't sell it to him," Quince said quickly. "Please, reconsider."

"I'm sorry," Leslie said. "My mind is made up."

"If you don't—" Quince stopped, then started again. "If you don't have any confidence in me, then hire another foreman. But I beg of you, don't sell."

"Quince, please," Leslie said. "Let's not get into an argument over it. I intend to sell, and that's final."

"But your father—"

"My father is deceased," Leslie said, almost screaming, "and I don't think it is fair of you to bring him into this conversation."

Quince sighed, and settled back into the sofa, just as Abner came into the office with his two associates. One was a large man with a round smiling face. The other, though much bigger than Abner, wasn't nearly as large as the first.

"Lady Leslie," Abner said, indicating the larger of the two men. "This is Dan Heckemeyer. And this," the other man stepped forward, "is Tony Norton. They are my associates, and will witness the reading of the will."

Leslie nodded at the two men, who then stepped to one side to await the reading.

Abner examined the seal on the envelope. "The seal was placed here on October 11, 1889, and is unbroken. I am now breaking it." He opened the flap and pulled out a paper, then looked up, dramatically. "The Will," he said.

Abner cleared his throat and examined the will, then began to read;

"I Stuart Northington Kendrake, Earl of Northington, being of sound mind and body, do hereby make and declare, this, my last will and testament, to wit:

"My title, Earl of Northington, which is of no value in America, and of only questionable value in England, being in England a title only, and without holdings, I bequeath to the next legally constituted Kendrake in the line of succession, who shall remain in England.

"To each cowboy in my service at the time of my demise, I leave the horse he rides for me, and all such tack and gear as he normally uses, which may be owned by me. To Rufus Butler, my cook and general handyman, I leave a horse of his choosing from the remuda, gear and tack, my Winchester, and the sum of two hundred fifty dollars in cash.

"To Quince Parker, my foreman, a man who was like a son to me, and in whom I have exhibited the utmost faith and trust, I leave five thousand head of cattle, and one thousand dollars in cash."

"Well, Mr. Goodpasture, at least I know five thousand head you won't be buying," Quince said.

"Oh?" Goodpasture replied. "Where are you going to keep them, on a cloud?"

"Gentlemen, please," Abner said, agitatedly, "don't interrupt the reading of the will. Surely Mr. Kendrake's memory deserves more respect than this."

"I'm sorry," Quince said. "You are right, of course."

Abner cleared his throat and went on.

"To my beloved daughter, Leslie, I leave everything else, to include all land, rolling and fixed equipment, buildings and outbuildings, and all such monies as may remain in my account or accounts at the time of my death." Abner picked up another sheet of paper and read from it. "Mr. Kendrake's accounts totaled $5,478.32 at the time of his death. Deducting Mr. Butler's two hundred fifty dollars, and Mr. Parker's one thousand dollars, there remains the amount of $4,228.32."

"There would have been more," Quince put in. "But we had a very hard winter, and Mr. Kendrake spent over seven thousand five hundred dollars, replacing stock."

"That's most convenient for you, isn't it?" Charles said.

"Charles, please," Leslie said. "I harbor no resentment. I think it is only fair that Quince receive a just settlement from my father's estate. Besides, the price you have offered me for the land is a very generous one."

"Yes," Charles said. He smiled. "And I think we should get on with our business now. That is, if you are finished, Mr. Poindexter?"

"Not quite," Abner replied.

"What else is there?" Charles asked.

"There is a codicile to the will which may bear on Lady Leslie's right to sell."

"What are you talking about?" Charles asked angrily. "Read it, man, read it."

Abner cleared his throat again, and read the last paragraph of the will. "As my daughter is, and has been in England, it would be irresponsible of me to leave her this inheritance, without constructing a means of preserving it. She is unschooled in the ways of cattle ranching, or business of any kind, and therefore, I leave as executor of the estate, my friend and confidant, Quince Parker. Quince shall have absolute and final authority with regard to all business dealings pertaining to Three Crowns, for a period of no less than five years from the reading of the will. This includes buying and selling of stock, equipment, or land. It is my hope that in establishing such a condition to this inheritance, I protect my beloved daughter from any evils which may befall her at the hands of unscrupulous businessmen."

"Do you mean that I *can't* sell Three Crowns?" Leslie said, white with shock.

"I'm afraid not," Abner replied, laying the paper on his desk and removing his glasses. He wiped them very carefully, then put them back into their case. "At least, not unless you have Mr. Parker's concurrence."

"But that isn't *fair*," Leslie said. "Why would he do such a thing?"

"As he explained in the will, Lady Leslie, he wanted only to protect you."

"But, but surely he didn't mean from Mr. Goodpasture?" Leslie said.

"Leslie, don't you understand?" Quince said. "That is exactly whom he *did* mean. Charles Goodpasture is the biggest crook in Wyoming."

"That kind of talk can get you into serious trouble, Parker," Charles said angrily, pointing a menacing finger at Quince.

"You are a crook, Goodpasture, and everyone knows it," Quince said.

"I, I don't suppose you will consent to the sale Charles and I have arranged?" Leslie said.

Quince smiled a slow, easy smile of victory. "No," he said. "I don't suppose I will."

"See here, Parker, this is an outrage!" Charles said. "Just what in the hell do you propose to do with that ranch?"

"The same thing I've been doing with it," Quince answered. "I'm going to raise cattle there."

"Mr. Parker, I did not come to America, only to have my life dictated by some, some *cowboy*!" Leslie said hotly.

"I'm only doing this for you," Quince said.

"Don't you understand? I don't *want* your help!"

"Well, according to the law, you have it, whether you want it or not," Quince said.

"Well, we'll just see about that, too," Charles put in. "As you are a party to the will, I feel there may very well be a conflict of interest in your administering the remainder of the estate."

"What do you mean?" Leslie asked. "You mean there is a possibility that the will can be broken?"

"I think a good lawyer can do it, yes," Charles said.

"That would take a court order," Poindexter said. "And the Circuit Rider won't be back until September."

"Oh, September?" Leslie moaned. "Does that

mean I shall have to wait until September before I can sell this ranch?"

"Even then, he may not rule in your favor," Poindexter warned. "It is a difficult thing to break a will."

"Leslie, you are welcome to stay on as a guest of Mountain Shadows for as long as it may take to resolve this."

"Thank you," Leslie said. She looked angrily at Poindexter, and at his law partners. "Now, Mr. Goodpasture, I believe you said that I would require a good barrister. Do you know a *good* barrister?" she asked. "I see none in this room," she added pointedly.

10

CHARLES HAD PLANNED a party to celebrate the transfer of Three Crowns, and even though the sale didn't take place, the invitations had already been issued, so the party took place that evening anyway. Phaetons, broughams, landaulets, and other elegant carriages were joined in the procession toward the big house by such common conveyances as buggies, buckboards, wagons, and even a few folk on horseback. As the mountains purpled in the evening shadows, the partygoers moved inside the big house.

Music spilled out of the house and rolled across the lawn to welcome the arriving guests. The music was not from the ordinary party band of five or six pieces, but from an entire orchestra, full of woodwinds, and brasses, strings, and an entire range of percussion instruments, hired by Charles and brought from Cheyenne in his train.

Inside the massive house the party seemed to flow and groups would form, chat for an instant, then explode with a burst of laughter and the participants would go to some other place and coalesce into new groups with just as short a life-span.

In the main dining room, a table which could

seat forty for formal dining was now laden with hors d'œuvres, glistening hams, and salads of every hue and design. Outside the house on the lawn, a spitted steer turned slowly over a huge barbecue pit, filling the air with a delicious aroma.

There were several bars working, one in the parlor, one in the game room, and another in the main ballroom. For those who didn't care to go to a bar, waiters glided from room to room, carrying silver trays laden with various drinks.

"Tell me, Lady Leslie," one of the guests was saying. "Does this party come up to the bashes you lords 'n ladies have in England?"

"Oh, this is much, much grander," Leslie said graciously.

"But we don't have the dukes and earls and such here," another said.

"Ah, but you have the same thing, only you aren't titled," Leslie said. "In England, anyone who owns an estate of five hundred acres or more would have to be titled."

"Five hundred acres?" one of the others scoffed. He laughed. "Well, hell, we've got chicken farms that big!"

"Precisely my point," Leslie said.

"Well, *Lord* Tate, would you care to mosey on back and get a bit to eat?" one of the men asked teasingly of another.

"Thank you, Sir Collins. I don't mind if I do." Both men laughed and started toward the table.

"Ah, there you are," Charles said, approaching Leslie, and the group surrounding her. "Come with me, I've someone I want you to meet."

"Excuse me," Leslie said with a gracious smile,

and she walked away with Charles. "Who is it?" she asked.

"No one," Charles said. He looked at her and smiled. "I could say I was just rescuing you from those men, but in truth, I was slightly jealous and wanted you for myself."

"Whatever your reason, I consider it a rescue," Leslie said. She looked around the room. "Where on earth did everyone come from? For as far as the eye can see out here there is nothing but open space. One might get the impression that the land is virtually uninhabited. But this crowd . . . everyone in the state of Wyoming must be here."

"Not only Wyoming, my dear, but from a few neighboring states as well," Charles said. "The biggest cattle barons in the West are here tonight. Look over there, that man is John Wesley Iliff. And there is Alexander Swan." Charles sighed. "He is a wild man, and mark my words, he is headed for ruin."

"Why do you say that?"

"He has no sense of value," Charles said. "He spends with reckless abandon, as if certain that there will never be a tomorrow."

"Ah, Charles, my dear fellow," someone said. Leslie saw a tall man, with a full head of snow white hair, and a bushy white beard. "So this is the delightful Lady Leslie?"

"Hello, Conrad," Charles said. "Lady Leslie, this is Conrad Kohrs. He owns a small farm in Montana, where he raises milk cows."

"Herefords, my dear fellow," Kohrs said. "Herefords. You see," he explained to Leslie. "I'm trying to convince the other addle-brained cattlemen around here that Hereford cattle are the cattle of the future. Longhorns are mangy, tough, evil-spirited things. Herefords are a much more docile breed, and I tell you the meat from a Hereford is far superior, too."

"That may be so," Charles countered. "But a longhorn can take care of himself. Herefords have to be tended and wet-nursed. And the public is so beef-hungry that they will buy anything we ship back to the East."

"Oh, speaking of the East, Augusta is going to New York in September for a visit to the Metropolitan Opera."

"Augusta?"

"His wife," Charles explained. "She is making a single-handed effort to bring a little culture to the range."

"Well, she'll never do it," Kohrs said. "Any more than I'm going to convince everyone to give up on longhorns."

"Maybe you should see the light and go back to longhorns," Charles suggested, "before you wind up broke."

"Oh, that doesn't frighten me," Kohrs said. "I guess I've been broke oftener than any man in Montana. Anyway, as I was saying, Augusta is going to New York in September, so if you are interested, Lady Leslie, drop us a line and she'll make arrangements for you to go with her."

"Why, I thank you," Leslie said. "I might consider it, if I am still here."

"Oh, there's Dudley Snyder," Kohrs said. "I wonder if I can convince him to switch to Herefords." Kohrs hurried over to the tall thin man, who was sipping water and looking on with disapproval at the quantities of whiskey being consumed.

"I'm a little surprised Snyder showed up," Charles said after Kohrs left, "he's such a teetotaler. But he's also a good businessman, and he wouldn't let the opportunity to find out what all the other cattlemen are doing pass by. Come along, let's get some fresh air.".

Leslie walked with Charles through French doors onto a veranda which completely encircled the house, and once outside, they strolled along the flagstone deck until they were behind the house. Here, the music and the noise of the crowd was subdued, and though there were many people present, Leslie managed to enjoy a sense of temporary isolation. She climbed up on the waist-high, wide-topped stone fence that guarded the edge of the porch, and sat there leaning against one of the many pillars that rose to support the roof. She looked out across the gently sloping lawn and into the clear night sky.

There was a quarter moon out, and it wasn't so bright that it obscured the stars, so Leslie could enjoy their diamond shine, scattered across the sky.

"It seems odd," she said, "to look at these stars and realize they are the same stars one sees in the night sky over England." She pulled her knees up and when she did so, her dress fell back so that her legs were exposed from her knees down. She wrapped her arms around her legs and rested her chin on her knees. The position was comfortable, and the cool breeze felt good against her legs.

Charles lit a pipe and the top of the bowl glowed red as he took a puff. "Look at that star," he said, pointing to one. "It looks like a gold nugget that someone just hung in the sky."

"That's Arcturus," Leslie said.

"You know the names of the stars?" Charles asked in surprise.

Leslie smiled. "Yes. I've always been interested in them. I think it is because I have been separated from those who are dear to me so often, and I would look at the stars, realizing that they could see the same ones and, somehow, it made us seem closer."

"Look!" Charles said. "One of them is falling!" he laughed. "I arranged that just for you."

"That is most kind of you," Leslie said with a little laugh.

"I've often searched for them when they fall," Charles said. "I would like to see one. I bet it would look like a diamond."

Leslie laughed. "No, not really. They are nothing but burned-out cinders. But I rather like the way you imagine them. To me they are more than just burned-out cinders. They are little pieces of heavenly bodies. Most people's view of a meteor is one of beauty, flashing through the night sky. I think they are just about the most beautiful thing in the world."

"No," Charles said easily. "I can think of something much more beautiful."

"What could be more beautiful?" Leslie asked.

"You," Charles said. He leaned forward and kissed her, with little fanfare and no warning. The move caught Leslie by surprise and she was unable to react until it was too late.

The kiss was not demanding in its hunger and urgency, as had been Quince's kiss on the trail on the way out to Three Crowns on that first day. But, like Quince's kiss, it was overpowering in the sensations it evoked. It was the kiss of one who was skilled, and thus immensely stimulating, even though devoid of the raw passion that had been present with Quince. It left Leslie's senses reeling and her mind spinning.

"Please," she said, turning her head away, gasping to recover her breath. "Please don't."

"Very well," Charles said. "I've no wish to force myself upon an unwilling woman."

"It's not that I'm unwilling . . . I mean ungrateful," Leslie said, correcting herself quickly, "for everything you have done. But I think I would rather we didn't do this."

What is it? Leslie asked herself. What was it about her body that would allow men to arouse her so easily? First it was Quince, and now Charles. Both had caused her body to flare into a quick heat of passion, to wish that it would go on, though all reason and propriety demanded that she stop.

This was something she had never experienced before. Perhaps it was the raw power of this great West, or the handsome virility of these magnificent men. She looked into the heavens and saw more flashes from the meteor shower.

Whatever it was, she thought, she was like those meteors. She could no more control her feelings than those meteors could remain fixed in place. And like the bursts of light of those remote flaming stars, her own passions flared with these two men.

The fire had burned down so that the flickering flames were gone, and there remained only the glowing red and orange of the embers. An open can of beans sat on a flat rock near the fire, and a small wisp of steam curled from the top. Two men sat near the fire waiting for the beans to warm. One of them leaned over to look into the can.

"Looks like it's about ready," he said. "We'll cut up a pepper or two and it'll be a fine meal."

"It's a hell of a way from being a meal, no matter what you do to it," the second cowboy snarled. Out in the darkness a calf, separated from the others by a casual shifting of the herd, bawled in fright, to be answered by the reassuring call of its equally anxious mother.

"Hell, I didn't say I would keep house for you, Simmons, I just said I would ride night-hawk with you," the cowboy over the beans said with a chuckle.

"How come you ridin' night-hawk, Quince? You are the top dog on this place. Hell, they's not a man-jack didn't hear about the readin' of the will today. A big portion of these cows is yours."

Quince chuckled again. "Maybe that's why I'm here," he said. "I gotta look out after my interest." He tasted a spoonful of beans. "Oh, I love 'em," he said. "They're great."

Simmons held out his plate, and Quince spooned

half the can onto it. Simmons took a mouthful, then made a face. "I'll tell you one thing, boss. You sure as hell are easy to please. If you ever get hitched up, your wife's gonna have an easy row to hoe."

"Yeah," Quince said. He took another mouthful. "*If* I ever get hitched up."

"You know, Quince, me 'n some of the other boys, well, this may not be none of our business or nothin', but, well, we was sort'a thinkin' that maybe you 'n Lady Leslie might hit it off."

"You're right," Quince said.

"You mean you hit it off?"

"No. I mean you're right about it bein' none of your business," Quince said.

"Well, don't get sore, boss. We didn't mean nothin' by it," Simmons said.

Both men heard it at the same time. It was a quiet sound, a subtle sound which the average person would have never discerned, but it stood out sharply on the senses of the men. The sound of horses' hooves, as distinguished from the sound of the hooves of thousands of milling cattle.

"You ain't expectin' no relief rider tonight, are you?" Simmons asked.

"No," Quince said, and the beans were tossed aside as both men moved quickly toward their rifles.

Quince made a silent motion with his hand to send Simmons around one side, while he started around the other, both men moving stealthily through the night, toward the sound of the intruder.

Quince ran through the night, crouched low, watching the ground before him in the dim moonlight, so that he didn't trip. Off to his right was the low, large mass of cattle, the herd he and Simmons were watching. Beyond the herd the quiet, looming mountains, so that the horizon was blocked out, and it was not possible to see in silhouette anyone who might be sneaking around.

Quince followed Tuttle Creek up to a higher elevation. It was this Tuttle Creek and its meager source of water which had helped to sustain the herd since Indian Creek was dammed. Wagon loads of water brought in from the river, a few strategic windmill wells and watering troughs, and this creek had kept the cows from hurting too badly, but even as he moved through it now, Quince couldn't help but noticing how little water remained. Within a month, it would all be gone.

Quince reached a rock outcropping about three quarters of the way up the draw, and he lay flat on it, and looked out over the herd. It was difficult to see anything more than a large, black mass.

"Quince!" Simmons yelled. "I see two men toward Devil's Butte!" A flash of fire and a rifle shot followed Simmons's call, and Quince knew that he had fired on the men.

The rifle shot startled the two horsemen into activity and they both left at a gallop. Their sudden movement, and the sound of their horses alerted Quince to their presence, and he, too, fired at them, not really trying to hit either of them, but merely trying to spur their retreat on.

"Yahoo!" Simmons yelled, firing again. "Look at them sons-of-bitches skedaddle!"

Quince hurried back down the creekbank until he returned to the fire. He had gone further than Simmons, so Simmons was already there by the time he returned.

"Who do you think that was?" Simmons asked. He was still pumped up with the excitement of the encounter, and his smile and wide eyes told Quince that Simmons had enjoyed the interruption to an otherwise boring duty. "Do you think they'll come back?"

"I doubt it," Quince said. "I'd say we frightened them off pretty good."

"Yeah, I'd say that, too," Simmons said. "Hey, you know who I bet it was?"

"Who?"

"I bet it was a couple of cattle rustlers. You know, nothin' big, just a couple of rustlers who thought they could cut out a dozen or so head."

"Yeah," Quince said. "You are probably right."

"As if no one would recognize the three crowns we got stamped right on the ass of every cow in this herd," Simmons said derisively. "You know the biggest trouble with cattle rustlers? They are dumb. They are just dumb sons-of-bitches, that's all. Hell, they ought to know better'n to mess with Three Crowns cows when me'n you is ridin' night-hawk."

"Yeah," Quince said, wondering if that was all there was to it. "Well, the shooting has the cows spooked. We'd better ride around a bit to calm them down."

"Sure thing, Quince."

"Oh, and Simmons, if you see anything strange, let me know."

"Strange? Like what? What do you mean?"

"I'm not sure," Quince said. "I just have an uneasy feeling, that's all."

11

THE FIRST PINK fingers of dawn touched the sage-brush, and the light was soft and the air was cool. Quince liked the range best early in the morning. He was camped in the cool shadow of The King, the largest of the three peaks which made up the Three Crown landmark of the ranch. The last morning star made a bright pinpoint of light over the purple mountains which lay in a ragged line far to the east.

The coals from his campfire of the night before were still glowing and he threw chunks of wood on them and stirred the fire into crackling flames which danced merrily against the bottom of the suspended coffee pot. A rustle of wind through feathers caused him to look up just in time to see a golden eagle diving on its prey. The eagle swooped back into the air carrying a tiny desert mouse which kicked fearfully in the eagle's claws. A rabbit bounded quickly into its hole, frightened by the sudden appearance of the eagle.

Quince poured himself a cup of coffee and sat down to enjoy it. It was black and steaming and he had to blow on it before he could suck it through his lips. He watched the sun peak above the Three Crowns, then stream brightly down onto the open range land.

Simmons had taken the last ride around the herd, and Quince heard his horse coming back in.

"I tell you, that coffee smells awful good," Simmons said, swinging down from his saddle and walking toward the fire, rubbing his hands together in eager anticipation. "I wouldn't mind havin' a biscuit 'n some bacon, either."

"Rufus'll hold breakfast for us," Quince said. "I've got some jerky in my saddlebag, if you'd care for some."

"No, thank you," Simmons said. "I've et enough range candy when I had to. I don't care to eat it when I've got a real breakfast waitin' for me."

Simmons poured himself a cup of coffee, and as Quince had before him, blew on it, and sucked it noisily through his lips.

"Everything all right?" Quince asked.

"Yeah, sure, we busted up whatever plan those fellas had in mind," Simmons said. "They ain't one cow missin' as far as I can tell." Simmons laughed. "Fact is, we may have gained on the deal."

"Gained? What do you mean?"

"Over there by the washout, I found tracks comin' *into* the herd. Cow tracks. You know, I think they meant to bring a leadin' steer in, have 'im mix with the herd, then just cut away ten or twenty beeves. I've heard of that."

"Yeah," Quince said. "They do that in the slaughterhouse. They have one steer who will mingle with the herd, then lead them right through the pens for slaughter."

"Only last night it didn't work," Simmons said.

"We surprised them before they got the job done, and we ran them off before they could get their Judas steer back. He's out there with our herd yet, 'cause there ain't no tracks goin' back."

Quince chuckled. "Well, we probably saved not only a few of our cattle but the other ranchers' cattle as well. Even Goodpasture should thank us."

"Goodpasture," Simmons said with a snort. "Hell, that son-of-a-bitch was probably *behind* it."

Quince laughed, then dashed the final dregs of his coffee into the fire. "He wouldn't be the first to start his herd by throwing a long rope. Ah, I see a couple of riders come to relieve us. Let's get back in. Rufus will throw breakfast away if we aren't there in time."

Quince saddled his own horse then, and he and Simmons rode back to the house, arriving just as the other hands were preparing to begin their daily chores.

"I thought I heard gunfire last night," Rufus said, stepping onto the front porch of the cookhouse just as Quince and Simmons were dismounting. Rufus was wearing an apron which was covered with the stains of hundreds of meal preparations. Flour was on his shirt, and even as he spoke, he was kneading dough.

"We spooked a couple of rustlers," Simmons said, smiling broadly. "You should've been there —though, bein' as you don't like guns, I reckon it's a good thing you weren't."

"Yeah," Rufus said. He looked at Quince, and in that brief glance he and Quince exchanged a world of information, though not a word was spoken. "I reckon you're right at that. Come on in. I've made up some gravy to go with your biscuits."

The two hungry cowboys went into the cook-house and Rufus went in behind them. He thought about what Simmons had said, and how Simmons, as well as most of the other people who knew him now, thought he never wore a gun because he didn't like guns, couldn't handle guns. They were right about one thing—he didn't like them, they had caused him an untold amount of grief in his life. But they were wrong about the other. Not only could Rufus handle a gun, he was probably as adept with a gun as any man in the West. Legends were spun about the gunfighter who had once shot it out with three men at the same time, and, though wounded, was the only one standing when the smoke rolled away. Young boys whis-pered his name in awe, mothers used it to frighten their naughty children, and would-be gunfighters challenged him to enhance their own reputation.

It was the result of one such confrontation, which had caused Rufus, who was then known as "Ruthless" Butler, to hang up his guns.

Ruthless was sitting at his usual table in the back corner of the Bull's End Saloon in Dodge City, when the young gunsel came in.

"Bartender," the young man called. "Is there a dog-eared, rum-pot, low-assed man hanging around here who calls himself "Ruthless" Butler? I'm told he frightens little children."

The young man laughed then, and his laughter sounded like crystal breaking. There was a degree of polish to it, like the elegance of delicately blown glass, but there was a harsh, brittle edge, too, as if the ingredients had some imperfection, so that the end result was flawed.

Rufus looked at the boy, for in truth, that was all he was. He was lean and blond, and would have been handsome, except for his eyes. His eyes were pale, blue, ice-cold, and totally without feeling.

The bartender glanced toward Rufus, and Rufus shook his head in the negative.

"I'm sorry," the bartender said. "He doesn't seem to be here."

"Oh?" the boy said. He turned so that his back was against the bar, and looked out over the room at the patrons who were there. "Perhaps one of you could help me," he said. "Does anyone know where I can find Ruthless Butler?"

"What do you want with him?" one of the patrons asked. The one who spoke was a large man, with a walrus moustache which he had to wipe clean every time he took a drink of beer.

"What I want with him is none of your business, fatso," the boy said.

"Fatso!" the big man exploded. He stood up so quickly that the table and chair tumbled over with a crash. "Why you drawed-up little son-of-a-bitch, I'll break every bone in your body!"

The boy had his gun out even before the big man had finished his threat, and he pointed it at the big man, and pulled the hammer back.

"Come ahead, fat man," the boy taunted. "I'd like to watch the expression on your face when you die."

The big man stopped short, and his eyes reflected his terror of the moment.

"Tell me you are sorry," the boy said.

The large man's temple throbbed, and his face reddened, as he stared at the boy with ill-concealed anger and hate.

"Say you are sorry," the boy said again, "and I'll let the hammer down slow and easy. If you don't say it, why, it just might come down too fast and . . ." the boy shrugged his shoulders and smiled, an evil, humorless, smile. "Why, who knows what could happen?"

The man stared at the boy for several seconds. During that time his temple seemed to throb even more, and his face reddened to purple, but he said nothing.

"Say it," the boy taunted.

"For God's sake, Ed, say it!" one of the other patrons suddenly said. "The boy is going to kill you!"

"Your friend is right," the boy said, and his smile grew even broader as he took deliberate aim.

"I'm sorry!" Ed said quickly.

"Well, now," the boy taunted. He let the hammer down easily. "Do you see how easy that was?"

Ed picked up his beer and drained the whole thing, then sat down, relieved to still be alive, but showing the effects of being broken by the boy.

"Now, I shall ask again," the boy said. "Where is Ruthless Butler?"

"Who wants to know?" Rufus finally asked.

The boy turned to look toward Rufus. Rufus was eating a plate of beans, and even now he was putting a forkful in his mouth.

"Mister, are you the one who just asked that question?" the boy asked.

"Yes," Rufus said. He touched at his lips with a napkin. "I asked, who wants to know?"

"I heard what you asked, mister. You don't learn too good, do you? I thought I made it clear that I ask the questions around here. Now I'm askin' you, old man, where is Ruthless Butler?"

"Who wants to know?" Rufus asked again, and this time Rufus grinned at the boy, a grin which could have appeared on the face of Satan himself, for it was totally without mirth. "You see," Rufus went on. "I may have to kill you, and I like to know the names of those that I kill."

"*You* may have to kill *me*?" the boy said. He laughed. "Why you stinking old rum-pot, what makes you think you could—" the boy stopped in mid-sentence, and the smile froze to become a rigid thing on his face. "You," he finally said. "You are Ruthless Butler."

"That's right, son."

Now the boy laughed. "Son," he said. "You call me *son*?" The laughter fell away, and he licked his lips as he looked at Rufus. "I don't reckon you'll be finishin' your supper now."

"Oh, I reckon I will," Rufus said. "You see, killin' always dulls my appetite, so if I don't eat now, I like as not won't eat 'till tomorrow."

"What if I kill you?" the boy wanted to know.

"Then these beans are apt to be a sight better than the supper they'll be servin' in hell," Rufus said. "Now, boy, what is it? Are you wanting to make your reputation?"

The boy laughed. "Somethin' like that," he said. "I've been lookin' for you for a long time."

"I haven't been runnin', son."

"That's the second time you've called me that," the boy said. "Don't call me that again."

"What will I be calling you?"

"Anything but son," the boy said. "My mother was always partial to Paul."

"Paul?" Rufus said, looking at the boy with a slight change of expression.

The boy grinned. "Yeah," he said. "That's my middle name of course. My first name is Clayton."

"What?" Rufus said in surprise. "My God, you're—" he started, pointing his finger at the boy, but the boy interrupted him with a quick, challenging shout.

"Draw, you mangy son-of-a-bitch!"

When Rufus saw the boy raise his gun and issue his challenge, he dipped his hand to his own gun. The boy fired first, and Rufus felt the bullet hit his shoulder, burning like a hot poker. Almost at the same moment, Rufus pulled the trigger and saw a hole appear right in the middle of the boy's chest.

The expression on the boy's face changed to surprise, then pain, and finally a kind of sadness, as he slid down from the bar, making one last effort to hold himself up, just before he fell.

"Why, boy?" Rufus asked, sadly. "Why did *you* of all people come after me?"

"Why not?" the boy asked. "One killin' is pretty much like another, isn't it?" The boy coughed then, and he looked at Rufus. His eyes, which had been cold and dispassionate, suddenly grew deep, and full of fear. "Pop," he said. "I . . . " His head jerked to one side, and the eyes, though still open, dimmed.

"What did the boy call you?" the bartender asked in surprise.

Rufus held his hand across the wound on his shoulder, while blood ran between his fingers.

"He called me pop," Rufus said. "I haven't seen him since he was six months old, so I didn't recognize him when he came in. He was my son."

"Hey, Rufus. Rufus," Simmons was calling. "Have you gone deef?"

"What?" Rufus asked, blinking his eyes to shove away the memory.

"I ast' you is there any more gravy back there? I swear, that was the best-tastin' stuff I ever put in my mouth."

"Yeah," Rufus said. "Yeah, there's some more gravy. Just help yourself."

Simmons went happily to the pan, and Rufus walked over to look through the window at the vastness of the country outside. But nowhere it seemed, not even here, was there enough room for him to hide from himself.

12

UNITED STATES DEPARTMENT OF THE INTERIOR
WASHINGTON, D.C.
July 23, 1892

The Honorable Lawrence Cauldwell
Commissioner, Water Resources
Wyoming District, Laramie, Wyoming

Dear Mr. Cauldwell,

This department is in receipt of a letter, dated the 3rd instant, in which the writer, Mr. Stuart Kendrake, raises the claim that the Platte-Indian Creek project has deprived him of the water which normally flows across the land.

You are directed to visit Mr. Kendrake, and explain that the clearing out of canals and channels will increase, and not decrease the flow of water. You will also assure him that there are no plans for a dam, as he has expressed some concern about an alleged dam at the conflux of Platte and Indian Creek.

An inspector will be in your area one month from now, and he will help you explain the project to those who are apprehensive about it.

Your faithful Servant,

Robt. Winters,
Under Sec'y.

Cauldwell put the letter to one side with trembling hands, and poured himself a stiff drink. What was he going to do when the inspector arrived? There was no dam authorized, and yet, the dam at Platte and Indian Creek was most obviously there.

Goodpasture, he thought. It was Goodpasture who had persuaded him to build the dam in the first place. It was Goodpasture who convinced him that in the long run, the dam was better for the ranchers, because it would preserve the water. It was Goodpasture who had said he would guarantee that there would be no trouble as a result of building the dam.

And now, it would be Goodpasture who would have to find a way out.

Cauldwell called Goodpasture's bank in Sweetgrass, and left word for Goodpasture to come to Laramie to see him on a matter of the utmost urgency. Later, he got a return call from Goodpasture's bank, informing him that Goodpasture would be there by four o'clock, and it was nearly that now.

Cauldwell finished his drink when the door to his office opened, and Goodpasture came in.

"See here, Cauldwell," Charles said angrily.

"You know better than to call my bank and demand to see me. There is enough talk about my benefiting from the water project as it is. If it gets out that you and I are in collusion, the situation would get worse."

"It may already be worse," Cauldwell said. "Look at that letter."

Charles saw the letter laying on Cauldwell's desk, and he picked it up and read through it.

"What is the problem?" he asked.

"What is the problem? I'll tell you what the problem is," Cauldwell answered, now more agitated than before because Goodpasture was unable, or, worse, unwilling, to see the potential danger. "What is going to happen when the inspector discovers a dam where no dam should be?"

"Give him the same story you've been giving the ranchers," Charles said. "Just tell him that you had to dam Indian Creek off, because it was diverting too much water from the Platte River."

"He won't buy it," Cauldwell said.

"He will have to buy it," Charles said. "It will be up to you to sell it to him."

"That's just it," Cauldwell said. "I'm afraid. If he starts asking me questions, I don't know if I can handle it."

"Don't be such a nervous Nellie and you'll handle it just fine," Charles said. Charles smiled, and took out his pipe, then, very slowly and deliberately, began tamping the bowl. It was as if by that action he was able to calm the fears of Cauldwell, and he took a few seconds attending to his task before he spoke again. And when he did speak, he spoke in a measured, calm, voice.

"After all," he said, lighting his pipe and taking audible puffs in-between words. "Mr. Kendrake is dead now, so we won't be hearing from him again, will we? And his daughter has been convinced to sell the ranch to me as soon as she can get the will set aside so that she may do so. So there is really no problem at all."

"Oh no? What about Quince Parker? I understand he intends to stay there, and with five thousand head of cattle of his own, he now qualifies as a legitimate rancher in his own right."

Charles smiled. "I have a feeling that we won't be having any problems with Mr. Parker. Very soon now, he's going to have more troubles than he can handle, and he's not going to have time to worry about the dam, water rights, or anything else."

"What kind of trouble?" Cauldwell asked.

"The worst kind of trouble a cattleman can have," Charles said mysteriously. "And if I were you, I wouldn't want to know any more about it."

"I don't, I don't," Cauldwell said, holding up his hands. "But, Mr. Goodpasture, what are we going to do about this?" He pointed to the letter.

"You just don't worry about that," Charles said. "When the time comes, I'm certain you will handle it."

"But I was counting on you for that, Mr. Goodpasture. I went way out on a limb for you, and I'm counting on your help."

Charles stood up to leave Cauldwell's office, but before he left, he looked back at Cauldwell, and pointed at him with his pipe. "Cauldwell, when it gets right down to it, I've already paid you for your services. A little sum of ten thousand dollars, I believe, for which you were so gracious as to sign a receipt."

"Oh, my God, the receipt!" Cauldwell said, putting his hand over his mouth. "I had forgotten that you made me sign that foolish thing. Please, you mustn't ever let anyone see that! That could put me in prison!"

"Yes, it could, couldn't it?" Charles said blandly. "I should think that would be enough incentive to ensure that the government inspectors cause us no problems. Now, you find a way to handle it yourself, Cauldwell, and quit crying to me. I'm out of this deal entirely. I bought myself out when I paid you the money." Charles smiled. "Good day, Cauldwell."

Charles left Cauldwell's office, then went down the street to the office of the Wyoming Cattleman's Association where he visited for several minutes with the veterinarian, then, after concluding his business there, he stopped at a florist's to buy two dozen long-stemmed roses.

Charles had not returned in time for dinner, so Leslie ate alone. She read for a short time after the meal, then she went to her bedroom where she put on her nightgown, but she didn't go to sleep.

Leslie left the room dark, save for the soft splash of moonlight, and she walked over to the windows and looked outside. A cluster of trees waved gently in the night wind, and the leaves of one of them caught a moonbeam and scattered a burst of silver through the darkness. The fragrant scent of carefully nurtured flowers floated in from a nearby garden, and the breeze caressed the silk of her nightgown, as delicately as the most gentle kiss.

Leslie felt the nipples of her breasts tighten in the breeze, and she felt a sensual awareness, a warming of the blood, and a churning of the loins which she couldn't quite understand. And then she knew why she was experiencing such feelings. She was thinking of Quince, and Charles, and of the kisses she had shared with the two men, and of the strange reaction her body had to the kisses. In both cases the kisses brought on a heat unlike anything she had ever experienced, a pleasant sensation, and yet, in each case, there was an extreme hunger for something more.

Leslie was innocent in that she was still a virgin. No man had ever known her, though there were many who had tried, and in the velvet-blue nights in the gardens of the houses where she had attended parties in England, some had gone so far as to touch her in those forbidden places, though she had always managed to stop before things went too far.

As Leslie thought of those times in the past, and of the more recent times when she had been kissed by Quince and by Charles, her skin grew unbearably hot, and she took the nightgown off and stood nude in the soft breeze by the window. It was a delightful feeling, a bold and wonderful feeling, and for a moment she had to control the urge to shout out in exultation.

Then, several moments later, while watching the silver moon sail across the night sky, she heard a very light knock on the door.

"Who is it?" she called quietly.

"It's Charles. I have brought you a bouquet of

roses from Laramie. I want you to have them while they are still at their loveliest."

"Roses, oh, thank you, Charles."

"May I come in?"

"Wait," she called, and she looked around quickly for her nightgown. Then, in a sudden rush of bravado, she came to a decision which would have shocked her, had she stopped to consider it. She decided not to cover herself at all. She took a deep breath, as if about to plunge into an icy stream. "Come in," she called.

The door opened and closed, and Charles stepped inside. As she was standing in the shadows, her condition was not readily apparent to him.

"I'll take them to the housekeeper and have her put them in water," Charles said. "But I wanted you to smell them tonight, for they will not be nearly so sweet in the morning."

"It was very nice of you to think of me in such a way," Leslie said. And as she spoke, she moved, ever so slightly, and her body was highlighted and made mysterious and intriguing by the subtle shadows and lighting of the night. Then, Charles saw that she was, unmistakably, naked.

"Leslie," Charles said. It was only one word, but it was spoken in such a way that it was eloquent for the information it provided. Here was a word of awe, and reverence, excitement and passion.

"Are you shocked?" Leslie asked.

"Yes," Charles said.

"Do you think it evil?"

"No," Charles said. He came over to her and

she could smell the scent of him. Mingled with the fragrance of the flowers from outside, and the roses he held in his hand, there was also a hint of pipe tobacco, leather, bourbon, and his own maleness. He began removing his clothes.

"You are sure you want to do this?" he asked.

"Yes," Leslie replied.

When the last of Charles's clothes lay in a pile on the floor, and he was as naked as she, she clearly saw that he was ready for her, and she went to him and put her arms around his neck and pulled his lips down to hers. She could feel the texture of his lips as she kissed him, and her mouth opened hungrily as if she would consume him.

Soon they were in bed with their naked bodies pressed together.

"This is my first time," she whispered, and Charles, surprised by the statement, pulled away from her for just a moment, but she, eager for him, pulled him back, and then all thought was suspended save their mutual quest for pleasure.

Now the passionate hungers so long enchained were being released, and Leslie writhed in pleasure as Charles paid homage to her body. White heat flooded through her, and when Charles moved over her and drove himself deep into her, the sharp pain she felt as he entered her quickly gave way to a feeling of intense pleasure. She was lifted to dizzying heights of sensation, going from peak to peak with such rapidity that it was difficult to tell when one peak was left and another attained. Finally, a shuddering moan told her that Charles had joined her in this maelstrom of sensation, and she locked her arms around his naked back, providing him with the cushion he needed to ride out his pleasure.

They lay together for several moments afterward, and they didn't speak and they didn't touch. Leslie was still coasting down from the dizzying heights of sensation, and her body was still sensitized and glowing, like the warmth that remains in an iron long after it has been taken from a fire.

Charles reached over and laid his hand gently across her hip, across the sharpness of her hip bone and the soft yielding of her flesh. It was a proprietary move, the move of one who is confident and possessive, and rather than resenting it, Leslie felt pleasure in it. She didn't mind belonging to him.

13

"Boss, boss, wake up. Wake up, boss, we got troubles."

Quince fought against the intrusion into his sleep, but the persistent voice continued, and was joined by a hand which shook his shoulder insistantly.

"Boss, are you awake?"

Other sounds began to penetrate into Quince's consciousness. He could hear the measured breathing and snoring of other sleepers in the bunkhouse, and, from outside, the steady drumming of a heavy rain.

Quince groaned once, and rolled over in his bed. He opened his eyes and saw a bubble of golden light coming from a candle which was being held by Simmons. The candle was the only light in the great, dark room, though a sudden bolt of lightning bathed everything in featureless, harsh, and white, for the instant of its flash.

"What?" Quince asked. He sat up and put his feet on the floor, forcing himself awake enough to deal with the problem. Another flash of lightning disclosed the sleeping forms of the other men, accenting the untimeliness of the hour. With no one in the Bighouse, Quince could have slept there if he had chosen to do so, and no one would have said anything about it. But he slept in the bunkhouse with the others because he preferred to sleep there. "Simmons, what time is it?" Quince asked.

"It's about four thirty in the morning, I reckon," Simmons said.

Quince reached for his trousers and began pulling them on. He knew that Simmons wouldn't awaken him at four-thirty in the morning unless there was a legitimate reason to do so. "What's up?" he asked.

"Rufus said I should let you see for yourself," Simmons said.

"Rufus? What does he have to do with it?"

"He's already up startin' the breakfast," Simmons said. "I stopped in to get a cup of coffee, and mentioned what I found to him. I was going to let it wait 'till mornin', but he says I should come get you now."

"All right," Quince said, pulling on his boots. He reached for his own slicker, which hung from a wooden peg over his bed. "I'm ready."

The cookhouse was only a few yards distant from the bunkhouse, and Quince and Simmons hurried through the dark and the rain until they reached that welcome haven.

Inside the cookhouse Quince was greeted with cheerful light, snug dryness, and the welcome aroma of brewing coffee.

"Here," Rufus said, setting a cup of coffee on a table in front of Quince. "Did Simmons tell you what's wrong?"

"No," Quince said. He wrapped his hands around the coffee mug, enjoying the pleasant warmth of the steaming coffee, then he lifted it to his lips and took a slurping drink.

"Good, for I told him to say nothing," Rufus said very mysteriously. "I want you to take a ride with me."

Quince gave a small smile. "I suppose it's important, or you wouldn't be asking me to go out in weather like this."

"I reckon it's 'bout the most important thing on this ranch right now," Rufus said. Rufus looked at Simmons. "Simmons, I got some biscuits in the oven, and some more rolled. When these is done, you take 'em out 'n put in the other pan."

"I don't know nothin' 'bout cookin'," Simmons complained. "I'm a cow-puncher."

"You know what a biscuit looks like when it's done, don't you?"

"Well, yeah, sure, but—"

"That's all you got to know," Rufus said, and he said it in a way that precluded any further discussion. "Come on, boss," he said. "As soon as we get there, you'll understand what has to be done."

Quince took one last swallow of his coffee then followed Rufus outside. Then ran quickly through the rain to the barn, then selected two mounts and saddled them.

The rain continued to fall as they rode. It slashed against them and ran in cold rivulets off the folds and creases of their ponchos. It blew in sheets across the trail in front of them, and drummed wickedly into the windwhipped trees and bushes. The lightning, when it flashed, lit up the landscape in stark, harsh white. It was followed immediately by thunder, snapping shrilly at first, then rolling through the valleys, picking up the resonance of the hollows and becoming an echoing boom.

They didn't speak during the ride; conversation would have been difficult if not impossible. Besides, Rufus, by his action, had indicated that he was going to show Quince something which spoke louder than words, and therefore Quince was willing to wait.

Finally, after a ride of some six or seven miles, and with a faint light beginning to crack in the east, they reached a draw where several cows had gone to seek shelter from the wind and the rain.

"What is it?" Quince asked. "What did you want to show me?"

Rufus sat in his saddle, looking over the large, black, mass, which was the herd. Then he saw what he was looking for, and, without a word, he pointed.

Moving along the perimeter of the herd, Quince saw the cow Rufus was pointing to. It was drooling from the mouth, and as it walked it would draw up first one foot and then the other.

"My God!" Quince said, leaping quickly from the saddle and starting toward the animal. He kneeled beside the cow and looked at its hooves. On the skin, just above the hooves, there were dozens of blisters.

"Hoof-and-mouth disease," he said.

"Simmons didn't know what it was," Rufus said. "But I knowed as soon as I heered him tell of it."

Quince felt sick, and he leaned against the saddle of his horse for a moment. "That means the whole herd will have to be destroyed, and buried in quicklime," he said.

"No, it don't," Rufus said quickly.

"What do you mean it doesn't? As soon as word of this gets out, I won't have any choice. I'll be *forced* to do it."

"Boss, they ain't no word of this gonna ever get out," Rufus said. "I done told you, Simmons don't know what's wrong with the cow, 'n none of the others have heard of it yet. All we got to do is kill this one animal."

"I don't know," Quince said. "An outbreak of this stuff could wipe out every animal on the range. I'd hate to think I was responsible for that."

"You ain't responsible," Rufus said. He too, had dismounted, and was now examining the cow. "This here ain't one of our animals."

"What do you mean?"

"Look at the brand," Rufus said.

Quince returned to the cow and looked on its flank. Instead of the familiar three crown brand, he saw a bar Z burned into the flesh.

"The Bar Z?" he asked. "I don't even know that brand."

"They's a fella runs that brand down in Texas," Rufus said. "His name is Zanders. I done some work for him oncet."

"*Texas*? What the hell is a Texas cow doing way up here?"

"And a diseased one at that?" Rufus said.

"My God, Rufus, I see what you mean," Quince suddenly said. "The other night when Simmons and I were riding nighthawk, it wasn't rustlers we spooked. They weren't trying to take any of our cattle, they just wanted to leave this one!"

"That's the way I got it figured, boss," Rufus said. "Somebody wants you outta business, so they run this here sick cow in, hopin' to infect all the others."

"Goodpasture!" Quince said angrily.

"That'd be my guess," Rufus said.

"All these animals have been exposed," Quince said. "They have to be killed. But we may be able to save the rest of the herd."

"Trouble is, how are we going to kill this many cows without arousing some suspicion?" Rufus asked. "There must be nigh on to a hunnert cows in this draw."

"I don't know," Quince said. He looked at the draw and at the cows which were herded together there. "Rufus, what do you think a couple of sticks of dynamite would do right there?" he asked, pointing to a rock overhang.

"It would bring that whole side of the mountain down," Rufus said.

"And with the cows trapped in the draw below them, it would kill them and bury them at the same time. God, I feel like I'm committing murder," he said. "But I don't have any choice."

"We have to keep them inside until we can blow the rocks," Rufus said.

"I know. Suppose you build a hasty barricade across the opening here, while I ride back to the ranch and get a couple of dynamite sticks."

"Alright," Rufus agreed, and without another word, he began his task.

The ride to the ranch and back took an hour, and by the time Quince returned, the rain had stopped, and the area was now lighted by the gray, drizzling light of early morning. Rufus, Quince noted, had done his job well, for a barricade of rocks, limbs, and sagebrush, kept the animals securely pinned inside the draw.

"Rufus!" Quince called. "Rufus, where are you?"

"He is up here, with me, Mr. Parker," a voice called, and Quince, startled by the outside voice, reined up sharply. When he looked up, he felt his heart sinking, for the man who spoke was Dr. Brewster, the veterinarian at the Laramie office of the Wyoming Cattlemen's Association.

"Dr. Brewster!" Quince said. "What are *you* doing here?"

"I think you know, Mr. Parker," Brewster said. "I was told by an anonymous source that there may be a danger of hoof-and-mouth exposure on Three Crowns, so I rode out here to see for myself."

"You rode out here in the middle of the night, in the middle of a rain storm to check on such a story?" Quince asked.

"I would have come out here in a blizzard if need be," Dr. Brewster said. "Something like this could infect every cow in Wyoming. I couldn't take any chances."

"And?" Quince replied.

"And I see that the source was correct," Brewster said. "There is evidence of the disease of in this herd. At least ten cows show the signs, and there may be many more."

"I know," Quince said with a sigh. "That's why Rufus and I were going to destroy these animals."

"Not just these animals," Dr. Brewster said. "You know the law."

"The law says I must destroy every infected animal," Quince said.

"Every infected and every *exposed* animal," Dr. Brewster said. "Three Crowns is open range, is it not?"

"You know I'd never have barbed wire on the place," Quince replied.

Dr. Brewster sighed. "Then I'm sorry, Mr. Parker. But that means you must destroy every animal on the place."

"What? But, that's ridiculous!" Quince said. "We've got some cows which are way on the other side of the range, perhaps thirty miles from here."

"They will have to be destroyed as well," Brewster said.

"No! You can't do that!"

"Mr. Parker, it is my *duty* to do that," Dr. Brewster said. "And the only way I can be prevented from doing my duty is to be shot."

"That can be arranged," Rufus said coldly, and Quince realized that those were the first words Rufus had spoken since he returned.

"What?" Brewster said with sudden fear leaping to his face.

"He's not serious," Quince said. "Listen, Dr. Brewster, is there any appeal I can make to save the rest of the herd?"

"You can appeal," Dr. Brewster said. "But by the time you got a ruling from the judge, it would be too late. No, sir, Mr. Parker. I'm afraid we are going to have to destroy your entire herd. I'll be back this afternoon with a crew. At least you don't have to pay to destroy your own animals."

"Yeah," Quince said dryly. "Aren't I the lucky one, though?"

"Then I must be on my way," Brewster said, looking nervously toward Rufus as if halfway expecting him to carry out his veiled threat to arrange to have Brewster shot.

"Say, Doc, how did you find out about this anyway? Who told you?"

"I'm sorry," Dr. Brewster replied. "But it has long been our policy not to disclose the source of our information. As you can well imagine, the individual owners are not always in a hurry to tell us when a disease occurs which might result in the destruction of their animals."

"Yes," Quince said. "I can understand that."

"So, in order to protect the greater whole, we offer a sizeable reward to anyone who reports a case, and, we guarantee their anonymity as well."

"When was you told?" Rufus asked.

"I was told at about midnight last night," Brewster said. "I came out here right away."

"Whoever it was sure found out in a hurry," Rufus said. "We didn't know about it ourselves until just a little over an hour ago."

"That's odd," Dr. Brewster said.

"Yeah, ain't it," Rufus replied.

"I have to go back to town," Dr. Brewster said. "Mr. Parker, have I your word that you won't try to move the herd?"

"You don't need my word, Brewster," Quince

said. "There's no way I could do it if I wanted to."

"No," Brewster said. "No, I guess not. Well, then I suppose I shall see you later."

"Yeah," Quince said. "I suppose so."

14

THE KILLING went on with grim efficiency. More than three hundred men, dressed in long, white coats, and wearing bandanas tied across their face, shot the animals, then dragged them into one of the several large pits which had been dug at various locations around the ranch. The cattle were tossed into the pits, then covered with lime. Then another layer was tossed into the pit, and covered with lime, until after some two weeks of around the clock work, the entire herd was destroyed.

Quince had watched a little of the operation during the first couple of days, but he was sick at heart, and unable to watch all of it. He stayed back at the ranchhouse and paid off the cowboys, who would now have to find employment somewhere else. Only Rufus remained with him, and when Quince told Rufus that he would have no money for wages, Rufus explained that he would take his pay out in grub.

On the fourteenth day Dr. Brewster arrived in a buggy, knocked on the door of the big house, and called for Quince.

Quince and Rufus were in the bunkhouse. They

had been keeping busy by making repairs, and painting. Work which had been passed over for years was being accomplished by their sudden outbreak of industry.

Quince heard his name called, and he put down his paintbrush and walked out onto the front porch of the bunkhouse.

"I'm over here," he said.

Dr. Brewster left the Bighouse, and started toward Quince. "I thought you would be in the Bighouse," he said.

"I don't own the Bighouse," Quince replied. "The fact is, I don't guess I own anything around here anymore."

"I'm awfully sorry about that," Brewster said. "A tragedy like this affects us all. But, just think how much worse it could have been if it had spread beyond the confines of Three Crown Ranch."

"Yeah," Quince said. "It might have even affected Goodpasture."

"And others," Dr. Brewster said. "I assure you, Goodpasture isn't the only other rancher who would have been hurt."

"What is that?" Quince asked, pointing at a paper Dr. Brewster held in his hand.

"This is a certificate of destruction," Brewster said. "I need your signature."

"Come on inside," Quince invited. "I've a pen in there."

Dr. Brewster followed Quince into the bunkhouse. The bunkhouse smelled of new wood and fresh paint, and Brewster looked around at the work Quince and Rufus had done. Even as he looked, Rufus was spreading a fresh coat of paint on the walls.

"My," Dr. Brewster said. "You have certainly fixed this place up nicely."

"Yeah," Rufus said. He stood up and looked around. "It's a little like the old maid aunts, all dressed up, and no place to go."

Quince signed the certificate and handed it to Brewster.

"What will you do now?" Brewster asked.

"I don't know," Quince said. He sighed. "I guess I'll sell the place to Goodpasture after all. I don't want to, and if it was mine, I wouldn't. But I owe it to Miss Kendrake to look after her best interests, and a ranch with no cattle isn't a ranch at all."

"No, it isn't," Dr. Brewster agreed. "And the thirty-five hundred dollars is little compensation for the loss."

"The thirty-five hundred dollars?" Quince said. "What thirty-five hundred dollars?"

"Mr. Kendrake was a member in good standing of the Wyoming Cattlemen's Association, with all dues fully paid."

"Yes, I suppose he was," Quince said.

"Then he is entitled to the compensation offered by the association of fifteen cents per head destroyed."

Quince let out a small, mirthless laugh. "Thirty-five hundred dollars?" he said.

"Yes, sir. The money will be paid within thirty days."

Quince ran his hand through his hair. "Thirty-five hundred dollars. A herd which was worth over three hundred thousand dollars is gone, and Three Crown Ranch is to be compensated to the amount of thirty-five hundred dollars?"

"I'm sorry, Mr. Parker," Dr. Brewster said. "I know it isn't much, but . . ."

"Don't apologize, Dr. Brewster," Quince said quickly. "That's thirty-five hundred dollars more than I thought we would get."

"Yes, well, in times like these I suppose any compensation is a blessing," Dr. Brewster said. He started back toward the front door, then stopped and looked back toward Quince.

"You know, what I can't figure out is how it got started here. It defies all logic for the disease to start here, and be isolated in such a way. Generally the disease starts near the seacoast, then moves inland. But there have been no other reported cases of it anywhere around here, and I'm puzzled as to how we were so lucky as to have it contained."

"Yes," Quince said sarcastically. "Weren't we lucky?"

Brewster nodded his head once in sympathy with Quince, then walked back out to his buggy climbed in, and drove away.

"Quince, you know damned well how come we got it when no one else did," Rufus said. "It was that damned mystery cow. And, if you ask me, that cow ain't that much of a mystery."

"I've written a letter to Zanders at the Bar Z in Texas," Quince said. "I'll be anxious to see what he has to say."

"Yeah," Rufus agreed. "Me too. Say, are you hungry? I think I'll fix us some grub if you don't mind."

"Yeah, I could use a bite to eat at that," Quince said. In the distance he saw a lone rider approaching, and he shielded his eyes with his hands and stared for a moment. "Well, I'll be damned," he said.

"What is it?" Rufus asked. He saw Quince staring toward the rider, then he amended his question. "I should'a asked, who is it?"

"It's Leslie Kendrake," Quince said.

"Good, good. I'll cook enough for all of us."

"I doubt that the lady is paying us a social call, Rufus."

"That ain't no reason we can't be polite," Rufus replied.

"You're right. There's no reason we can't be," Quince said. He looked down at himself. "In fact, I think I'll just put on a clean shirt."

When Quince reappeared on the porch of the bunkhouse a few moments later, washed up, hair combed, and shirt clean, Leslie was just arriving. Quince started toward her to help her dismount, but she slid off quickly and easily.

"You handle a horse very well," Quince said with genuine admiration.

"Thank you," Leslie said. She looked around. "I see you've been painting a few things."

"Might as well," Quince said. "We've no cows to punch."

"I know," Leslie said. "Quince, I'm so sorry."

Quince gave a half-smile. "I would think you

should be," he said. "They were mostly your cows."

Rufus stepped out onto the front porch of the cookhouse. "Miss Kendrake, you'll be stayin' for lunch, I hope?"

"I . . ." Leslie started, as if she were going to refuse the offer, then her face broke into an easy smile. "I'd be happy to," she said.

"Good, good," Rufus said. "I could set it in the Bighouse if you wish."

"Is that where you take your meals?" she asked Quince.

"No," Quince said. "I'm sleepin' and eatin' out here, same as always."

"Then I shall eat where you eat," Leslie said. A freshening breeze was answered by the windmill, and the blades began spinning with a quiet, clacking sound. A rope snapped against an empty wagon, and the loft door of the barn slammed shut.

"How loud all the noises seem when a ranch is quiet," Leslie said.

"This ranch is quiet, alright," Quince said. He walked down to the split rail fence which surrounded the lawn. Red, white, and blue petunias waved their heads in the breeze, poking up from the freshly trimmed grass, at the foot of the fence row. "Rufus and I are the only two left on the place. There are a few horses left in the remuda, a handful of chickens, and that's about all."

"Will you be leaving now?" Leslie asked.

"Is that why you came over here?" Quince snapped. "To claim the spoils?"

"No," Leslie said, clearly hurt by Quince's outbreak. "That isn't why at all, and you know it."

Quince sighed, and pinched the bridge of his nose between his thumb and forefinger. "I'm sorry," he said. "I had no right to snap at you."

"It's alright," Leslie said. She put her hand on his arm to comfort him. "I know you have had a difficult time of it. You have every right to be upset."

"I have no right to be short with you," Quince said. "The truth is, I probably will leave. I see no reason why I shouldn't agree to the sale now. There's nothing left here."

"Don't worry about selling it," Leslie said. "And you can stay here as long as you like."

"What?" Quince asked in surprise. "I don't understand. I thought you were so anxious to sell the ranch to Goodpasture."

"I don't need to sell it to him," Leslie said. "It will soon be his anyway."

"It will? Why? What do you mean?"

Leslie smiled, though there was a touch of sadness to her smile. "Quince, you may offer me your best wishes," she said. "For I am soon to marry Charles Goodpasture. And when I do, why, this ranch shall belong to him as well as me."

"Marry?" Quince said weakly. "You are going to marry Goodpasture?"

"Yes," Leslie said.

"I see." Quince looked quickly at the ground.

"Quince," Leslie said. "Quince, I want you to be happy for me. I don't want us to fight again, ever."

"Why should you be so concerned?"

"Because," Leslie said. "You were like a son to

my father. In a way, that should make you like my brother. I never had a brother, but if I did, I would have wanted him to be just like you."

Quince looked at Leslie for a long moment, and his eyes spoke volumes, but finally the hurt and turmoil passed away, and he allowed a slow smile to spread across his face. "Then I surely will wish you all the best," he said. "For in truth, I do want you to find happiness, Leslie."

The clanging of the dinner triangle arrested their attention then, and Quince offered Leslie his arm to escort her back to the cookhouse.

Inside a tablecloth had been spread on one of the tables, and fresh flowers decorated the center. Rufus was standing behind a chair, holding it out for Leslie.

"Oh, how nice everything looks," she said. "And I'm truly glad I accepted your invitation, for everything smells just wonderful."

"I've made fresh rolls," Rufus said. He looked at Quince. "Biscuits, to you," he said. "And a nice stew."

"Why didn't you fix a steak?" Quince asked.

"Oh, a stew is just fine, thank you," Leslie said. "To be honest, I find American steaks are a bit tough."

"American steaks?" Quince asked. "Isn't a steak a steak?"

Leslie laughed. "Not entirely. You see, most of the steaks out here are from longhorn cattle. In England, we raise Hereford cattle. The meat is much more tender, and, if I may say so, much better tasting."

"Hereford cattle? But you can't raise Herefords out here," Quince said. "They aren't hardy enough."

"Mr. Kohrs is raising them," Leslie said. "He has a ranch up in Montana, and he was telling me all about them when he came to Mountain Shadow for a party."

"Do you have many parties there?" Quince asked.

"Yes," Leslie said. "Charles entertains frequently." She laughed. "He is trying to make me feel at home, I know, but we never had this many affairs in England."

"Well, leave it to Goodpasture to put on the dog," Rufus said.

"We mustn't criticize Mr. Goodpasture, Rufus," Quince said. "He is going to marry Leslie."

"What?" Rufus expostulated. "Miss Kendrake, excuse me for buttin' in where it ain't none o' my business, but I can't believe you're that big a fool!"

"I beg your pardon," Leslie said coldly. "Who are you to criticize my choice of a husband?"

"I'm someone who wants to be your friend," Rufus replied. "And I've got no personal interest like Quince has, so I reckon I'm free to speak up if I feel like it."

"You certainly are *not* free to speak up," Leslie said.

"Yes, ma'am, I reckon I am free," Rufus said. "You see, this here is still a free country, 'less I've been mistaken all this time."

"Then . . . then if you value my friendship and wish to keep it, you will not speak so of the man I intend to marry."

"I value your friendship all right," Rufus said. "I just don't want you to make a mistake, that's all."

"Quince didn't react so negatively."

"Quince knows he can't," Rufus said. "You see, whether or not you know it, Quince is—"

"Rufus!" Quince said sharply. "Rufus, I think we've spoken enough on this subject."

Rufus looked at Quince, and then at Leslie. He shook his head slowly and sadly, then helped himself to a plate of stew. "I reckon I'll bide my tongue," he said. "I'm nothin' but a fool anyway, 'n they say there ain't no fool like an old fool."

The conversation turned to other things then, and before the meal was over the three had even managed to find a few things to laugh over. And yet despite the lightness of the conversation, the heaviness of the news Leslie had brought hung over them like a cloud, and Quince couldn't help but feel a small tug of hurt in his heart.

After the meal, Quince and Leslie took a walk about the place. Quince led her down a small road to a shady glen beside a pond. The pond was down, and cracked mud surrounded it. Lily pads floated on the water, and dragon flies flitted about, gleaming purple in the sun. Frogs and crickets croaked and creaked from the cattails alongside.

"The pond is drying up," Quince said. He picked up a pebble and tossed it into the pond, causing ripples to spread over the quiet surface. The ripples caused the lily pads to bounce up and down, and a frog deserted one of them, leaping into the water with a plop. "It's probably just as well that we don't have any cattle. We wouldn't have water enough to support them in another week anyway."

"Where does this water come from?" Leslie asked, pointing to the pond.

"When Tuttle Creek is up, it feeds water into here," Quince said. "But it's gone down now, and the water it left is drying up. Before Indian Creek was dammed, this pond stayed full for the whole year," He laughed. "Your pa even fished here some."

"Did my father take to being a cowboy?"

Quince laughed. "Well, your father wasn't exactly a cowboy," he said. "A cowboy is someone who punches cows."

"*Punches?* You said that while ago. What does that mean?"

"That's just an expression," Quince said. "What I really mean is that a cowboy is someone who rides herd, tends to the herd, from horseback. He ropes them, and brands them, and drives them into pens, and watches over them on the range, that sort of thing. A cowboy is a hired hand. Your father was a cattleman, and he was a good one."

"You're just trying to make me feel good, I know," Leslie said. "Charles told me my father was a popular man, and a good man, but even he admitted that my father wasn't a very good rancher."

"Goodpasture is full of—" Quince started, then paused. "I don't want to be critical of him before you now, but, I would say that there are many who wouldn't agree with Goodpasture's appraisal. Your father came out here and turned barren wasteland into one of the most productive ranches in the state."

"But Charles said that Three Crowns is just a small, relatively unimportant ranch."

"I'll admit that Mountain Shadow is much larger, but Three Crowns, is not small and unimportant. It is a ranch a person could be proud of, and I'll say this as well—Stuart Kendrake never threw a long rope in his life."

"Threw a long rope?"

"He never took a cow, or an acre of land, that wasn't his by right," Quince said.

"Are you implying that Charles has?"

"Yes," Quince said. "But many ranchers have, so this is not singling out Goodpasture alone. But it makes your father's record all the more admirable."

"Oh, I wish I could have known him," Leslie said.

"I wish you could have, too," Quince replied. "He was a wonderful person, and you would have been very, very proud to be called his daughter."

"I am proud to be called his daughter," she said.

Quince reached out to her then, and gently, cupped her chin in his hand. He tilted her face up so that she was looking into his eyes, and in that gaze alone the most eloquent love poem was spoken, though in truth not a word was said.

Leslie held her breath for a long moment, feeling her senses beginning to reel, knowing she should break and run, but unable to do so. She watched as his lips came to hers, watched as one mesmerized, unable to think, unable to move, unable to do anything save wait and watch.

Quince's mouth came onto hers, and she felt as

if a thousand butterfly wings had brushed against her lips. Her head began to spin, then she felt Quince's tongue darting about, touching her tongue lightly, spreading a warmth rapidly through her body.

The sensations nearly overwhelmed her. Leslie raised both her arms, pulling herself closer to him, pressing her pliant body against his, losing herself in the kiss. The kiss deepened and she tested it to see how far it could take her. A moment later, with her senses reeling and her self-control slipping away, she found it necessary to pull back.

"I, I've never been kissed like that before," she said.

"You don't love him, Leslie," Quince said urgently. "You *know* you don't love him."

"I do," Leslie said.

"No you don't," Quince insisted. "You couldn't love him and kiss me like that. Don't you realize that?"

"Oh, Quince! I'm so confused," she said. She put her hand to her forehead and turned away from him. "Please, don't say anything else to me. I, I have to get back."

"Leslie, think about it," Quince said. "All I ask is that you just think about it."

"No!" Leslie said. She started back for the house at a run, rushing quickly through the tall grass and the sunflowers which slapped at her. Tears burned in her eyes, and she fought hard to repress the choking sob which was caught in her throat. Her chest ached, and she didn't know if it was from holding back the sob, or from heartbreak.

"Miss Kendrake, what is wrong?" Rufus asked.

"I . . . nothing . . ." Leslie said. "Really, nothing is wrong. I just need to get back, that's all. Thanks for the meal."

Leslie knew that her eyes shone with unspilled tears, but she had no time for explanation, so she mounted her horse, then urged him into a quick gallop. She saw Quince coming out of the breaks just as she passed through the gate on her way back to Mountain Shadow and Charles Goodpasture.

15

"WHERE HAVE you been?" Charles asked. There was a degree of sharpness in his voice, and when Leslie looked at him in surprise, he looked aside, then apologized. "I'm sorry," he said. "I didn't mean to be so harsh. But it is late, and you did miss dinner."

"I ate dinner at Three Crowns," Leslie said.

"I'd rather you not go over there."

"Why not? After all, I do *own* the place, don't I?"

"Well, yes, but, well, the truth is, I don't trust that Parker fellow."

"My father looked upon Quince Parker as his son," Leslie said. "I can't believe his confidence could be that badly placed."

"I'm sure your father's confidence wasn't badly placed while he was alive," Charles said. "But now Quince Parker sees an opportunity to grab everything for himself, and greed does strange things to a man."

"What is there to grab for himself?" Leslie asked. "All the cattle are gone. All I saw was two men working hard to take care of a ranch."

"Well, perhaps you are right," Charles conceded. "After all, without cattle the ranch has no particular value to him now, other than a place to live, anyway. But still, as a favor to me, I would prefer that you not see him again."

"And I would prefer to pick my own friends," Leslie said.

"Oh," Charles said then, changing the subject abruptly, but willingly, as the conversation wasn't going his way. "Speaking of friends, some of my friends are here and I would like you to come into the parlor to meet them."

Leslie smiled then, and the smile softened the otherwise tense moment. "Of course," she said. "I'll be glad to meet them as soon as I have changed."

Leslie stood in her room at the mirror, and studied her reflection. How different her world was now than it had been in England! There she had been a schoolgirl, with only the most remote notion of life, and now she was experiencing life to its fullest. And yet, one thing persisted. As a schoolgirl, she was often perplexed by life, there, because it had never been experienced and thus represented an unknown quantity, here, because it had been experienced, but the mysteries had not been revealed.

She was confused about a number of things now, just when she thought she had sorted things out. Charles had asked her to marry him, shortly after his visit to her room, and she had quickly agreed. After all, when Charles had made love to her she had been lifted to the heavens in the sweet rapture of the moment. Surely, that could not be if she didn't love him. Surely, she had made the right decision in telling him she would marry him.

And yet, Quince had been able to do the same thing with *just a kiss*. And if he could lift her to such rapture with a kiss, how much sweeter would it be if she allowed him to make love to her?

Leslie felt herself flush in quick embarrassment. How could she do this? How could she stand there and calmly contemplate making love to Quince Parker when she was engaged to marry Charles Goodpasture? She closed her eyes tightly, and clenched her fists, and tried to will Quince's features out of her mind. But an odd thing happened. For when she closed her eyes, instead of going away, his face seemed to grow bolder, and larger, until she felt as if she was swimming in his eyes.

"Go away," she said quietly. Then, louder, "Go away. *Go away, go away, go away!*"

Leslie heard a pounding on her door.

"Leslie, are you all right?"

"What?" Leslie called, arrested by the knock, and brought back to an awareness of where she was and what she was doing. The vision of Quince popped out of her mind.

"I heard you calling out," Charles said from the other side of the door.

"Oh, I'm sorry," Leslie said. "There was a spider in my room, and it frightened me. I'm all right now."

"Very well," Charles said. "Please, do hurry, dear. We're keeping our guests waiting."

They aren't *our* guests, yet, they are *your* guests, Leslie thought, but she didn't voice her thought. Instead she merely called out, "I'll hurry."

* * *

Quince got up in the gray light of early morning and left the house, even before Rufus was awake. He hurried to the barn and saddled his horse, then rode out the back trail and up Three Crowns, toward the smallest of the three peaks, the one called Princess. When he reached the top of Princess he dismounted and walked out to a rock ledge and stared down at the ranch and at the buildings below.

He thought back to the many times he had come up here, early in the morning, and sat on this very rock and looked down at the wispy pall of wood smoke which lay in a place . . . a place where he could reason things out.

It was here that Quince formulated the plan which brought water from Indian Creek onto the land. And it was here that he had worked out a new plan of inter-connecting ponds and creeks, fed by deep wells and springs, to construct a water system which was independent of Indian Creek.

The new water system Quince had devised would be able to support only half the number of cattle which the Indian Creek system had supported. But that was all right, because Quince was going to have to sell off half the cattle in order to have enough money to pay for the new system anyway. Of course, all that planning was before the outbreak of hoof-and-mouth disease had completely wiped out the Three Crowns herd.

Now what did he have to offer Three Crowns? And what did he have to offer Leslie Kendrake?

Nothing, that's what, he thought bitterly. But then, what difference did it make anyway? Leslie

Kendrake was engaged to marry Charles Goodpasture. She wasn't for the likes of him.

Still, Quince felt that he owed it to the memory
of Stuart Kendrake not to give up yet. He owed
much to Kendrake, because Kendrake had not only
saved his life, he had also provided Quince with a
new direction and a purpose in life. For Quince
now had the ambition of some day owning his own
ranch. Oh, he knew it wouldn't be as fine, or as
grand as Three Crowns, but it would be his.

Quince had dreamed that 'dream often, and
thoughts of it had sustained him through the long
hours of nighthawk duty, and on the trail rides
when he sat in the saddle for many hours at a
stretch eating dust, sweltering in the relentless
heat, or freezing in the brutal cold. It was a pleasant dream, generally peopled by faceless ranch
hands and an equally faceless wife—for a wife,
someone to share in the building of the ranch,
always figured prominently in Quince's dream.
Though he had never met any woman whose features could make up the face of the girl.

Until now. For now, even as the thought of his
dream came back to him, the features of his imag-
inary wife were highlighted by the tawny hair and
golden eyes of none other than Leslie Kendrake.

"Don't be a fool," Quince said aloud, and the
voice sounded thin and weak in the great openness. But he spoke aloud purposely, to drive such
a foolish thought from his brain. Leslie Kendrake?
She was beautiful, she was even titled, and she
was engaged to a man who, as of now, personified
all the troubles which faced Quince.

A letter had come back from Zanders in Texas,

explaining that he had, in fact, been wiped out by an episode of hoof and mouth disease. But he could not explain how one of his diseased cows had reached Wyoming, for, under government supervision, all of his animals had been put to death. He was terribly sorry that, somehow, one of his cows had escaped, and wound up in Wyoming to infect the Three Crowns herd.

In answer to the question about Charles Goodpasture, Zanders said that he had, indeed heard of him, as had nearly every other rancher in the West. But he had never had any business dealings with the man, and had never sold him any cattle.

Quince was disappointed in the letter. He had hoped that it would have provided him with all the evidence he needed against Goodpasture, but it said nothing. Other than his own feeling that the mysterious rustlers he and Simmons had spooked had actually inserted the diseased cow, he had nothing to go on.

Quince sighed. What good would it have done him to find proof anyway? With Goodpasture's resources, Quince would have never made a lawsuit stick. He would have had the personal satisfaction of knowing that Goodpasture was the guilty party, but, in truth, he already knew that. And, there was little satisfaction in knowing that, so, he reasoned, what good would it do him to have the proof he needed anyway?

Quince saw the back door of the cookhouse open. Rufus stepped out to toss away a pan of water. From this height Rufus was not only small by distance, but foreshortened as well, and he looked a little like an ant scurrying around.

Quince pulled his pistol and pointed it straight up. He pulled the trigger, and felt the gun jump in his hand as the cartridge exploded with a loud, booming sound. The sound of the gunshot came bouncing back from the next peak, and then the next and then the next, so that, by echo at least, Quince's one round became a volley.

Rufus looked up toward the top of the mountain, and when Quince saw him he waved at him. Rufus waved in return, then Quince got on his horse and started the long ride back down to the ranch.

Bacon and eggs were waiting for Quince when he stepped into the cookhouse a while later, and Quince hadn't realized how hungry he was until that moment.

"Did you think the Indians were attacking?" Quince joked.

"No Indian would be damnfool enough to show hisself on the skyline like you done," Rufus said. "Someone who is good with a rifle could'a picked you off easy."

"Ahh, who is that good?" Quince asked.

"Me," Rufus said easily.

"I'll take your word for it," Quince said, laughing. "I don't want you to feel that you have to prove it to me."

"I don't," Rufus said. He poured himself another cup of coffee, and looked at Quince through squinting eyes. "Boss, what are you going to do now?"

"About the only thing I can do, I guess," Quince answered. "I'm going to buy cattle."

"From Goodpasteur?" Rufus asked. "'Cause he's

near 'bout the only one 'round here with cattle enough to sell. And the truth is, he probably won't cotton to sellin' it to you, any more'n you'd like to buy it from him."

"I know," Quince said. "In fact, he might not sell any to me at all."

"I guess we're gonna have to go down to Texas to get our cows," Rufus said. He shook his head slowly. "I oncet swore I would never go to Texas again, but I reckon if you ask me to, I will."

"Texas seems to be about the best bet, I guess," Quince agreed. He sighed. "The problem is, after paying off the men and our debts, I've only got a couple hundred dollars left from the money Mr. Kendrake left me. I don't think we can count on getting any money from Leslie Kendrake, so all we have to go on is the thirty-five hundred dollars Brewster said we would get."

"I got two hundred fifty you can have," Rufus offered.

"Rufus, I can't take your money."

"Why not? I didn't earn it. Kendrake left it to me. Besides, I'll go along with you on just about anythin' you say. Hell, I'd even tend sheep if you wanted me to."

"You know, I might be able to go into Cheyenne and borrow money," Quince said. "Mr. Kendrake borrowed there a couple of times. I could borrow money for the water system, and use our money for the sheep."

"Sheep?" Rufus said.

Quince laughed. "Sure, didn't you just say you would tend sheep if I wanted you to?"

"I wouldn't of said it, if I thought you was gonna take me up on it," Rufus said. "But I've done it before, and I reckon I could do it again."

"*You've* tended sheep?"

"Yep."

"I wouldn't have thought that in a million years," Quince said.

"The fact is, Quince, there ain't much I *haven't* done," Rufus said. "I wasn't always a cowboy. I soldier'd some with Genrul Terry, I prospected for gold, I tuk me an Injun squaw 'n trapped furs one winter, and oncet I was shanghaied onto a Clipper ship in San Francisco, 'n wound up sailin' round the world." He smiled. "That's where I learned about the Englishmen callin' cookies biscuits."

"You were a sailor?"

"Yep," Rufus said. He took another swallow of coffee. "An' after I sailored some I wound up with Buffalo Bill's Wild West show," he concluded.

"How come you never told me all this before?" Quince asked, amazed at the diversity of Rufus's background.

"There never seemed no need," Rufus said easily. " 'Sides, it ain' somethin' I'd share with ever'-one."

Quince knew that in that simple statement Rufus had just paid him the supreme compliment, and that knowledge made him feel warm inside. He wanted to say something deep and meaningful, to express his own feelings for this loyal friend, but he knew that to do so would embarrass them both. So, he just smiled, and said, jokingly, "Your secrets are safe with me, pardner."

16

THE CATTLEMEN'S BANK of Cheyenne was a three-storey brick and wood structure, and one of the most imposing buildings in the entire city. Twice in the past, Stuart Kendrake had borrowed money there, because this bank was totally independent of Charles Goodpasture. In fact, the president of the bank, Gerald Finely, was known to be antagonistic toward Goodpasture, and frequently made loans to people Goodpasture's banks had turned down, just because Goodpasture *had* turned them down.

Quince knew Finely. He had met him in the past, but always as an employee of Kendrake. This was the first time Quince had ever gone to see Finely on his own accord, and now, he stood on the board porch in front of the bank, took a deep breath, then pushed his way inside.

"Today is the 4th of August, 1892" a sign said just above the small table which was covered with counter checks. On the wall opposite the table, a clock ticked loudly, and the hands showed the time to be two-thirty in the afternoon.

Quince stood just inside the bank for a moment and looked around. There were three men tellers in their cages, and a small line of customers stood in front of each cage. Quince didn't want to barge into Finely's office, so he stood in one of the lines until finally he reached the teller.

"Yes, sir?" the teller asked.

"My name is Quince Parker, from Three Crowns ranch in Sweetgrass," Quince said. "I would like to speak to Mr. Finely, please."

"Just a moment," the teller said, and after closing the wire screen across the cage, and locking his money drawer, he stepped into the area behind the cages and stuck his head in through the door of an office. A moment later he returned. "You may go on in," he said.

Finely was standing behind his desk with his hand extended, and a smile on his face when Quince walked in.

"Quince Parker," he said. "You are a sight for sore eyes. I haven't seen you in quite a while. Have a seat, have a seat."

Finely's office was dominated by a large desk, and a huge, dark green safe. The name "Standard" was printed across the front of the safe in old English lettering. The letters were in gold, but the last "d" was missing, and could be read only because it was a darker and cleaner shade of green than the rest of the door.

On the wall there was a calendar which was a month behind, and a wall clock which was fifteen minutes ahead. There was a gun case with three rifles, and just above it a stuffed moose head, moth-eaten and with one eye missing. Quince found a seat on an overstuffed horsehair sofa.

"I'm so sorry about Lord Kendrake," Finely said.

"He was not only a valued customer, but a friend as well." Finely's eyes twinkled in humor. "And an ally against that blackguard, Goodpasture."

"Mr. Kendrake always spoke highly of you, and of this bank as well," Quince said.

"Well, tell me, Parker. What is happening at Three Crowns? Who is running it now?"

"I am," Quince said. "His daughter inherited it, but as she has recently come from England, Mr. Kendrake thought it would be better if I administered the ranch."

"Good thinking, good thinking," Finely said. "How old a girl is his daughter?"

"She's about twenty," Quincy said.

Finely's eyes flashed again. "Twenty, you say? And pretty too, I'll bet."

"She's beautiful," Quince said, and even as he spoke, he could hear the almost reverent sound of his own voice.

"Yes, well, I certainly wish you all the good luck," Finely said.

"Good luck?"

"With Kendrake's daughter."

"I . . . uh . . . am afraid that I've already had all the luck I'm going to have with her, and that was bad. She's going to marry Goodpasture."

"What?" Finely asked, sputtering in surprise. "Kendrake's *daughter* is going to marry Goodpasture? How can you let her do such a thing?"

"I'm afraid I have no power to stop her," Quince replied.

"It almost makes one glad that Lord Kendrake isn't around to see it," Finely said. He rubbed his chin with his hand. "Such a shame, such a shame."

He looked back at Quince, and now, with the amenities out of the way, he was ready for business. "What can I do for you, Quince?"

"Mr. Finely, I need to borrow some money," Quince said.

"You want a personal loan, do you?"

"No, it's not for me," Quince said. "It's for Three Crowns." Quince reached into his inside jacket pocket, and pulled out a piece of paper. "Let me show you what the money will be used for," he said.

On the paper, he had drawn a map, and on the map, he had laid a grid of innerconnecting ponds and canals. "I'm going to drill at least ten more wells," he said. "Those wells, and the two natural springs we have, plus the water we get from Tuttle Creek for nearly nine months of the year, will supply us with enough water to be forever independent of access to the river. We will be able to support a rather sizeable herd with our own water resources."

"I see," Finely said. "How expensive will this operation be?"

"I've got enough money to do this, since Rufus and I will do most of it ourselves. I need a loan from you to replace the herd."

"Replace the herd? What do you mean? What happened to your cattle?" Finely asked.

"We had to destroy them," Quince said. Quickly and simply, without expressing his own suspicions on the subject, Quince told Finely about the disease which had wiped out his entire herd.

Finely lit a cigar during the telling of the story,

then leaned back in his chair and exhaled a long cloud of blue smoke.

"So you want to borrow enough to restock, is that it?"

"Yes," Quince said.

Finely smiled. "Well, I see no problem. I guess we can let you have the money right away."

"You can?" Quince replied, amazed that it had gone so smoothly. "Why, that's wonderful!"

"I'll just have to have Miss Kendrake's signature on a few papers, and we are all set."

"Miss Kendrake's signature?" Quince asked, feeling his elation slip away from him.

"Yes. She owns the property, doesn't she?"

"Of course she does," Quince said. "But I am the administrator of the property."

"Do you have specific authorization to borrow money against it?"

"Well, no," Quince said. "But I know Stuart Kendrake would have wanted me to do this if it was necessary for me to save the property."

"I'm inclined to agree with you," Finely said. "But, unfortunately, Lord Kendrake is dead, and we can't interpret his wishes. We can only follow what was laid down in black and white, in the will. My hands are tied, Mr. Parker. Surely you can see see that."

"Yeah," Quince said sadly. "Yeah, I guess I can see that."

"But I really don't see the problem anyway," Finely went on. "All you need is Miss Kendrake's signature and I'll give you the money."

"You don't know Leslie Kendrake," Quince said.

"You mean she won't sign?"

"That's exactly what I mean."

"Not even to save the ranch?"

"She has no real desire to save it at all," Quince said.

Finely sighed, and stood up, a signal that the meeting was over, as no further progress could be made. "I'm sorry," he said. "I really wish I could help you."

"Well, perhaps some other time," Quince said, smiling weakly. He reached out and shook Finely's hand again, then, trying to hold his face impassive to mask his disappointment, he left the bank.

The Crystal Palace saloon, right across the street from the bank, was featuring free sandwiches with beer. Quince had not eaten lunch, and this seemed the most inexpensive way, so he crossed the street to avail himself of the opportunity.

It was darker inside the saloon, and a little cooler. There weren't many people, as it was still early afternoon and the evening crowds had not yet collected. Quince looked around, and saw several round tables covered with green felt, behind which sat the dealers, waiting for the evening games to start. Most of the dealers were counting their chips and the bright red, white and blue stacks caught the dim light vividly, contrasting sharply with the light absorbing felt. Some of the dealers were dealing hands methodically, flipping them over to look at them, then pulling them back to deal again.

The bar was of burnished mahogany with a highly polished brass footrail. Crisp, clean white towels hung from hooks on the customer's side of the bar, spaced about every four feet. A mirror was behind the bar, flanked on each side by a small statue of a nude woman set back in a special niche. A row of whiskey bottles sat in front of the mirror, reflected in the glass so that the row seemed to be two deep. A bartender, with slicked-back black hair and a handlebar moustache, stood behind the bar polishing glasses.

"I'll have a beer," Quince said, and he started preparing a generous sandwich for himself.

The bartender drew a mug and set it in front of Quince. Quince blew away some of the foam, then took a deep, thirsty swallow. It was as cool and refreshing as a mountain stream, and he drank the whole mug without putting it down.

The bartender set another one in front of him, and Quince picked it up and took another long drink before he turned and looked around the place. It was nearly deserted.

"Is it always this dead?" he asked.

"It's only three o'clock, fella," the bartender answered. "What do you expect? It'll pick up."

"If you're looking for some action now, I might be able to accommodate you," one of the dealers said. The dealer was at a nearby table, and he was wearing a green visor. He fanned the cards out in front of him, then flipped them all over neatly and closed them up again. "Perhaps you'd be interested in a little highcard?" he asked. "One time for ten dollars."

Quince took another long drink from his beer and eyed the man closely. "I might," he said.

The dealer shuffled the cards. "I haven't seen you around here before."

"I haven't been around," Quince answered.

"Where are you from?"

"Are we going to play, or are you going to talk all day?" Quince wanted to know.

"Oh, you are anxious, huh? Good, I like your kind," the dealer said. He spread the cards out on the table. "All right, mister, draw one."

"I think I'll take the ace you have up your sleeve," Quince said.

The smile left the dealer's face. "Are you accusing me of cheating?"

"Not at all," Quince said easily. "But as long as I have the choice of cards, I'll take the one I just saw you slip under your shirt cuff."

Quince's eyes were crystal clear, and they held the dealer's eyes unwaveringly.

The dealer cut his glance away. "Get out," he said. He started to fold the cards up, but Quince reached down with one hand and grabbed the dealer's wrist in a viselike grip. He pulled the card out and flipped it over. It was the ace of spades.

"Now you can draw," Quince said.

The dealer picked up a blue chip. "Here," he said. "You can cash it at the bar."

"Don't you want to play again?" Quince asked.

"Cash your chip, mister, and be lucky I don't have you thrown out of here," the dealer said.

Quince took his chip over to the bar and handed it to the bartender. The bartender took it, and gave him a ten dollar bill for it.

"Thanks," Quince said. He started to eat the sandwich he made earlier.

"Don't bother with that," a man said.

"I beg your pardon?"

"I said don't bother with that," the man said again. He had come into the saloon just in time to witness Quince's play with the high-card dealer. He smiled, and stroked his chin whiskers. "Let me buy you a good meal over at the Cheyenne Club."

"Who are you?" Quince asked.

"Kohrs is my name," the man said. "Conrad Kohrs."

"I'm Quince Parker, Mr. Kohrs," Quince said, taking Kohrs's extended hand. "I'm foreman for Three Crowns."

"Ah, Three Crowns, yes," Kohrs said. "I had the pleasure of meeting your mistress at one of Charles Goodpasture's parties. Leslie Kendrake, I believe her name was. A lovely young woman, if memory serves me."

"Your memory serves you quite well," Quince said. "But tell me. Why would you be interested in buying a meal for me at the Cheyenne Club?"

"I like the way you handle yourself," Kohrs said. "You see, I came in here for a very specific kind of of fellow, and I think you may be that fellow."

"I'm not sure I follow you."

"I wanted a gambler," Kohrs said. "Someone I could back in a small game of chance to be held at the club tonight. So I came in here to look over the professionals, in order that I might select one. But when I saw you I changed my mind. I don't want any of these people. I want you."

"I'm afraid you would be disappointed," Quince said.

"I don't think so," Kohrs said. "I think you are

a fellow with a keen eye, a bit of courage, and an obvious streak of honesty. How about it? Will you be my man?"

"What, exactly, do you need?"

"I need you to play a game of cards for me," Kohrs said. "I'll back your play."

"Why don't you play your own cards?"

"My dear fellow, you simply don't understand," Kohrs said. "Jason Kyle is a very old and very dear friend of mine. But when Jason and I play cards," Kohrs shook his head sadly. "Well, I'm afraid that Jason is just too competitive. He takes it very personally, and the next thing you know there is bad feeling between us. So, the way to overcome that is very simple. Jason hires a player, a 'second' if you will, and I do the same. This has worked out quite well in the past, but he recently acquired a riverboat gambler of no mean skill, and with quite a reputation. So far, I've been unable to find anyone good enough to beat him."

"Mister, it sounds to me like you need a professional card shark, and I'm not your man," Quince said.

"You may not be a card shark, but you are a gambler," Kohrs said. "Aren't you gambling on bringing water back to Three Crowns?"

"What?" Quince asked, shocked by the statement. "How did you know that?"

Kohrs laughed. "It isn't all that mysterious," he said. "I happened into the bank right after you left, and Finely told me."

"I thought a man's banking business was supposed to be private," Quince said with obvious anger.

"Please," Kohrs said, soothingly. "Don't be upset with Gerald. There was a good motive for his telling mè of your loan application." Kohrs took out a long, slender cigar, ran his tongue along the side, held it up to smell its aroma, then lit it. "You see," he went on between lighting puffs. "I might be able to help you."

"Help me? How?"

"We can talk about that later," Kohrs said. "In the meantime, suppose you come to the club with me, and let me buy you that dinner I promised. Then we can discuss whether or not you would be willing to engage Kyle's man in a little game."

Quince chuckled. "Mr. Kohrs, it's your money," he said. "If you are willing to back me in a game against Mr. Kyle's man, then who am I to argue with you? Besides, Mr. Kendrake took me to the Cheyenne Club once, and I said then I'd never turn down an opportunity to return. You've got yourself a deal."

"Good, good," Kohrs said. He took a cigar from his jacket pocket and handed it to Quince. "Have a cigar."

"Thank you," Quince said, accepting the smoke. "I believe I will at that."

17

THE CHEYENNE CLUB was built in 1880 to give the cattle barons of the West a place befitting their wealth and status. The three story mansard-roofed building looked more like a mansion than a private club, and it featured two grand staircases, a smoking room, a reading room, a dining room, hardwood floors, and plush carpets. It also boasted the finest wine cellar west of the Mississippi River, and served these wines with meals which featured caviar, pickled eels, French peas, and Roquefort cheese.

The Club was limited by charter to two hundred hand-picked members, and the members often dressed for dinner in white tie and tails. It was a place which had entertained visiting Presidents and royalty, and was known far and wide as the "Pearl of the Prairies."

"Good evening, Mr. Kohrs," a dignified-looking gentleman greeted, as Kohrs and Quince stepped inside. The gentleman took both men's hats.

"This is my guest for the evening," Kohrs said. "His name is Quince Parker. Quince, this is Phillip Owens. He is our club steward."

"Welcome to the Cheyenne Club, Mr. Parker," Owens said.

"Say, isn't that Teddy over there?" Kohrs asked, beaming broadly. "By golly, I think it is."

A vigorous looking, thick-necked, mustachioed man, wearing pince-nez glasses, walked over to greet Kohrs. "Connie," he said. "It's bully to see you."

"What are you doing out here, Teddy? I thought you were back East for good now."

"I'll never go back for good," the man said. "But I am back there, I'm on President Harrison's Civil Service Commission now. Who is your friend?"

"Oh, I'm sorry," Kohrs said. "Quince Parker, I want you to meet as fine a Westerner as you'll ever meet, even if he is from New York. This is Teddy Roosevelt."

"Quince Parker, eh?" Roosevelt said. "Aren't you the foreman of Three Crowns?"

"My God," Quince said. "Am I wearing a sign or something? Everyone knows me."

Roosevelt laughed. "Well, maybe you are more popular than you thought. You ought to consider going into politics with that kind of popularity. But, if you ever see me running for something, don't run against me."

"Don't worry about that," Quince said. "I have no interest in such a thing."

"Well, then as we will never be adversaries, we can be friends then, eh what?" Roosevelt said, laughing out loud. "The truth is, I know your name because I'm out here to look into the performance of Lawrence Cauldwell. A complaint was filed with our office, informing us that a dam was built at the junction of the Platte River and Indian Creek. When we asked Cauldwell to explain why, he replied that it was to preserve the natural water rsources."

"Mr. Roosevelt, if you believe that, you'll believe anything," Quince said.

Roosevelt took his glasses off and polished them, squinting as he did so. Despite his obvious strength and vigor, he was a man, Quince noted, with remarkably weak eyes.

"I was rather afraid of that," he said. He put the glasses back on, then looked at Quince more closely, as if seeing him for the first time. He held up a finger and wagged it back and forth slowly. "I don't like to take action against anyone unless such action is the only thing remaining which will produce the desired result. Then, if action is to be taken, it should be swift and decisive. In fact, I have a motto, you know. Don't hit at all if it is honorably possible to avoid hitting, but never hit soft."

"Mr. Roosevelt, those are pretty good words to live by," Quince said.

"They have always served me well," Roosevelt said. "Well, you gentlemen have a good time tonight. I must be on my way. And Mr. Parker, I assure you that unless Mr. Cauldwell can justify his action in the building of that dam, he will be gone forthwith."

"And the dam, Mr. Roosevelt?"

"Ah, the dam," Roosevelt said. "Therein is the rub. My commission allows me to take action against Cauldwell only. I have no jurisdiction over the dam. Its fate must be decided by another department."

"Then you can't be of much help to me, can you?"

"I can't provide you with short term help, Mr. Parker. But if Mr. Cauldwell is guilty of misconduct in building the dam, then that should be ample justification for the eventual dismantling of the dam. The mills of the gods grind slowly, but they do grind exceedingly fine."

Roosevelt gave both men one final smile and handshake, then went on his way.

"He seems like a nice enough man," Quince said. "But I don't have any hope of his being able to do anything."

"Oh, don't sell Teddy short," Kohrs said. "He is a most exceptional man, I assure you. You know, when he first came out here, eight years ago, all the cowboys made fun of the 'four-eyed tenderfoot' from eastern society. But they didn't do so for long. One night in a saloon, a fella who was toting a gun began to pick on Teddy. Teddy calmly walked up to him, knocked him down, and took away his gun."

"Barroom heroics," Quince said.

"No," Kohrs said. "Not just barroom. As a rancher, Roosevelt worked as hard as any of the men on his ranch. He would sit in the saddle for forty hours at a stretch during round-up time. He brought in stray calves for branding, he delivered feed to cattle during blizzards, and he mended fences."

"Maybe I was a bit hasty," Quince said. "If he's all you say he is, then I'd say he's a good man to have on my side."

"You won't find a better man," Kohrs said.

"Connie, have you brought someone to take on my man?" The speaker was tall, with brown hair and dark eyes. He had distinguished-looking side whiskers, and a full mustache, and he looked a little like he was enjoying a joke at someone else's expense. He was walking across the carpeted foyer to greet the two men.

"Yes," Kohrs said. "I believe I have the man right here, but I intend to let him enjoy his meal before we begin. Quince Parker, this is Jason Kyle."

"Let the condemned man enjoy his last meal, eh?" Kyle said, laughing at his joke. "Well, eat heartily, Mr. Parker."

"Mr. Kohrs," Quince said. "I'd like to play now."

"I thought you missed your lunch," Kohrs said.

"I did," Quince said. "But my reckoning is that if I can't help you, then I have no right to feed at your trough."

Kyle laughed. "A noble sentiment, and well spoken," he said. "Connie, I like your man. He has spunk, even if he doesn't have any sense. Come on, Chester is waiting for us."

A long layer of blue tobacco smoke hung just beneath the ceiling of the Smoking Room. Open windows allowed a slight breeze to enter, and the breeze caused the smoke to drift and curl through the room and collect in a small cloud above a table, where there sat a man, quietly shuffling cards. The man was stiff, and unhumorous, with sharp gray eyes, a grim mouth, and a sad face. He looked like an old man until Quince examined him more carefully, then he saw that the man was actually no older than Quince himself.

"Chester, Mr. Kohrs has brought in another victim," Kyle said, laughing. "His name is Quince Parker."

"Are you any good, Mr. Parker?" Chester asked. The words were flat and mechanical, without the slightest change in expression in Chester's face as he spoke.

"I've played a little," Quince said.

"I am the best," Chester said. Again, it was a flat, declarative statement, spoken in such a way that it seemed to be informative, rather than braggardly. "Have you ever heard of me?" he asked.

"No," Quince answered. He extended his hand, but when Chester made no effort to shake it, he withdrew it. "Should I have?"

"Not necessarily," Chester answered easily.

Kyle placed several stacks of chips on the table, and Chester took two piles. "Mr. Kohrs, do you have enough confidence to back your man for this much?" he asked.

"No limit," Kohrs said.

Chester smiled for the first time. "I'll make it easy on you," he said. "We won't bring any more money into the game than there is on this table right now."

"I hate to sound like a fool," Quince said. "But I don't know what these chips are worth. How much money is on this table?"

"About ten thousand dollars," Chester said. "But don't let me make you nervous."

Quince smiled at the cadaverous man, then picked up a new deck of cards and broke the seal. "Do you suppose I could have a beer?" he asked.

Almost instantly, one of the uniformed attendants placed a beer before Quince. He shuffled the cards, and the stiff new pasteboards clicked sharply. His hands moved swiftly, folding the cards in and out, until the law of random numbers became king of the table. He shoved the deck across the table, and Chester cut them, then pushed them back.

"Five card stud?" Quince asked.

"That'll be fine," Chester answered.

Chester won fifteen hundred dollars in the first hand, and a couple of hands later was four thousand five hundred dollars ahead.

"That's it," Kohrs said. "Take your money off the table, Kyle. You won again."

"Your man still has five hundred dollars on the table," Kyle said. "I'd like to take that too, unless you need to keep a grub stake."

"What do you say, Quince?" Kohrs asked. "Do you want to stay in for the last five hundred dollars?"

"It's your money, Mr. Kohrs," Quince said easily.

"Well, what do you think? Can you win at least one hand?"

"I can try," Quince said.

"All right, give it a try."

"It's your game," Chester said, shoving the deck over to Quince.

"One hand of showdown," Quince said.

"Showdown? That isn't skill, that's luck."

"Mine hasn't been good," Quince said. "That should comfort you."

Chester smiled again, though the smile was little more than a twitching of his thin lips. "No," he said. "No, it hasn't, has it?"

Quince dealt five cards to each of them and took the pot with a pair of fours.

"Well," Chester said. "You aren't exactly spilling over with luck, are you? How about another hand for a thousand?"

Quince won that hand with a king high.

"Want another one?" Quince asked.

"One more time," Chester agreed. "No better hands than you are getting, you couldn't possibly win three in a row."

Quince did win with a pair of tens, and Chester threw his cards on the table in disgust. He slid the rest of his money to the center of the table. "High card for all of it," he suggested.

Quince fanned the cards out and turned up a seven. Chester flipped over a four. "Damn!" he bellowed out, and he got up from the table and walked away.

Those who had gathered around to watch the game, now released their pent-up tensions, and erupted into noisy shouting and laughter.

"Kyle's man has been beaten," someone said. "Did you hear? Someone finally beat Kyle's man."

There were several expressions of congratulations, then a general rush to the bar where the men began replaying the games in their talk, telling how they would have played certain hands.

Quince raked all the money in and began stacking up the chips.

"Well, you had yourself a pretty good few minutes there," Kohrs said. "You beat Kyle's man, and I won myself four thousand dollars."

"Five thousand," Quince said.

"No," Kohrs put in. He slid one stack of chips out of the pile. "Twenty per cent is yours. You just earned yourself one thousand dollars."

"Thanks," Quince said, hefting the chips, feeling their weight and potency.

"Now," Kohrs said. "Are you enough of a gambler to invest that money in your own plan?"

"What do you mean?" Quince asked.

"You were willing to let the bank back your play at Three Crowns. Are you willing to back your play with your own money?"

"This isn't enough," Quince said.

"I'll make up the difference," Kohrs put in. "But you have to put that one thousand dollars, plus any other money that you have, into cattle. How much more do you have?"

"I have just under a thousand dollars," Quince said, and in that figure he realized that he had added in Rufus's money as well.

"Good. If you put that thousand, and this thousand, into the pot, I will loan you the rest of it."

"Mr. Kohrs, have you heard about the recent problem we had with hoof and mouth disease? When I buy cattle, I'm going to have to start fresh."

"I know," Kohrs said. He smiled broadly. "That's why I'm willing to back you. You see, there is a condition to my helping you."

"What's that?"

"You must stock your range with Herefords, rather than Longhorns."

"Herefords? But they aren't hardy enough. They won't survive the winter."

"Mine have," Kohrs said. "I'm not saying it doesn't take work, but if you are dedicated, you can do it. Now, what do you say? Will you try it with Herefords?"

Quince looked at Kohrs for a long moment, then remembering Rufus' comment, he broke into a smile. "Hell, Mr. Kohrs, I'd try it with sheep if I had to."

"Lord no, don't do that," Kohrs laughed. "In fact, don't even mention that word in here, or we could get thrown out," he teased. "Now, how about that dinner I promised you? Are you ready for it?"

"I'm starving," Quince said, rubbing his stomach.

"Good. I've had the cook prepare us a good Hereford steak. I want you to see what you will be raising. Once you taste it, you'll wonder how anyone ever ate Longhorn in the first place. Are you game for it?"

"I'm game," Quince said.

18

"PLEASE, SENORITA, you must choose the pattern and the material for your dress. There is but one more month until the wedding, and we haven't even started making the dress yet."

"I know," Leslie said. She looked at the bolts of material which Maria and the seamstress had placed on her bed, and she ran her hands across them, feeling the textures of the silk and the lace. "But I just can't make up my mind."

"Would you like us to select the pattern for you, *señorita*?" the seamstress asked sweetly. She opened the pattern book. "Here is a lovely one."

"No, I'll do it," Leslie said. "After all, it is *my* wedding day. Don't you understand? Everything should be perfect on a person's wedding day."

"*Si, señorita,* I understand," the seamstress said, closing the book hard enough to let her impatience with Leslie show through. "But, you should understand, too. I must get started on this dress right away, or I cannot possibly be finished in time for the wedding."

"Then, then we shall just postpone the wedding," Leslie said. She smiled brightly. "Yes, that's it. We'll just move the wedding back to a later date."

"Oh, I don't think *Señor* Goodpasture is going to like that," Maria interjected. "He wanted it to be even earlier than it is."

"Well, he will simply have to like it," Leslie said. "For it is impossible for me to get ready as soon as next month, and I shall explain it to him, I am sure he will understand when I tell him."

"I hope so, *señorita*," Maria said.

Leslie left her bedroom then, and walked quickly down the long hall toward the parlor. She had seen Charles go in there, just before Maria and the seamstress had come to see her. This would be a perfect opportunity for her to speak to him, to explain how difficult it is for a girl to get ready for such an important event.

Surely Charles would understand her concern. Surely, he wouldn't make her go through with it before she had time to get everything ready. After all, everything should be perfect on a girl's wedding day.

And yet, as Leslie turned the arguments over in her mind, they sounded weak, even to her. She knew that it wasn't really to give her more time to select the dress. It was simply to give her more time. For, already, Leslie was beginning to have second thoughts about marrying Charles.

Leslie pushed the door to the parlor open, and barged inside. "Charles, I want to talk to you about—" she stopped in mid-sentence, for there were two men in the parlor with Charles. One was Morrison, the foreman of Mountain Shadow, and the other was a man everyone called Smitty. Leslie had asked once if his name was Smith, and when he replied, "Isn't everyone's?" everybody laughed. She didn't get the joke, and was a little embarrassed by it, so she had generally avoided Smitty, and the other cowboys, as much as possible. "I'm sorry," she said. "I didn't know you were busy."

"That's quite all right, dear," Charles said. "I think you should listen in on this anyway." He smiled. "After all, you will soon become the mistress of this place, you should have some idea as to what is going on."

"Well," Leslie said. "If you are certain I won't be in the way."

"You won't be in the way at all," Charles assured her.

Leslie smiled at the two men, then sat on a large leather sofa to listen to the men talk.

"Now," Charles said to Morrison. "You were telling me about Cauldwell."

"He's been fired," Morrison said. "This fella Roosevelt come all the way out here from Washin'ton, 'n fired him."

"Well, it's no wonder," Charles said. "Cauldwell made a mistake when he built that dam. A bad mistake, and several ranchers were hurt because of it."

Morrison and Smitty looked a little surprised at Charles's comment, then, glancing over at Leslie, they recovered quickly.

"Uh, yeah," Morrison said. "That was a bad thing he done."

"We were talking about Lawrence Cauldwell," Charles explained to Leslie. "He was the Government agent who built the dam where your father was killed. I might add that he built that dam over the objections of just about everybody, and now, at last, the government seems to have caught up with him."

"Well, will the dam be torn down?" Leslie asked.

"Yes, I'm certain it will," Charles said.

"In that case, Three Crowns could become productive again," she said.

Charles smiled, a patronizing smile. "Oh, I hardly think so," he said. "It will be at least three years before the government ever gets around to it. No, for the foreseeable future, Three Crowns' worth is still relegated to providing grassland for Mountain Shadows."

"Boss, we're missin' more cattle from the north rangeland," Morrison said.

"How many are we missing?"

"I can't rightly tell," Morrison said. "But we was runnin' more'n ten thousand head up there, and damn me iffen we aren't down to under eight."

"And me'n some of the other boys found tracks where the cattle was drove off," Smitty said.

"Boss, it looks to me like you're gonna have to hire this fella Tom Horn," Morrison said.

"Tom Horn's services aren't available," Charles said. "I've already looked into it."

"How about Emil Bates?" Smitty asked.

"Emil Bates? I don't know," Charles said. "I don't know much about him."

"They ain't too much anybody knows about 'im," Smitty said. "Only that he's a hired gun, 'n he'll clean out a pack of rustlers quick as he would a pack of wolves."

"Do you know how to reach him?" Charles asked.

"Yep."

Charles ran his hand through his hair and sighed. "Very well," he said. "I really didn't want to have to resort to this, but I can see that I have no choice. You may hire Mr. Bates."

"Oh, by the way," Morrison said. "You was wantin' to know about Parker? Well, I found out what he's been doin' ever since he got back from Cheyenne."

At the mention of Quince's name, Leslie's interest perked up, and she looked toward Morrison to hear his report.

"What has he been doing?" Charles asked, failing to notice Leslie's aroused curiosity.

"He's been diggin' wells, Mr. Goodpasture. You should see them. They's windmills all over the place, and pipe laid to hell 'n gone. He and this Rufus fella been over there workin' like a couple of scalded-ass beavers. Oh, beg' pardon, ma'am," Morrison said to Leslie, excusing himself for the oath.

"It looks to me like they are tryin' to bring water back to the rangeland. You don't think they can really do it, do you, Mr. Goodpasture?"

"Gentlemen, I would never sell Quince Parker short on anything," Charles said. "After all, it was he who diverted Indian Creek in the first place. Yes, I think there is every possibility that he will be successful. But, what are his plans beyond that?"

"I been keepin' my ears open, boss, and I ain't heard nothin'," Morrison said.

"If you ask me, they ain' nothin' he can do after this," Smitty said. "I think he 'n Rufus is just putterin' around, tryin' to find busy work."

"Well, the busier they keep themselves, the less trouble they make for us, or anybody else. We'll just let them pass their time in whatever fashion they see fit. Now, is that all, gentlemen? I think Miss Kendrake wants to talk to me."

"Yeah, boss," Morrison said. "Come along, Smitty, we got work to do."

Morrison and Smitty touched their hands to hats which had not been removed during the entire conversation, then made their exit.

"I'm sorry to break in like that," Leslie said.

"It's quite all right," Charles said. "Now, what is on your mind?"

"Charles, we must delay the wedding."

"Delay the wedding? Why would we want to do that?"

"I've too much to do," Leslie said. "My dress hasn't even been started yet, I have all sorts of arrangements to make . . . it's just impossible to get ready in time."

"Don't be silly," Charles said easily. "You can get ready in time. If you need more people to help you, why, I'll simply hire them, that's all."

"But you don't understand—" Leslie started.

Charles smiled at her. "Oh, I think I do understand," he said. "You are just nervous, that's all. Darlin', everyone is nervous before they get married. Hell, even I'm nervous."

"Oh, I suppose you are right," Leslie finally said,

realizing that she was fighting a losing battle.

"I know I'm right. Listen, I'll tell you what. Why don't you accept Augusta Kohrs' invitation to visit her at their ranch up in Montana? Kohrs' spread covers more than a million acres, and his wife lives like a queen. I think it would be good for you to visit her, to see what the life of a mistress of a big ranch is like."

"Perhaps I will," Leslie said.

"Good, good," Charles replied. "I'll get a message up to Mrs. Kohrs to be expecting you, and I'll arrange for your tickets."

"Thank you," Leslie said. She started to leave the parlor, and Charles picked up some papers to do some work. Leslie stopped at the door and looked back toward him.

"Is there anything else?" Charles asked.

"No," Leslie said. "No, I guess not."

As Leslie walked back down the hall, she met Maria and the seamstress. "Did he agree to the delay?" Maria asked anxiously.

"What?" Leslie replied, having momentarily forgotten why she had gone to see him in the first place. "Oh, uh, no," she said. "No, the wedding will go on as planned."

"And which dress, *señorita?*" the seamstress asked again.

Leslie sighed. "Oh, I don't care," she finally said. "You and Maria pick out one for me."

"Very well, *señorita*," Maria said.

"You won't be sorry," the seamstress said. "We will make a dress so beautiful that *Señor* Goodpasture will lose his breath when he sees you wearing it."

"*Si, señorita,*" Maria said. "I promise you, it will be most beautiful."

"I'm sure it will be," Leslie said. She looked back down the hall toward the closed door of the parlor. "Maria," she said. "If Mr. Goodpasture asks about me later, please tell him that I have gone for a ride."

"*Señorita,* he does not like you to go for rides alone. He feels it is dangerous," Maria said. "Perhaps you should tell him beforehand."

"I will do no such thing," Leslie said rather sharply. "And I trust that you will say nothing either."

"*Si, señorita,* I will say nothing," Maria said. "But if *Señor* Goodpasture discovers that I knew, and said nothing, he will be greatly angry with me."

"Very well, then, if he asks about me, tell him you don't know where I am."

"*Si, señorita.*"

A blazing hot sun, the mark of late August, beat its relentless heat onto the prairie below. Leslie almost regretted having gone for a ride, but she felt she had to get out of the house, to be on her own, to have time for her own thoughts. If anyone had asked her where she was going, she would have told them, nowhere in particular, and in fact, she would have believed that herself. But, perhaps subconsciously, she found herself clear of Mountain Shadow range and riding on Three Crowns land.

Leslie wasn't looking for them—or, perhaps she was looking for them and didn't realize it, but suddenly she found herself coming upon a wagon and two men. The two men were Quince and Rufus.

Quince and Rufus were both on their knees, work-ing on some kind of valve. A pipe ran from the valve back to a nearby windmill.

"It seems to me like we need a little grease and the valve will open easy enough," Rufus was saying.

"Hello," Leslie called.

Quince looked up and smiled broadly. "Well, you have arrived just in time," he said.

"Just in time? Just in time for what?"

"You are going to witness a miracle, Miss Ken-drake," Rufus said. "Water shall flow where no water flowed before."

"I'll go release the brake on the windmill," Quince said. "You turn the valve."

"No," Rufus said. "This whole thing was your idea, you should have the privilege of turning the valve. I'll release the brake."

Rufus walked back to the windmill, pushed a wooden handle up, and the blades started spin-ning. The sucker rod started moving up and down then, and there were a few clanks and rattles as Leslie saw the pipe at her feet jump slightly.

"She's got pressure!" Rufus yelled.

Quince turned the valve, then a stream of water, one inch thick, started spewing out of the pipe, and running into the dry creek bed. Quince washed his hands in the flow of water, then cupped them and brought them up for a drink.

"Taste it!" he said happily. "I tell you, there's no sweeter water in the world!"

"You did it!" Leslie said happily, and she, Rufus, and Quince held hands and danced a small jig around the gushing water, as if they were children, playing ring around the rosey.

"We've got 'em like this all over the range now," Rufus said. "Three Crowns has water! Three Crowns is a ranch again!"

"Not quite a ranch," Quince said. "We need cattle."

"How will you get them?" Leslie asked.

"I'll buy them," Quince said.

"Where will you get the money?"

"I've got some."

"You have very little," Leslie said. "I received a statement of accounting from my barrister, listing the known expenditures you've entailed."

"I know," Quince said. "I submitted that list to him, asking that you share in the expenses, since it is your ranch. He said that you were opposed to operating the ranch, and therefore you were not responsible for any debts incurred by me. I had to pay everything from my own pocket."

"Which brings us back to my question," Leslie said. "How do you propose to buy cattle when you have no money with which to buy cattle?"

"I've found someone who will loan me the money," Quince said, simply.

"Don't take the loan," Leslie said.

Quince sighed. "Leslie, I know you've been against me from the beginning, but I'm not going to just roll over and play dead. This ranch can work, and I can make it work."

"Oh, I quite agree," Leslie said.

"So, if you don't mind, I will just—" Quince paused. "What did you say?"

"I said, I quite agree," Leslie repeated, smiling. "You can make it work, and I think you should."

"You think I *should?*"

"Absolutely," Leslie said. "That's why I don't want you to borrow the money from the source you had in mind. I want you to use the money my father left me."

"Leslie, do you know what you're saying?" Quince asked, scarcely able to believe his ears over the good fortune.

"Yes," Leslie said. "I'm telling you to try and make a go of Three Crowns."

"But, what about Goodpasture?"

"Oh, I expect he will be quite displeased with it all," Leslie said. "But this is my land, and I'll do with it as I wish."

Quince smiled so broadly that Leslie thought he was going to break out laughing. "Hot damn," he said. He stuck his hands out and took Leslie's in his, and once again they danced a little jig. "Hot damn!" he said.

Even as they danced, a sudden wind blew up from the west, from the line of purple mountains, and Leslie could feel and smell in the breeze the dampness of an upcoming rain. They looked toward the west, and saw a great, billowing rain cloud bearing down on them.

"Isn't that just the way it is, though?" Quince said. "Here we've broken our backs for three weeks to get water, and on the day we succeed it rains."

"You 'n the lady better go find some shelter somewhere," Rufus said. "I'll look after the wagon."

"Come on, Leslie, sometimes these summer storms can be real humdingers," Quince said. He helped Leslie get her poncho on, then he put one on, and spread them both to provide as much protection for the horses as he could.

"Let's go," he called out, and he led the way, moving off in a fast trot.

The dark, ominous clouds moved closer to them, preceded by swiftly moving tumbleweed and a rolling column of dust. Quince and Leslie leaned forward in their saddles and hurried on.

Moments later the rains came, hitting them full force. At first, Quince thought he would try and make it all the way back to the Bighouse, but the rain was coming with such velocity that the drops were actually stinging. Then, a few minutes after the rain started, it began to hail, and the horses grew frightened. That was when Quince saw the line shack.

"Over here!" he called against the force of the storm.

There was a small lean-to for the horses, and Quince tied them there; then, taking Leslie by the hand, they darted through the storm to the small, weather-beaten shack.

"Who lives here?" Leslie asked as they pushed the door open and stepped inside.

"You do," Quince said.

"What?"

Quince laughed. "Well, you own the place," he said. "No one lives here. This is a line shack. The cowboys stay here when they are out on the range."

"It's cozy enough," Leslie said, looking around. "It isn't even leaking."

Quince laughed again. "When line shacks are being used regularly, they are often in better shape than the bunkhouse. You see, the cowboys have to spend several days at a time in them, and they get bored, so they make any necessary repairs. Also, a cowboy living alone in a line shack comes to regard it more or less as his own, and he'll do everything he can to make it comfortable." He held his arm out to take in the interior of the little building.

"Now, look at this one. It has real glass in the window, a real tick mattress on the bed, a table and four nice chairs, a combination cooking and heating stove—why this one even has a shelf full of books."

"Look at this lovely cabinet," Leslie said. She examined it more closely. "Why, it's hand-built!" she said in surprise.

"Everything you see here is," Quince explained.

Leslie opened the cabinet door, and saw several cans of fruits and vegetables. "Well, we certainly shan't starve, shall we?" she said.

"I should think not," Quince said. "We could stay here for days."

"Oh, I hope not," Leslie said.

"I can think of nothing I'd rather do," Quince said, and though he tried to make the statement light, he was unable to, and for a moment there was a pregnant pause. Finally Leslie, unable to hold his glance, looked away.

"I'll make us some coffee," she said.

"Yes," Quince replied. "Yes, that would be good, thank you."

19

THE RAIN CONTINUED to fall, and as Leslie puttered about the kitchen, Quince stood on the small front porch of the cabin, and watched the rain move across the mesa, and slash into the prairie. A prairie dog, driven from one hole by quickly rising water, bounded along through the rain and disappeared down in another.

Though Quince was sheltered from the direct effect of the rain, he was being splashed with the spray, but he made no attempt to escape. He loved the rain. It blanketed all sight and sound and formed a curtain behind which his soul could exist in absolute solitude. Only those with whom he really wanted to share could penetrate it.

The front door opened, and Leslie came onto the porch to join him. She was carrying two steaming cups, and she handed one to him. "I hope you like it straight," she said.

"I do," Quince replied. He took the cup and looked at it. "This isn't coffee."

"No," Leslie said. "I found some tea, wasn't that wonderful?"

Quince smiled. "If you say so." He took a sip.

"Now confess, it isn't bad, is it?"

"It's all right," Quince said. He smiled. "Right now, I'd probably drink hot water and be grateful, though."

"Then don't complain about my tea," Leslie teased. She looked out over the rain-swept prairie. "Oh, I know it is inconvenient, but I just love the rain. I think that is what I miss most by being out here. You know, it rains so often in England."

"Well, it may rain more in England, but I'll bet we have bigger storms."

"You have wonderful, glorious storms," Leslie said, and she hugged herself as she leaned out to let some of the rain splash in her face.

"You'll catch a cold," Quince warned.

"Ha," Leslie replied. "I'm not as wet as you are. Look at you, standing there dripping water like a wet mouse. Come on in the house, let me dry you off. I found some empty flour sacks which will make marvelous towels."

Quince stepped into the room, and Leslie started to close the door.

"No," Quince said. "Don't close it, please."

Leslie smiled and left the door open. "Take off your shirt," she said. "I'll hang it by the stove to dry."

"What about you?" Quince asked. "You are as wet as I am. Aren't you afraid you'll catch cold as well?"

"Well, now, you can at least take off your shirt. I can't very well do that, can I?"

Quince stripped his shirt off and handed it to Leslie, and seeing his broad shoulders, his flat stomach, and the droplets of water clinging like tiny diamonds in the mat of hair on his chest, she

felt a sudden and unexpected charge of sexual exci-
tation.

"Uh, perhaps you'd better wrap up in one of
these sacks," Leslie suggested, reddening.

"Why?" Quince asked.

"I, I wouldn't want you to get too cold."

Quince reached out and put his hand on Leslie's
upper arm, then pulled her to him. "That isn't
what's troubling you and you know it," he said.

"Please," she said. "Please, Quince, don't do this,
you'll only make matters worse, don't you un-
ders . . ."

But Leslie's entreaties were stopped by a kiss as
Quince moved his mouth over hers.

The kiss took Leslie's breath away. Twice before
she had been kissed by this man, and twice before his kisses had been fire and ice, sending her
into dizzying heights of rapture. Again, as she had
the last time, Leslie began to test the limits of the
kiss, to see how far it would take her. She gave
herself up to it, then felt her self-control completely desert her. Her head spun faster and faster
in dizzying excitement, and for one almost fright-
ening moment, she was afraid she was going to
pass out.

The sensations so overwhelmed Leslie that for a
moment she lost sight of who and where she was,
and she let herself go limp against Quince.

Quince's hands went to the fastenings of her
bodice, and slowly, but without awkwardness or
hesitation, he opened her dress. Then, gently, ever
so gently, he slipped it across her shoulders, down
her waist, and over her hips, until she was standing nude and damp before him. Then his hand

burned a searing path down her body and across her stomach, which was drawn in tightly now with eager anticipation. When Quince's hand stopped, it was between her legs, at the center of all her feelings.

Leslie's knees turned to water, and she began to fall, then, as if in the same motion, she toppled and was caught up and carried in Quince's arms over to the bed.

Quince placed Leslie gently upon the bed, and she lay there, floating now in the partial trance which was brought on by her extreme sensual arousal. She watched as Quince removed his trousers, feeling her blood run hot, and aware of a sweet aching in her loins. Somewhere, from the innermost recesses of her mind, she knew this was wrong, that she shouldn't be doing this, and she tried to say no, but whether the word was ever spoken or not, she didn't know.

Quince moved onto the bed with her, bathing her lips, face, neck, and shoulders in his kisses, setting fire to her with his eager but gentle hands. Finally, though nothing was said, they knew they were ready for each other, and they came together.

Leslie gasped as he thrust into her. It was a gasp of delight, for what she was feeling was an exquisite pleasure, silken sensations unlike anything she had ever dreamed of. She clawed at his bare back with her fingernails, and as she did so, she gave as well as took, so that she was not only being made love to, she was making love in return. She took his lips and tongue eagerly and gave herself up to him to receive him deeply into her, moving in a headlong rush toward something mysterious and wonderful, waiting for her in all its potentiality.

Then it started, a tiny sensation that began deep inside her, buried in the innermost chamber of her soul. It began moving out then, spreading forth in a series of concentric circles like waves emanating from a stone cast in a pool. The waves began moving with more and more urgency, drawing her up tighter and tighter like the mainspring of a clock until finally, in a burst of agony that turned to ecstasy, her body attained the release and satisfaction it had sought. There were a million pins pricking her skin, and involuntary cries of pleasure came from deep in her throat. She felt as if she lost consciousness for just an instant, and brilliantly colored lights passed before her eyes as her body jerked in orgasmic, convulsive shudders.

There were two more after that: one nearly as strong, and another, not quite as strong but intensely satisfying in its own right. Then, when she felt Quince reach his own goal, it was as if she was struck by lightning when a new, unexpected orgasm burst over her, sweeping away all that had gone before it and bringing her to a peak of fulfillment so intense that every part of her being, from the tips of her toes to the scalp of her head, tingled with the kinetic energy of it. She hung precariously balanced upon the precipice for several seconds, and during those rapturous moments her body became so sensitized that she experienced not only her own sweet pleasure, but felt, through Quince, the muscle-jerking spasms of pent-up energy that were his release. The waves of pleasure that swept over him moved into her own body so that his climax and hers became one massive burst.

As Leslie coasted down from the peak, she descended not like a stone, but floated like a leaf, meeting new eddies of pleasure, rising back up a bit before slipping farther down. Finally, after all the peaks and valleys had been explored, and there was nothing left but the warm, well-banked coals of the once blazing fire, they lay there side by side, without touching and without speaking. The door to the porch was still open, and it was still raining, and the rain made music. It was perfectly orchestrated, from the rhythmic percussion and harmonic bass notes of the large booming drops to the delicate trills and melodious tinkling of the water which ran off the roof and cascaded across the eaves of the porch.

They didn't speak, because they wanted to preserve this moment, lock it forever in their hearts as a time when realities had been set aside, so that a pure, unrestrained truth could surface. And the pure truth was that despite the fact that Leslie was engaged to Goodpasture, despite the fact that even now her seamstress was making her wedding dress . . . she and Quince were in love.

Finally, after the rain had stopped and darkness had fallen, after the blanket of silence was invaded by noises from outside, the calling of frogs, the hooting of the evening owls, the distant bark of a coyote, they knew they had lost their moment. Leslie slid her hand across the bed and placed it into Quince's hand. Quince held it for several seconds, then squeezed it tightly.

"It hurts," Quince finally said.

"I know," Leslie replied, realizing that Quince had just said goodbye to their moment, too.

20

IT WAS NEARLY ten o'clock by the time Leslie returned to the main house at Mountain Shadows. She was surprised by the number of saddled horses gathered in front of the house, and also by the number of men who were gathered in the brightly lit foyer, just inside.

"Smitty, you take three men and ride the eastern range, and check the river bank for any sign that you might—" Goodpasture was talking from about the sixth step on the grand staircase, and he stopped in mid-sentence when he saw Leslie come through the front door. His face grew very red, and he compressed his lips in a tight line as he stared at her.

"Hello, Charles," Leslie said.

"It's Miss Kendrake," a voice said.

"She's back," another added. And then someone voiced the question that was obviously on everyones' minds.

"Where have you been?"

Leslie looked puzzled. "Why, I simply went for a ride, then had to seek shelter from the rain, that's all."

"Gentlemen," Charles finally managed to say,

barely choking the words out. "I thank you for
your concern and your offer to help. But as you can
see, Miss Kendrake is home now, and she is quite
safe." He forced a tight smile. "And I know you
share my relief and joy that all is well. I bid you
all goodnight, now."

"Goodnight, Mr. Goodpasture," the men said.
"Goodnight, Miss Kendrake." One by one the men
filed by Leslie, some of them mumbling a goodnight, some nodding at her and touching their hat,
a few making no sign of recognition at all. Within
a moment the last cowboy had left the foyer, closing the door behind him, and Leslie was standing
alone just inside the door. Charles was still on the
sixth step of the stairs, having neither moved nor
spoken since he had dismissed the cowboys.

The clock ticked loudly.

"Ah, *caramba*, you are back!" Maria said, coming
through the door which led back into the kitchen.
She took several steps down the hall, smiling
broadly and holding her arms out toward Leslie.

"Maria," Charles said. He spoke only the one
word, and it was softly spoken, though with a
brittleness which caused it to fall from his lips
like ice.

Maria was stopped by the word as surely as if he
had physically restrained her. Her smile of joy and
relief over seeing Leslie fell away, to be replaced
by a quick look of apprehension.

"I . . . I'm glad you are back, *señorita*," Maria
said. She wiped her hands nervously on her skirt,
then turned and hurried back down the hall and
through the kitchen door. The kitchen door closed
with a bang.

And again there was silence, except for the loudly ticking clock.

"Charles, I'm . . . sorry," Leslie finally said. "I wouldn't have wanted you to worry so."

"Don't you ever do this to me again," Charles said quietly.

"I'm sorry," Leslie said again.

Charles descended the stairs and walked toward her. For one split instant, Leslie was actually frightened, because she didn't know what he was going to do.

He put his arms around her.

"Leslie, darling, you have no idea how frightened I was," he said, and now the venom was gone from his voice. "I was so afraid that I thought I was going to go out of my mind."

"But what were you afraid of?" Leslie asked. "You know that I'm a good rider."

"Darling, do you think a fall from a horse is the only danger which could befall you?" Charles asked. "You could have been attacked by a bear, or a mountain lion, or a pack of wolves. You might have been fair game for a roving band of Indians or outlaws. You could have gotten lost, and wandered around until you died of thirst or starvation. My God, girl, you don't *know* the dangers which could have befallen you. And to think that you were out on the range at night, completely alone!"

Leslie took a deep breath, then plunged ahead with her next statement.

"I wasn't alone," she said.

Charles still had his arms around her, and when Leslie made the statement that she wasn't alone, she felt Charles's body stiffen. Finally, slowly,

Charles dropped his arms and backed away. He looked at her.

"What did you say?"

"I said I wasn't alone," Leslie said. She tried to make the comment casual, as if it were perfectly ordinary. "I was with Quince Parker."

"You were with Quince Parker?" Charles asked. The same, tight-lipped expression she had seen on his face when he saw her step through the door now returned. "What were you doing with him?"

"Really, Charles. Quince Parker is my foreman."

"I don't like that man," Charles said. "And I don't want you to be around him."

"I can't see that it is any of your business *who* I am around," Leslie replied in quick, snapping anger.

"It is my business because you are my fiancée," he said. "Soon to be my wife."

"Perhaps not," Leslie said.

"What?" Charles replied, showing genuine surprise at her remark. "Leslie, what are you saying?"

"Charles, perhaps you were too hasty in asking me to marry you. Or perhaps I was too hasty in accepting. But the plain fact of the matter is, I am having second thoughts about marrying."

"Darling, you can't *mean* that," Charles said, and he put his arms around her again, and pulled her to him, holding her in his embrace. "Please, Leslie, don't say anything like that."

"I, I want you to release me from my promise," Leslie said.

"No," Charles replied. "No, darling, I could never do that." He squeezed her even more tightly, and for an anxious moment, Leslie feared that he might never let her go again. But the feeling passed, because he did release her. Then he put his hands on her shoulders, and looked at her with deep, impassioned eyes.

"I need you, Leslie," he said.

In truth, Leslie was somewhat surprised by the intensity of Charles's reaction. And this caught her off-guard, so that she wasn't quite as sure of herself as she thought she would be.

"I just feel we moved too fast, that's all," Leslie said.

"Leslie, is there someone else?" Charles asked.

"There . . . there may be," Leslie said. She braced herself for what she must say. She was going to tell Charles outright that she loved Quince. And then she planned to tell Quince. Leslie's own personal code of ethics decreed that she should be free of any obligation to Charles, before she could speak of love to Quince, so Quince knew nothing of her plan.

"Is it Quince Parker?"

"Yes," Leslie admitted.

"Leslie, you don't love him, you know you don't," Charles said. "If you thought you were too hasty with me, then, you are being equally hasty with Parker. He is a young, handsome man, and, I suppose, quite a dashing figure. But you have already seen how immature and headstrong he can be. Surely, you couldn't love a man like that, Leslie."

"Oh, Charles," Leslie said. Tears flooded her eyes, and she was unable to choke back a sob. "I think I do love him, but I am so *confused*."

"Of course you are, darling," Charles said. He sighed. "Look, I'll tell you what I'll do." He put his hand under her chin, and turned her face up to him. Two tear tracks trailed down her cheeks, and he brushed them both away, gently, with his thumb. "I'll release you from your obligation to me."

"You . . . you mean end the engagement?" Leslie asked.

"Yes," Charles replied. "As of this moment, we are no longer engaged," he said. He smiled, a sad kind of smile, which did more to move Leslie than any of his words had. "But, as of this moment, also, I become once again the serious suitor, bidding for your hand."

"Oh, Charles, I don't know," Leslie said. "What would that accomplish?"

"It would give me the same chance as Quince Parker," Charles said. "And that's all I want, Leslie. Just give me an equal chance with him. After all," he smiled. "Am I not being fair to him? All I'm asking for is an even break."

"Charles, I'm so confused—"

"Well, of course you are," Charles interrupted. "And I'm not making it any better. I'll tell you what. Let's just not discuss it until after you get back."

"After I get back?"

"From Montana. Remember? You are going up to visit Augusta Kohrs."

"Yes," Leslie said. "Yes, I think I would appreciate the chance to get away and think things over."

"Fine, fine," Charles said. "And whatever you decide when you return, you will have my blessing. I hope you decide to marry me, but if not? Well, if not, you will have my best wishes. Now, that's fair enough, isn't it?"

Leslie smiled through her tears. "Yes," she said. "That seems fair enough."

"Good, good. Now you just think about the fine time you will have there, and everything else will fall into place. I'll make arrangements for you to go later this week."

"All right," Leslie said. She started toward her bedroom, but after a few steps she stopped and looked back at Charles. "Charles, would you promise me something?"

"Of course, my dear. What is it?"

"Would you promise that, even if we are married, you will let Three Crowns continue as a ranch, and not assimilate it into Mountain Shadows?"

"Well, darling, that seems a little impractical, doesn't it?"

"How do you mean, impractical?"

Charles laughed. "After all, one can't ranch without cattle, and there are no cattle at Three Crowns, nor water for them, even if there were."

"Oh, but there is water," Leslie said. "Charles, you should see what Quince and Rufus have done! They've put in windmills, and laid pipes, and now the streams are flowing again. And I told Quince to buy cattle with the money my father left me."

"You are going to restock the ranch?" Charles asked.

"Yes," Leslie said.

Charles ran his hand through his hair in a quick, nervous, almost agitated motion, then suddenly he smiled.

"I hope he is successful," Charles said. "And I

will do anything I can do to help make him successful."

"Oh, Charles, you will?" Leslie asked.

"Of course I will. Leslie, I don't want anything to come between us when we do get married. I don't want you to ever think that I may have been less than fair with anyone. So you can count on me to provide whatever assistance Parker may need in making Three Crowns a productive ranch again."

Leslie laughed, then ran back the few steps which had separated them, threw her arms around his neck, and kissed him. "Thank you, Charles. Oh, thank you."

"Well now," Charles said, smiling broadly at the kiss. "That almost makes it worth while."

Quince saw the cluster of lights as he returned to the bunkhouse of Three Crowns. It had been an hour's ride back from where he left Leslie, just outside the front door of Goodpasture's house, and during that hour Quince had thought of many things.

Why hadn't he spoken his thoughts to Leslie? Why hadn't he told her that he loved her? Why hadn't he made her admit that she loved him? Why, in fact, hadn't he come right out and asked her to marry him? That was clearly on his mind, and he felt it had been on her mind as well.

But he hadn't said anything. And neither had she. And the whole thing may have been in his imagination.

But what about their making love in the line shack? That wasn't in his imagination. That had clearly and decidedly taken place.

She did love him. He was sure of it. And if she didn't say anything to him, then it wasn't her place to say anything to him. And he, being merely a foreman, had no right to say anything to her. Not, that is, until he could bring Three Crowns back into productivity again. Then, and only then, could he tell her what he felt.

But what if she went through with her plans to marry Goodpasture? Quince grunted aloud. He hadn't thought of that. He couldn't think of that. Well, he would just have to believe that she wouldn't marry him. Because if he couldn't hang on to that belief, then he had nothing to work for anyway, and he may as well leave.

"Don't worry," he said to his horse. "She won't marry Charles Goodpasture. I know she won't."

Quince unsaddled his horse, threw some oats and hay into the feed trough, then walked the short distance between the barn and the bunkhouse. Above him the moon hung like a great, silver plate, and scattered all through the heavens was a fine sprinkle of blue dust as the stars winked from the night sky. Quince stopped and looked up for a moment. The canopy of stars which covered him when he slept out on the prairie was always beautiful to him, but this night it seemed more beautiful than ever. He shrugged, then went inside.

"I held back some supper for you," Rufus said. "It's fried chicken, so it'll be just as good now as it was when it was cooked."

"Thanks," Quince said. He walked over to the stove and peeled back a towel which Rufus had placed over the plates of food. He picked up a drumstick and took a bite from it.

"All the creeks are full," Rufus said. "'Course, the rain helped out considerable, but the pumps is all a-workin', cause water is spillin' outta the pipes good 'n steady."

"Rufus, I'm going to marry Leslie Kendrake," Quince said.

Rufus beamed brightly. "You are? Well, now I expect that's about the best news I've heard this day, and I mean it beats the news of the water flowin' again."

"I thought you'd be pleased," Quince said.

"Pleased? Hell, I'm that tickled I'm near 'bout to bust out singin'. When are you goin' to do it?"

"I don't know," Quince said.

"Yeah, well, she has to break off the engagement with Goodpasture and all. I suppose it's understandable her not wantin' to pick a date just yet."

Quince finished the drumstick, put the bare bone down, and drew out another piece. "She, uh . . ." he said, studying the piece of chicken intently to keep from having to look directly at Rufus. "She, uh, really doesn't know it yet."

"Doesn't know the date you mean?" Rufus asked, confused by Quince's strange remark.

"Not exactly," Quince said. Quince tried to avoid Rufus's direct questioning. "Uhmm, this is good chicken." He took a big bite.

"Never mind the chicken," Rufus said. "Quince, what are you talkin' about?"

"She doesn't know the date because she doesn't know she's going to marry me," Quince said.

"You mean you say you are going to marry her, and you haven't even asked her yet?" Rufus asked, the tone of his voice clearly reflecting his exasperation.

"Yep."

"Well, why didn't you ask her?"

"I couldn't," Quince said. "I was afraid she would say no."

Rufus grunted in disgust. "Well, I can tell you one thing, pard. She'll damn sure never say *yes* iffen you don't ask her."

"I'll ask her," Quince said.

"When?"

"When I've got something to offer her," Quince said. "When I've made this ranch productive again." Quince smiled broadly. "And we are going to do that, pardner. You and I are going to do that."

"You bet we are," Rufus replied, and he smiled just as enthusiastically as Quince. "And say, didn't Miss Kendrake say we could use Three Crowns money to stock the ranch?"

"Yep."

"You know what that means?"

"What?"

"It means we can stock the ranch with longhorns," Rufus said. "You don't have to take that Kohrs fellow up on his crazy notion of runnin' nothin' but Herefords."

"I don't have to, but I will," Quince said quietly.

"You will? Why?"

"A couple of reasons," Quince said. "The stock I buy with Leslie's money will be Leslie's stock. The money I borrow from Kohrs can be used to replace my own herd."

"What difference does it make?"

"I said I wanted to have something to offer Leslie before I ask her to marry me," Quince said. "I can't offer her her own cows."

"All right, I might go along with you on that. But you said there were two reasons. What is your other reason?"

"If Kohrs is right, Herefords are going to be the cattle of the future," Quince said. "I figure that if we get in on the ground floor now, we'll have a leg up on the beef market when buyers start gettin' particular enough that they want Herefords instead of longhorns."

Rufus smiled. "I guess that's why you're the boss 'n I'm the cook," he said. "I hadn't figured that, but you are pure-dee right."

"Listen, Rufus, I'll be going up to Montana later this week to pick up the cattle. I want you to hire us a new crew while I'm gone. Do you suppose you can handle that?"

"They'll be here when you get back," Rufus promised. "But what about you? Won't you need someone to help you bring the cattle down?"

"I'm going to bring them down by railroad," Quince said. "I'll only need one or two people, and I'll hire them up there."

"I can get Simmons back easy enough," Rufus said. "He's been laying around in town, spendin' his pay ever since we let him go."

"Then he should be about out of money and ready to come back," Quince said with a grin.

"That's the way I have it figured," Rufus said. "Oh, and I'd better restock the kitchen. Let's see, we'll need beans, flour, bacon," Rufus got up and started toward the pantry mumbling to himself, and Quince knew that he had lost him for the rest of the evening. But that was all right with Quince, because he wanted a little time to be alone with his own thoughts anyway.

Quince walked through the door of the bunkhouse and ambled down to the fence. He leaned on the fence and looked out across the vast, rolling valley. The distant mountains, which were a purple blue by day, were now no more than a darker line on the horizon. There was land enough out there to support more than thirty thousand head of cattle. And now, water as well.

"Mr. Kendrake, damn, I wish you were here for this," he said, almost prayerfully.

21

THE SIGN on the front door said, "Open at Four", but as Charles had a key to Rosita's, he let himself in without regard to the sign.

Rosita was down on her hands and knees behind the bar, taking inventory of her liquor supply, when she heard the front door.

"Manuel? que' le te parece. . . . . . ,"

"It isn't Manuel," Charles interrupted.

Rosita raised up and looked over the bar to see Charles standing just inside the door. The door had been shut once again, and Charles was locking it behind him. The shades were drawn and the room was in shadows, but even so, Rosita's eyes were flashing as if with an inner light.

"So," Rosita said. "You have come to see me. Why? Did the English lady kick you out of her bed?"

Charles turned to look at her, and he wagged his finger mockingly. "Ah, Rosita, why are you so angry? Can't you be happy that I am here?"

"Happy? Why should I be happy?" Rosita said. "Am I your whore, that you come to see me only when you want a woman?"

"No," Charles said. He walked over and placed

the palm of his hand on her cheek. "You know you are more than that to me, Rosita. Much more."

The gentleness of his touch, and the unexpected tone of his voice disarmed Rosita, and though she was prepared to be very angry with him, she couldn't be now. She took his hand in both of hers, and pulled it around to her lips to kiss it.

"It has been so long," she said. "And I was afraid that I would never see you again." She smiled, happily. "I am glad you are finished with the English lady."

"Rosita, I intend to marry Lady Leslie," Charles said.

"Marry her? But, Charles, no," she said. Her eyes flooded with tears. "You have told me it is Rosita you love. How can you marry another?"

"Rosita, you must know by now that I could never marry you," Charles said. "You could never be mistress of Mountain Shadow."

"And your English lady can?"

"Yes," Charles said. He smiled. "But you wouldn't want to be the mistress of Mountain Shadow anyway," he said. "I know you. I know you would prefer to stay here."

"If we were married, I would do both," Rosita said.

"Oh, no," Charles replied. "There is no way you could be my wife, and still run this saloon."

"But half is mine," Rosita said. "And I am paying you for the other half. You wouldn't take it away from me?"

"No, I wouldn't take it away from you," Charles said. "That's why things are better off, left as they are. You stay here, I will get married, but still, I will come to see you."

"I will only be your whore?" Rosita asked sharply.

"How can you say that, Rosita? A whore I can visit anytime, and pay a little money, and forget. I have given you all this," he held his hand out in a grand, sweeping gesture. "And I come to see you again and again. One does not do this with a whore."

"You have found another," Rosita said. "Perhaps I will find another as well."

"I'm sure you can, Rosita. Anyone who comes in here would be pleased to jump into your bed. But is that what you really want?"

"Perhaps. But I do not jump into bed with just anyone. Already, I have been seeing someone."

"Good for you," Charles said, saying the words in such a way as to show that he didn't believe her.

"You don't believe me."

"Yes, I believe you," Charles said. But he spoke the words in the same tone of voice.

"Shall I tell you who it is?" Rosita challenged.

"If you wish."

"It is Quince Parker," Rosita said.

"Quince Parker?" Charles laughed. "You're right, Rosita, I *don't* believe you."

"I will prove it to you," Rosita said. "The first time was on the night of the Fiesta for the 4th of July. You were supposed to see me, but you didn't. Quince Parker had a fight with the English lady, and he came here. I was angry because you did not come, so I invited him up to my room,"

Rosita said, finishing with a rush, because half way through she lost her bravado and became genuinely frightened at how Charles might react.

Charles realized by her action then that she was telling the truth. At first he felt a quick surge of anger, but then a glimmer of light flashed in the deep recesses of his mind. Here was information that he might be able to use.

"Are you telling me the truth?" she asked.

"*Si*," she said.

"Have you seen him since?"

"*Si*," Rosita lied. She knew that she was either going to make Charles jealous, and thus aware of what he was giving up for the English lady, or she was going to make him dangerously angry. But it was worth the risk, for she could not afford to lose Charles entirely. She took a deep breath and plunged on. "He has come to see me many times since then and always, we go to my room and make love." She closed her eyes and made her face into what she believed was an expression of rapture. "He is *uno muy bueno* lover."

"Do you really think so?"

"*Si*."

"Rosita, I don't believe you," Charles said. He did believe her, but he was playing a hunch now, putting into motion a plan which he had begun to develop, even as she told him the story. "I don't think Parker has ever been in your bed."

"It is true," Rosita said.

Charles laughed. "No, it isn't. Don't think I don't know what you are trying to do. You are trying to make me jealous."

"No, I'm not," Rosita said.

"Yes, I think you are," Charles said. "But it won't work, because I don't believe you. Unless you knew of some way you could prove it to me."

"*Caramba*, how can I prove it to you?" Rosita asked, angrily. "Do you think I invite people to *watch* when I make love?"

"You could," Charles said.

"What? Are you loco? Why do you say such a thing?"

"Rosita, if you can have Quince Parker making love to you at 9:30 in the morning, I will give you the title to this place, free and clear."

Rosita was shocked by Charles's statement. This wasn't going as she planned, not at all. She had hoped to make him jealous by bragging of her affair with Quince Parker, but he wasn't jealous at all. In fact, she had no idea what he was.

"You mean, you want me to make love with Quince Parker?" she asked in disbelief.

"Yes."

"But, why? I don't understand."

"You don't have to understand, Rosita," Charles said. "I only want you to do it. Can you?"

Rosita sighed, and looked at the floor. She was quiet for a long moment, and then tears began to flow down her cheeks.

"No," she said. "I can't do it."

Charles laughed. "What do you mean you can't do it? You were a whore when I found you, Rosita. You would go to bed with any man who gave you money. Why is that any different from what I am asking you to do?"

"Because I lied to you," Rosita said. "I was trying to make you jealous. Quince Parker came to my bed on the Fiesta Day, just as I said. But he has never been back since that time."

"Then get him back."

"How can I do this?"

Charles reached for his special bottle, uncorked it, poured himself a glass, and took a swallow while he thought about it. "I have an idea," he finally said.

"What?"

"You will send him a letter, and tell him that you want to see him here, tomorrow, at nine o'clock."

"Why do you think he would come, just because I send a letter?" Rosita asked.

"Because, you will tell him that it is very important that he come see you. Then, when he gets here, tell him you wish to make him a loan to buy cattle for his ranch. Take him to your room, and then . . ." Charles stopped in mid-sentence and smiled. "Well, Rosita, once you have a man in your room, do I have to tell *you* how to get him in your bed?"

Rosita smiled. "No," she said. "That, I can do."

"Well, all right then, there's no problem, is there? All you have to do is get him in a compromising position by nine-thirty tomorrow morning and I will turn over the deed to this building, free and clear."

"Charles," Rosita said. "Why would you want to do this? I thought you said you wanted things to stay as they have been between us."

"I do."

"But you want me to go to bed with other men?"

"No, not with other men, just with this one man,

and just this one time," Charles said. "You must believe me, I have my reasons."

"If that is what you want, that is what I will do," Rosita said sadly.

"Look at it this way," Charles said. "You've sold your body before, but never for so much, no?"

The exotic idea of selling herself for so much, had, in its own way, a strange and exciting effect on her, acting somewhat as an aphrodisiac. She smiled seductively at Charles.

"You are right," she said. "Never have I sold myself for so much money. But now, if you wish, come with me. You, my love, I will give myself to, so that we can seal our bargain."

"That's not a bad idea," Charles agreed with a smile of his own, as he followed her upstairs.

22

QUINCE had just finished breakfast, and was repairing the corral fence, when Manuel rode up the next morning. Manuel slipped off his horse, wiped his perspiring face with a red- and white-dotted handkerchief, and sighed.

"*Caramba*, it is going to be hot today," he said.

"Yes," Quince said. He pointed to the pump.

"The water is cool and sweet. Help yourself."

"*Gracias*," Manuel said. He walked over to the pump, saw a tin cup hanging there, then jerked the handle up and down a few times to fill it. He drank thirstily, with water trickling down his chin and wetting his already sweat-wet shirt.

Manuel let out a long, appreciative sigh, hung the cup back on the pump, and wiped his hands on his shirt.

"What can I do for you?" Quince asked.

"*Que?*"

"Why are you here?" Quince asked. "Are you looking for a job?"

"A job? No, *señor*," Manuel said. "I could not be the cowboy. The work it is too . . . too . . ." Manuel shrugged his shoulders, "how you say . . ."

"Hard?" Quince said, laughing.

"*Si*, hard," Manuel said. He took an envelope from his jacket pocket. "*Señorita* Rosita, she give this to me and say I should give to you?"

"What does it say?" Quince asked, taking the letter.

"I don't know, *Señor*. English, I do not read so good. Spanish, I do not read either."

Quince opened the envelope and pulled out the letter.

> *Señor* Parker,
> Please come to visit me at my place at nine o'clock this morning. It is very important for you to come.
>
> > Rosita

"Are you going to go, *Senor*?" Manuel asked.

"I thought you said you couldn't read," Quince said.

"I cannot," Manuel said. "But *Señorita* Rosita say, she ask you to come."

Quince ran his hand through his hair and looked back toward town. Though the town itself wasn't visible, the Front Door, the mountain which protected Sweetgrass from the brutal winter winds, was.

"I don't know, Manuel, I have a lot to do around the place here. I'll be bringing new cattle in soon."

"*Si*, the cattle," Manuel said. "It is the cattle she wants to talk about."

"Rosita wants to talk to me about cattle?" Quince asked. "What for? What does she have to do with cattle?"

"I don't know, *Señor*," Manuel said.

Quince chuckled. "Well, I have to admit that, now, I'm curious. All right, Manuel, I'll come see Señorita Rosita."

"*Gracias, Señor,*" Manuel said, smiling broadly. "Now I do not have to face the anger of a woman who is scorned."

"Nine o'clock, huh?" Quince said. "I'd better get going, I guess."

"Hurry, Andrew, I don't want Lady Leslie to miss her train," Charles said. Charles and Leslie were standing by the carriage, and Andrew was carrying the last of Leslie's suitcases, and loading them into the carriage boot. Andrew was mumbling under his breath as he walked.

"It seem to me like she takin' enough to move up there for good."

"I'm always afraid I'll go somewhere and leave what I need most at home," Leslie said, apologizing for her voluminous luggage.

"Yes'm, I knows how it is," Andrew said. "I'm that way too."

Leslie laughed at Andrew's remark, but Charles, checking his watch in irritation, hurried him on.

"Charles, I thought you told me the train doesn't leave until ten o'clock."

"It doesn't," Charles admitted. "But there is someone I want you to meet in town before you leave."

"Oh? Who?"

"It is a woman," Charles said. "A business acquaintance of mine. Her name is Rosita Mendoza."

"Rosita? I've seen that name before," Leslie said.

She smiled. "Oh, I know where I've seen it! Isn't there a pub in town called Rosita's?"

"Yes," Charles said. "Only we call them saloons, rather than pubs."

"The baggage is all loaded now, Mr. Charles," Andrew said, grunting as he placed the last piece on the rack behind the seat.

"Fine, fine," Charles said. He helped Leslie into the carriage, then climbed in behind her. Andrew got on the driver's seat then, and clucked to the team, and the carriage started rolling, briskly, but sedately, with the wheels crunching against the finely crushed gravel which made up the curved driveway in front of the house.

"Charles, why would you want me to meet a pub-mistress, or saloon keeper, or whatever you call them here? I have nothing against such persons you understand, but, little in common as well."

Charles cleared his throat, as if composing his thoughts. "I've been thinking about our conversation," he said.

"Our conversation?" Leslie laughed. "Which conversation? We've had many."

"You know the one I mean," Charles said. "The one where I agreed to free you from your promise to marry me."

"Oh, Charles, you aren't going back on that now, are you?" Leslie asked anxiously.

"No, dear," Charles said, reassuringly. "But, as I am to try and win you anew, I want to ensure that there are no hidden obstacles which may turn up to haunt me. And that's why I want you to meet Rosita. You see, you may hear my name linked with hers because, well not only is she a business acquaintance, I financed her saloon, but I also used to visit her occasionally."

"What do you mean, visit her?" Leslie asked, though in fact, she knew what he meant, and asked the question merely because she was enjoying his obvious embarrassment.

"You know," Charles hedged. "I *visited* her. I wasn't married, I had not yet met you, and she was a rather pleasant diversion."

"I see," Leslie said. Leslie smiled, then asked, impishly. "Wouldn't you rather I wait outside, in the carriage, while *you* visit her?"

"No, of course not," Charles said. Then, seeing her smiling, he smiled as well. "You are teasing."

"Of course I'm teasing," she said. She put her hand on his arm. "You are sweet, Charles, but you don't have to do this."

"I know I don't have to, but I want to."

"Did you love her?"

"No," Charles said. "Not that she isn't a fine person in her own right. But I didn't love her, and I haven't seen her since you've come into my life."

"Then if it is important to you that I meet her, I shall," Leslie said.

"Thank you," Charles said. "I knew you would understand."

"Well, after all, you have been very understanding to me," Leslie said. "So why shouldn't I be understanding to you?"

Andrew couldn't help but overhear the conversation, and he shook his head in disapproval. But he said nothing aloud, for it wasn't his place to mix in with the affairs of rich white folks.

* * *

Rosita's was closed, and the sign was up when Quince arrived, but Rosita had been looking for him, and the moment Quince stepped onto the boardwalk, she opened the door and motioned for him to come inside. With the same motion, she waved Manuel away, so she and Quince would be alone. "Good, good, you have come," she said. She stepped back to let him enter. The shades were all pulled, and the interior was in shadows, so that it was considerably cooler inside than out. Quince stood just inside the door and let his eyes adjust to the darkness, before he moved further in.

"Why did you want to see me?" Quince asked.

Rosita smiled. "You have not come back to my place since the fiesta," she said.

"I know."

"I have missed you."

"Rosita, is *that* why you sent for me?" Quince asked, a little irritated.

"Is that not a good enough reason?" Rosita asked. She leaned forward to rest her hands on the table, and as she did, her blouse fell forward, showing much of her breasts. "Did you not enjoy Rosita?"

"Yes," Quince said.

"But not enough to come back?"

"I've had other things on my mind," Quince said.

"And another girl, yes?" Rosita challenged.

"Yes," Quince said resolutely.

"I know the other girl," Rosita said. "It is the English lady. But you are *loco*, Quince Parker. She is *Señor* Goodpasture's woman."

Quince smiled. "No, he just *thinks* she is."

"It is true," Rosita said. "You will see that it is true."

"Rosita, I really didn't want to come here to talk about my personal life," Quince said, again allowing his irritation to show. "Now, what do you want?"

"I want to loan you money," she said. "I want to loan you money for to buy cows to make the ranch go again."

"Why would you want to do that?" Quince asked.

"I am angry with Goodpasture," Rosita said. "I do not want to see him get his way with everything. If you make the ranch go again, he will be upset, no?"

"Yes, he would be *very* upset."

Rosita smiled broadly. "Then, that is my wish, Quince Parker. I want to upset him. Will you take my money?"

"What conditions do you attach to the loan?" Quince asked.

Rosita smiled broadly. "Only one condition, Quince Parker. The condition is that you make the ranch go and make Goodpasture be *muy* upset. This you will do?"

"This I will try to do," Quince agreed.

"*Bueno.* Now, come up to my room and we will close the deal."

"Come up to your room? Why?" Quince asked.

Rosita laughed, and, playfully, chucked Quince under the chin. "*Loco* one. Do you think Rosita is so ugly she must use tricks to get a man in her room?"

"No, of course not," Quince said.

"Then do not think I will trick you. I ask you to come to my room because that is where the money is. I will give you ten thousand dollars."

"Ten thousand dollars!" Quince said. "Why, with that money, I wouldn't have to borrow any from Kohrs."

"Then you will take the loan from me?"

"Yes," Quince said. "Since we seem to have a common goal, Rosita, I would be glad to take the money from you."

"I am glad," Rosita said. She pulled the sleeves of her blouse down from her shoulders, and let it roll down so that her breasts were exposed, almost to the nipples. She smiled, seductively. "Now, come to my room and we will make the deal."

There was a table in the center of Rosita's room, with a bottle and two glasses. Rosita went right to the table, and poured them both a drink.

"Oh, no thanks," Quince said, holding his hand out. "It's too early in the day for me to have anything to drink."

"But it is *Señor* Goodpasture's whiskey," Rosita said.

Quince laughed. "No, I remember what happened the last time I drank his whiskey."

Rosita smiled, seductively, and pulled the neck of her blouse down so that her breasts were now completely exposed. "*Si*," she said, "I remember too. Are you sure you do not want the same thing to happen again?"

"Rosita, what are you doing?" Quince asked. "I thought we had some business to discuss."

"Feel my breast," Rosita said, taking Quince's hand and placing it on the golden mound of flesh.

Despite himself, Quince couldn't help but react to the contact. Her skin was burning hot, and the flesh was firm, yet resilient to his touch. The nipple was hard, yet tender, and he could feel her heart pounding as he touched it.

"There," she said. "Can you not feel my desire for you?"

"Rosita, I've already told you," Quince said. "I love another."

"She is not here now," Rosita said. "I am."

"That doesn't matter. I can't be untrue to her."

"Ask yourself where she is," Rosita said. "She is with Goodpasture, is she not?"

"I suppose she is, but that doesn't change anything," Quince said. "I know that she loves me."

"If she loved you, she would be with you," Rosita said. "As I am." Rosita pulled Quince's lips down to her, then she opened her mouth and sent her tongue against his, darting in and out like the rapidly flicking tongue of a serpent.

"Rosita, don't do this," Quince said. "You are an exceptionally beautiful woman, don't you know you can have anyone you want?"

"I want you," Rosita said. She shoved her blouse down, and then pushed her skirt over her hips, and let the dress fall on the floor, so that it became a shimmering pool of cloth, from which rose the naked Venus.

Quince felt Rosita's nakedness leaning into him. Her breasts mashed against his chest, her loins ground against him, and, even through his clothes, he could feel the heat of her desire.

And he could feel something else as well. For despite his protestations to the contrary, he had

been so overwhelmed with her overt sexuality, that
he was now showing unmistakable signs of arousal.

"Please, Rosita," he said, almost gasping the en-
treaty. "I'm only human, don't you know what you
are doing to me?"

"*Si*, I know what I'm doing to you," Rosita said.
"I can *feel* what I am doing to you."

Quince felt her hands then, cool, and soft, and
skilled, as they opened his pants and let them slide
to the floor to lie in a heap next to her discarded
dress. Then, with a shock of surprise, he realized
that Rosita had already made connection, even as
they were standing.

"My God, woman, what is this?" Quince asked,
feeling himself totally losing control of the situation. It had been she who initiated it, but he was
now as caught up in the maelstrom as she was, as
committed to the quest for fulfillment, and as totally obvious to everything as was she.

That is why he didn't hear the outside door
open, or the sound of feet coming up the stairs. He
should have heard it, because the door to Rosita's
room was wide open, and he and Rosita were standing, connected in a writhing, lovers' embrace, just
inside her room.

"Oh, I'm so sorry," Charles suddenly said. "I saw
the door standing open, I thought it would be all
right to come on up."

"What the—?" Quince yelled, and then he saw,
standing in the door with a face twisted in shock,
not only Charles Goodpasture, but Leslie Kendrake
as well.

23

THE LAST THING Leslie said to Charles, just before she boarded the train was, "We'll get married as soon as I return."

Charles kissed her happily, and put her on the train, apologizing for his "inadvertent" contribution to her embarrassment, and assuring her that she was making the right decision in reinstating the wedding.

Leslie didn't know if she had made the right decision or not. Whatever the case, she was certain of one thing. She never wanted to see Quince Parker again!

Even as she thought of the humiliating scene she had witnessed, she fought hard to choke back the sob which rose in her throat. It was now clear to her that Quince Parker didn't love her, he merely used her. That was why he didn't speak of love to her on that long ride back to Mountain Shadows. That was why he didn't ask her to give up Goodpasture and marry him. He had no intention of loving her or marrying her. He had meant only to use her, as he was using Rosita.

Leslie pressed her forehead to the window and watched the desolate country flash by outside. The train was travelling at sixty miles per hour, and the sagebrush nearest the track whipped by so fast that it was a blur. Further out from the track the country rolled by more slowly, yet even these distant objects confirmed the train's great speed. An antelope bounded up, challenged the train to race, lost ground quickly, then pulled away, abandoning the challenge.

There was something comforting about watching the scenery slide by outside. The vastness of the land, the immense openness, seemed to belittle mere man, and make all individual troubles unimportant. It was a measure of perspective which allowed Leslie to regain at last some peace of mind. Finally, the relaxing motion of the train, the rhythmic clacking of the wheels, and the sedating display of scenery, put her to sleep, and her turmoil subsided.

Leslie changed trains at Ogden, and took the luxurious *Rocky Mountain Flyer* north. She had ridden comfortably enough enroute to Ogden, but from there north she rode in the lap of luxury. The *Rocky Mountain Flyer* boasted two libraries, a hair-dressing salon, and two organs. The parlor car was resplendent in plush upholstery, rich hangings and hand-carved inlaid panelling.

"Lady Leslie," a uniformed steward inquired as soon as Leslie's luggage was stowed, and she had settled into a large, overstuffed chair.

"Yes?"

"Welcome aboard the *Rocky Mountain Flyer*, Lady Leslie." He handed her a menu. "There are seats available in the dining car at eleven, noon, and one o'clock. Which would you prefer?"

"I think I will take the one o'clock seating," Leslie said.

"Would you care to select from the menu?"

Leslie's trip West had prepared her for the veritable feasts offered to first class passengers on the elite trains, but the *Rocky Mountain Flyer* exceeded all her expectations. The menu featured blue-winged teal, antelope steaks, roast beef, boiled ham, broiled chicken, corn-on-the-cob, fresh fruit, hot rolls and cornbread.

"I'll have broiled chicken, please," she said, returning the menu to the steward.

"An excellent choice, Lady Leslie," the steward said. "The dinner seatings will be announced by the porter's chimes. Yours will be the third seating."

"Thank you," Leslie said.

After the steward left, Leslie looked through the large windows. The scenery had changed somewhat since leaving Wyoming. It was still vast, but the mountains seemed closer, and more overwhelming, while in the meadows and plains alongside the track, wildflowers grew in colorful profusion. There were more towns and settlements along the railroad here, too, and as the train passed each station, it attracted the curious at trackside, and Leslie saw dozens of children waving gaily as they sped along. At first she returned their waves, but soon grew tired from the sheer effort of it, and she settled back to read one of the books from the library.

By one o'clock, when the third call for lunch was issued, Leslie was ravenously hungry.

The elegance of the dining car was in keeping

with the rest of the train, and Leslie saw richly
panelled walls, plush drapes and upholstery, and
flower-bedecked tables. She was met by a waiter
as soon as she stepped through the door.

"Your name, miss?"

"Leslie Kendrake."

"Of course, Lady Leslie. Right this way, please,"
the waiter said, smiling, and led her through the
car of diners to her table.

When the meal was served, she was glad to see
that its preparation matched her appetite, and she
ate heartily. She was also aware of something else.
This was the first meal she had eaten alone in
several weeks. In fact, this was the first time she
had been alone in several weeks, and she was
enjoying it. It was a pleasant, almost an invigorat-
ing experience, to be her own company for a
change.

Leslie had not realized how much she missed
being by herself until these last few hours. It was
a condition she was used to because as a student
in school she had no one upon whom she was dependent, and she had taken a great deal of pride
in her self-sufficiency. She was happy to discover
that she was still capable of enjoying a bit of solitude. In fact, she wished this train trip could go
on longer, much longer, even indefinitely. At that
moment, she could think of no greater joy than to
be a passenger, alone and unbothered, floating
through space without time, substance, or reason,
forever.

Quince was quiet when he returned to Three
Crowns. Four of the old hands were back, includ-

ing Simmons, and they greeted him happily when he came into the bunkhouse. Quince returned their greeting, but he went almost immediately to his bunk and lay down with his hands folded behind his head. It wasn't the way of the cowboy to sidle up to someone who had, by his action, expressed a desire to be alone, so most of the cowboys let Quince lie in peace.

"Simmons, why don't you take the boys out and show them the water system?" Rufus suggested. "One of the things you boys are going to have to be familiar with is how to keep the water flowing."

"Right, boss," Simmons said, and though the other cowboys could remember when Rufus was only a cook, they didn't question it when Simmons referred to him in such a way. It was obvious, even to them, that Rufus had moved up in the scheme of things.

Simmons and the others left, and a moment later, Rufus heard them riding off. He worked for nearly half an hour on a piece of harness, musing over it and studying it as if it presented a very perplexing problem to him. Finally, he sighed, and laid it on the table.

"What's wrong, Quince?" he asked.

Quince didn't answer.

"I know it ain't in the way of things to be talkin' 'bout ever' little thing that could trouble you, but there seems to be somethin' wrong."

"I'm the biggest kind of a fool God ever let walk on this earth," Quince finally said. He was still staring at the ceiling, and he didn't look over toward Rufus as he spoke.

"What makes you think that, pard?"

"I've just driven away the only woman I could ever love. She'll never speak to me again, and I don't blame her. The fact is, I don't know if I could even face her after what I've done."

"You want to tell me about it?" Rufus asked quietly.

Quince sighed, then sat up, swinging his legs over the side so that his feet were on the floor and his arms were resting on his legs. He clasped his hands in front of him as he spoke. "It isn't a pretty story," he said, then he told about going into Sweetgrass in answer to Rosita's letter. And he told how Rosita took him to her room, and practically threw herself at him, finally succeeding just as Goodpasture and Leslie came up the stairs.

"Of all the times for Leslie to happen in," he said.

"She didn't just happen in," Rufus said.

"What? Why of course she did."

"You're just too damned close to it," Rufus said. "You are so close you can't see that you was took by Goodpasture."

"What do you mean?"

"Hell, he set you up," Rufus said. "Like as not he paid Rosita a good bit of money to do what she done. Or he had some other hold over her. You are still young, and in some ways, Quince, you are as innocent as a babe in the woods."

"Damn, if that's true . . ." Quince started, but his statement was interrupted by the loud banging open of the front door.

"Boss, Rufus, come quick!" one of the cowboys said. "It's Simmons, he's been gutshot!"

When Quince and Rufus arrived at the place

the cowboy took them, they saw Simmons lying near one of the newly irrigated streams. Someone had removed his saddle and had placed it under his head, and the saddle blanket was thrown over him. His face was ashen-white, and gripped with pain. The others who had ridden out with him were either standing or sitting by him, and another man, dressed in black, was standing a short distance away, looking impassively toward the scene.

"Emil Bates," Rufus said under his breath.

"Emil Bates? The hired gun? What's he doing here?" Quince asked.

Quince walked over and squatted down beside Simmons. He looked into his face, and as soon as he did, he realized that there was nothing he, or anyone else, could do.

"You wasted a ride out here," the man in black said. "Unless you wanted to hear his last words."

"What are you doing here, Bates?" Quince asked.

Bates pointed downstream a short ways, and Quince saw half a dozen head of cattle, watering at the creek. "I come to bring back some of Mr. Goodpasture's property," Bates said. He smiled, and tipped his hat back, and studied Quince closely. "You know who I am, huh?"

Quince looked into Bates's face. His eyes were so pale a blue that they were nearly without color. His hair was the color of straw too long in the sun, though, oddly, his pale face showed little sign of exposure to the sun. His smile, if it could be called that, was a study of malevolence.

"Yeah, I know who you are," Quince said. "You are a paid butcher."

"I prefer to think of myself as a policeman," Bates said. "The only difference is that I don't get paid by the government."

"You get paid by anyone who wants some killing done," Quince said. "So, you're working for Goodpasture now, eh?"

"Yes," Bates said. "He's been losing too many animals, and he has hired me to stop the thieves."

"Well, what has that got to do with Simmons?" Quince asked. "He sure as hell isn't one of the thieves."

Bates smiled again, the same, malevolent grin he had on his face earlier. "Oh, but he is," he said. He pointed toward the cows. "You will notice that three of them are hobbled," he said. "And one of them has Three Crowns branded over Mr. Goodpasture's brand."

"I don't believe it," Quince said.

"It's true, boss," Simmons said. He coughed when he spoke, and Quince could barely hear him. The cough brought on a new spasm of pain, and Simmons groaned.

"What? But why, Simmons? I don't understand."

"Boss, I finally figured out how come we to lose all our cows to hoof-n-mouth," Simmons said. "I figured it must be that cow that got run in on us that night, you remember . . . when we thought someone was rustlin'?"

"Yeah, I remember," Quince said.

Simmons coughed, again, and again there was a

spasm of pain. "Well, I got to thinkin' about that,
'n I started puttin' two 'n two together. Who do
you think would want somethin' like that to happen to us? Goodpasture, that's who. So, when I
seen his cows drinkin' our water, I figured, why
not just brand us a few to help us get our own
herd started, you know what I mean? And I had
just hobbled me a few'n was startin' in, when this
fella appeared."

"Did he shoot you in cold blood?" Quince asked,
looking toward Bates with ill-concealed anger.

"No," Simmons said. "He braced me when he
seen me, 'n damn fool that I was, I thought I
could take him. I drawed on him, boss, he kilt me
fair 'n square."

"You two men, go back to the Bighouse and get
a wagon," Quince ordered. "We need to get Simmons into town to a doctor."

"That's a waste of time," Bates said.

"It's my time, and I'll waste it," Quince said. He
pointed toward the cows. "Now, you collect your
damn cows and get them the hell off this land, or
I'll start taking them one per minute, for rent."

Bates grinned again. "Try it," he said.

There was the sudden, and unmistakable sound
of a rifle being cocked, and Bates and Quince
looked toward the sound. Rufus had walked back
to one of the horses and pulled the rifle from the
saddle scabbard. It was pointed toward Bates.

"Hey, old man, I don't know who the hell you
are," Bates said.

"I'm the cook," Rufus interrupted.

Bates laughed. "The cook?"

"Yeah," Rufus said. "And I'm gonna' fry your

bacon, if you don't do what Quince told you to do."

"Old man, don't you know I could pull this gun and shoot you before you could even pull the—"

The rifle went off, and a puff of dirt popped up right between Bates's legs. The bullet whizzed on by, humming like an angry bee, and even before the echo died, the rifle was cocked again.

"Do what the man said," Rufus said again.

"I'm tellin' you to watch your step!" Bates said, and he pointed his finger at Rufus.

That was the opportunity Quince was looking for, and with his left hand he lifted the pistol from Bates's holster, while he made a fist of his right hand and crashed it into Bates's face. Bates went down like a sack of flour, clawing desperately at the empty holster.

"You son-of-a-bitch, I'll *kill* you!" Bates shouted in a choking rage. He tried to get back up, and Quince hit him again. When Bates tried to get away from Quince's pummelling blows by crawling away on his hands and knees, Quince kicked him in his exposed posterior, and Bates fell forward, sliding on his nose.

The men laughed at Bates's predicament, despite the danger of the moment, for everyone there knew that Bates would carry out his threat if he could.

Quince ejected the cartridges from Bates's pistol, then threw the pistol on the ground beside him.

"Now, pick up your gun and get out of here," he said. "And don't ever let me see you on Three Crowns land again."

Bates slipped his gun back into his holster, mounted his horse, and amidst the hoots and shouts of the cowboys, rode out at a gallop.

"How is Simmons?" Quince asked, after Bates was gone.

The cowboys looked at each other in quick embarrassment. They had so enjoyed the spectacle of Bates that they had forgotten about Simmons. One of them dropped to his knee beside Simmons and looked at him closely. He reached down and put his fingers on Simmons's neck, then looked up at Quince and shook his head sadly.

"He's dead, boss," he said.

Quince sighed. "Rufus, see to getting him back and getting him buried," he said. He walked over to his horse and swung into the saddle.

"Where you goin'?"

"I'm going to take these cows back to Goodpasture," he said.

"You want me to go with you?"

"No. I think I'd better have this out now, or we'll be in the midst of a range war before we know it."

"All right," Rufus said. He was still holding the rifle. "But I think you ought to go armed."

"I'd rather not," Quince said. "I'm no match for Bates in a gunfight, and I don't want to be tempted to try."

"Good luck to you then," Rufus said.

Quince rode over to the handful of strays, cut the hobbles and started driving them toward the big mountain from which Mountain Shadow took its name.

24

THERE WAS a party going on on the front lawn of Mountain Shadow. Tables were set up on the neatly clipped turf, and they were all covered with white linen, and spread with an array of food, drinks, china, and crystal. Well-dressed men and women were standing around in groups, and waiters flitted about, carrying trays of drinks. A chamber orchestra was playing on the porch.

The original intent of the party had been to introduce Leslie to anyone who might not have met her, and Charles had merely forgotten to cancel it when Leslie left to go to Montana. Outside the fact that there were a few jokes made about the guest of honor not being present for her own party, there was little note taken of her absence, because Charles's parties were events in and of themselves, and her absence did little to dampen the spirits of the revelers.

At first, only a handful of the guests noticed the approach of the rider, a man who was dressed in jeans, shirt, and hat, and who was driving about half a dozen cows. Those who noticed him paid little attention to him, as they assumed he was merely one of the ranch hands. Most looked away, to redirect their attention to the conversation at hand, or to enjoy the music or the food and drink of the party.

But suddenly there was a crashing sound, the bawl of a confused steer, and the scream of a frightened woman! Everyone looked back around then, and they realized with shock that the cowboy was driving the cattle right through the lawn party! Tables were knocked over, and chairs were brushed aside, as the party guests scattered to avoid the animals. A huge silver punchbowl, the centerpiece of the largest table, was turned over, spilling its dark, red liquid upon the lap of one of the women guests.

Charles stood there in confused shock, but then he recognized the cowboy, and he shouted in anger.

"Parker! Parker, what the hell do you think you are doing?"

Quince Parker was the man driving the cattle, and he stopped his horse, and hooked one leg across the pommel of his saddle, then sat there, looking challengingly down at Charles.

"I'm just being neighborly," he said. "I'm bringing your cows back."

"Well, you didn't have to bring them back like this, did you?" Charles asked, sputtering in his anger.

"Oh, I thought they were awfully important to you," Quince said. "I figured they would have to be, or you wouldn't have had your hired gun murder one of my men."

There was a murmur of surprise from the group.

"Murder?" a woman said questioningly.

"What's he talking about?" a man asked.

"Yes," Charles said. "I'd like to know what you are talking about myself. Who was murdered?"

"Ben Simmons," Quince replied. "It seems a shame you don't even know his name, as you are responsible for his death."

"Parker, you are either drunk or insane," Charles said. "You should know better than to make crazy accusations like that. What do you mean by it?"

"You had your hired gun kill my man," Quince said, "all over a misunderstanding about a few cows. These cows," he said, pointing to the animals, which by now had wandered through the lawn and were on their way to open rangeland, and company more to their liking. "Emil Bates pulled the trigger, but you paid him, so there's no difference in my book. You are as guilty of murder as Emil Bates."

"Emil Bates?" one of the other ranchers said in surprise. "Charles, is he telling the truth? Have you hired Emil Bates?"

"Well, I . . ." Charles started, then he hesitated.

"Tell them, Goodpasture," Quince said. "They are all dressed up in suits and ties, drinking your wine, listening to your music. Tell them that the courtly gentleman who is such a gracious host is also the same man who would hire a rattlesnake like Emil Bates."

"You're lying, Parker," one of the other ranchers said. "I've known Charles Goodpasture for a long time, and I know he wouldn't have anything to do with someone like Emil Bates."

"Am I lying, Goodpasture?" Quince asked.

"I, I didn't tell him specifically to kill your man," Charles mumbled.

"Charles," the rancher who had defended him said in surprise. "I can't believe this. You have actually hired Emil Bates?"

"Yes," Charles said.

"Do you know what kind of a man Bates is?"

"He's a vigilante for hire," Charles said.

"He's a killer," another said gruffly.

"I heard he once burned out a settler's family," somebody else said. "They were squatting on some rancher's range, and he burned them out, and killed the husband, wife, and four kids."

"I heard it was six kids," another put in.

"However many it was, he killed them all. He's torched more houses than the Indians."

"There were only two kids," Bates said, suddenly appearing from the direction of the bunkhouse. "And they had plenty of warnin' to get out of the house."

"Oh, my God! It's him!" one of the women said, and a ripple of shock passed through them. Bates stood just beyond the part of the fence which had been knocked down by the cattle when they exited the lawn, and he was smiling at the guests, as if in secret amusement over their fear and disgust with him. He was still wearing the same black shirt and black pants he had on earlier, and he was still wearing his gun belt. The gun was strapped low, and his right arm was hanging loosely, with the hand open and curved. The fingers worked open and shut, slowly.

"You, you *admit* it?" one of the ranchers asked.

"Sure, I admit it," Bates said easily. "Why shouldn't I admit it? A jury found me innocent." His evil smile grew broader. "Fact is, nearly everyone of my killings have had the same verdict from the jury. It's called 'justifiable homicide.'"

"You're a killer!" someone shouted, but when Bates's eyes flashed, and he looked toward the assembled guests, all looked down at the lawn, and no one would own up to the remark.

"Perhaps he is," Goodpasture said. "But, as he said, he has been justified in all his killing. He is a rough man, yes, but you must remember the type of people with whom he must deal. Killers and thieves all. If you are going to survive in this kind of world, then you have to be tougher than they are. And if you are going to survive as a rancher, then you must take tough, yes, even drastic measures, sometimes, and that is just what I am doing. I've had a tremendous loss in stock, due to thieves, lately. I had to do something to look after my interests, so I hired Bates. I hired him, and I will pay for his services. But in effect, he will be working for all of us."

"He's not working for me," one of the ranchers said self-righteously.

"Isn't he? Mr. Vogel, didn't you tell me yourself, not thirty minutes ago, that you are losing more cattle to thieves than to any other cause?"

"Well, yes, but I'm not ready to go out and hire an Emil Bates to take care of it."

"Well, I am," Charles said. He looked at all of them, challenging them with flashing, angry eyes. "Do you think I intend to wind up broke and destitute like Swan, or Frewen, or DeMores? Once, they had ranches as big or bigger than Mountain Shadow, and they were respected names throughout the country. Well, that's not going to happen to me, gentlemen. No, sir, that's not going to happen at all. I built this ranch on sheer gall and guts, and by God, I'll hold it together the same way. If it takes a man like Emil Bates to frighten away the thieves, and the poachers," he said, looking over at Quince, "then I'll hire a man like Emil Bates. And if any of you had any sense, you would realize that Quince Parker is trying to cause all the trouble he can cause, because his bubble is about to break."

"What do you mean?" someone asked.

Charles smiled at Quince.

"Mr. Parker was Lord Kendrake's foreman. Oh, he had Lord Kendrake buffaloed for a great number of years, even to the point that Kendrake treated him as he would his own son. Well, that was what Parker wanted, because the result was that Parker cheated Lady Leslie out of the right to make a profit from her rightful inheritance. But he wasn't content with that," Charles went on. "Oh, no. He wanted all of her inheritance for himself, so he tried to marry her."

"Maybe you have him wrong," one of the women said. "Maybe he really loved her, and was hurt when she agreed to marry you."

"Madam, I am sorry to destroy your romantic image," Charles said. "But the only thing Quince Parker knows about love is what Rosita Mendoza has taught him down at her establishment."

There was a gasp of shock from most of the ladies, and a few ill-concealed laughs from the men, who had already heard the story about Quince and Rosita.

"I'm sorry if one of your men got killed," Charles said. "But I'm sure it wasn't cold-blooded murder."

"Naw, it wasn't, and Parker knows it wasn't," Bates said: "The fella pulled his gun on me, 'n he admitted the same to Parker before he died. Didn't he, Parker?"

"What difference does that make?" Quince asked.

Bates smiled. "Well, now, that just makes it another case of *justifiable* homicide."

"Well?" Charles asked. "Did it happen that way?"

"Yes," Quince admitted. "But Ben Simmons was no more of a gun fighter than you are. When he went up against Bates, it was the same as if he was unarmed."

"Not the same," Bates said. "You never can tell, he coulda got lucky." He looked at Quince with his pale, colorless eyes, and the smile remained fixed in place, like a permanent thing. "Just like you. You might get lucky, too, you know."

"What do you mean?"

"Go for your gun," Bates said quietly. He moved his hand out just a little, holding it poised in place just ready to draw. "Go for it. You might be lucky."

There was a gasp of horror from some of the party-goers.

"Bates, no," Charles called. "I don't want this."

"This one ain't for you, Mr. Goodpasture," Bates said quietly. "This one is for me. I want to kill this son-of-a-bitch for my own self."

"Oh, I think I'm going to faint," one of the women said, but so fixed upon the events unfolding before them were the others that no one paid any attention to her pronouncement. In fact, even she forgot to do it as she watched the life and death drama being played out by these two desperate men.

"I had a notion you were going to try something like that," Quince said. "So I took the precaution of not wearing a gun."

"You ain't wearin' a gun?" Bates said angrily.

"Nope."

"Then get one, mister," Bates ordered. "Get one now, 'cause I intend to kill you, just like I said I was goin' to."

"No," Quince said. "I won't give you the opportunity to kill me with your justifiable homicide."

"Then I just may shoot you outta that saddle, anyway," Bates said.

"No, I don't think so," Quince said. "You see, I took a precaution against that, too."

"What do you mean?" Bates asked, puzzled by the strange statement. "How are you going to stop me from killin' you iffen I feel like it?"

"Because I have hidden two armed men and their rifles are trained on you right now," Quince said. "If you make a move for your gun, they will both shoot at once. One of them is bound to get you."

Bates looked around in surprise, then, he looked back at Quince. "I don't believe you," he said.

"Go for your gun," Quince challenged. "See if you can get it out before they kill you."

Bates stood there a moment or two longer, opening and closing his fingers, and looking with a nervous jerking motion from side to side. He began to sweat.

"What's the matter, Bates?" Quince asked easily. "Are you afraid?"

"Tell them to come out in the open," Bates said. "Tell them to come out so I can see them. I'll take both of them on at once, and we'll just see how afraid I am."

"I won't do that," Quince said. "But I'll tell you where they are. One is behind that boulder over three. Can you see the end of the rifle barrel? It's pointed right at you."

Bates looked toward the boulder, and licked his lips. "No, I don't . . . yeah," he said. "Yeah, I think I do. That's a cowardly trick, you gutless son-of-a-bitch."

"Perhaps so," Quince said. "But it's keeping me alive, isn't it? The other man is in the hayloft of Goodpasture's barn."

Bates looked toward the barn.

"Where are they?" someone in the party said. "I don't see them."

"I see the one in the barn, but I don't see the one behind the rocks," another said.

"You're crazy, the one behind the rocks is almost in the open. It's the one in the barn I can't see."

"I can't see either one of them."

"Hell, I can see both of them. There's one, see?" someone said, pointing. "And there's the other."

"Oh, yeah, I see them now. At least, I think I do."

"Well, Mr. Goodpasture," Quince said. "Now

that I have returned your property, and in the process provided a little entertainment for your party, I think I'll be going."

"I would appreciate it if you would," Charles said with quietly controlled anger.

"And in the future," Quince said. "I will hold any of your cattle that stray onto Three Crowns land for twenty-four hours. After that time, I will put my brand on them."

"You mean the Three Crowns brand?" Charles asked, with a big smile. "Because that's soon going to be my brand, anyway."

"No," Quince said. "I mean my brand. I'm using the diamond brand."

"The diamond brand? That's too close to my brand. Connect the Mountain with the shadow, and you could turn my brand into a diamond."

"Yeah," Quince said with a smile. "Couldn't I?"

Quince swung his leg back across his saddle, then touched his hand to his hat in a mock salute. "I'll be going now, Goodpasture," he said. He looked at those tables which had not been turned over by the cows. "Sorry I can't stay a while longer. It looks like a swell party. Oh, and Bates, if I were you I'd stay right where you are for about five minutes after I've left. Otherwise my men might get a bit itchy in the fingers."

Quince wheeled his horse about, then rode off at a gallop. Bates stood rooted to the spot for a few minutes longer, still glancing nervously first toward the rocks and then toward the hayloft of the barn.

A few of the men in the party began easing slowly toward the rocks, while on the opposite side,

a few started toward the barn. Then the ones nearest the rocks let out a yell.

"Hey! There's nobody here!"

"There's nobody in the barn either!" the men
from the barn yelled.

Bates let out a bellow of rage, and pulled his
gun, turned and fired three times toward the rocks,
with his bullets smashing and whining as they rico-
cheted from the rocks and out into the valley beyond. Then he turned and fired three times into
the hayloft of the barn, screaming out his rage with
every shot.

Bates continued to pull the trigger, though now
the hammer clicked harmlessly against empty
chambers.

A nervous ripple of laughter spread through the
assembled party guests, then the laughter spread
untiu all, even the women, were laughing almost
hysterically.

"I've never seen *anyone* aced the way you were,"
someone called derisively.

"There was nobody there," another said, laughing and wiping the tears from his eyes. "There never
was anyone there. He ran as cool a bluff on you as
I've ever seen run on anyone."

"That's quite a gunfighter you've hired yourself,
Charles," another man called. "He does pretty good
against rocks and empty barns."

"You wanna try a few shots at a windmill, Don
Quixote?" someone hooted, and everyone laughed
again.

Bates had reloaded his gun by now, and he
turned it against the party. He shot a couple of

glasses off one of the tables, sending a shower of whiskey and glass spraying. Another bullet carried the hat from a woman's head, and she screamed and fainted.

"Now," he said, menacingly. "The next son-of-a-bitch that makes a remark gets one right between the eyes."

"Bates, I'm not paying you for this sort of thing," Charles said nervously.

"You ain't payin' me for nothin' anymore, Goodpasture," Bates said, "'cause I'm takin' this on as a charity case. I'll kill Parker for you for free."

"No!" Goodpasture said. "Don't be a fool! If you kill him now, everyone here will know it was murder!"

"If that's the only way I can get the son-of-a-bitch, then that's what it will be," Bates said. "But I'm goin' to get 'im." He walked over to one of the tables and took two bottles of whiskey, one already open but nearly full, and the other, as yet unopened. He turned the open bottle up and took several long swallows. "Uhmm," he said, taking the bottle down and wiping his mouth with the back of his hand. "Now, that's real sippin' whiskey. Yessir, you rich bastards really know how to live."

He turned and walked slowly back toward the bunkhouse, carrying the full bottle of whiskey in his left hand, holding it low so that it just cleared his knee, and with his right hand turning the open bottle up to take generous sips as he walked along.

"What, what are you going to do about him, Charles?" one of the ranchers asked quietly.

"Do? What can I do?" Charles replied. "You

heard him. He quit. I don't have any more control over him now than you do."

"Someone should do something," the man said.

"Yeah," another agreed. "Someone should do something."

"What do you suggest that we do?"

"I don't know," the man said. "But someone should do something."

A moment later they heard a horse, and looked around to see Emil Bates riding away. They breathed a collective sigh of relief, then gradually, the conversation began again.

"Music!" Charles shouted to the bandmaster, who, along with the members of the band, had watched the entire proceedings in stunned silence from the front porch of the house. "I didn't bring you all the way out here so you could stand around and gawk!"

The bandmaster slapped his baton against his podium several times, and the musicians hurried back to their chairs. He raised his baton, held it for an instant, then brought it down sharply, and the music began once again.

Gradually the flow of liquor and food helped to relax the guests, so that within half an hour, the entire incident had become little more than an interesting interlude to an otherwise routine party.

Only Charles Goodpasture still felt uneasy about what might yet happen as a result of the afternoon's confrontation, and he walked over to a sycamore tree and leaned against it, looking off into the distance. He felt himself losing control of the situation, and he did not like being in a situation over which he had no control.

His stomach began hurting, and he started into the house to take some baking soda and water. He wished the party was over, and the people were all gone. Then he thought, to hell with them. If he didn't return to the party, the guests should just get the hint and go home anyway. And if they didn't, it would not really matter, because he was through for the day. One of the advantages of being wealthy was that you could afford to offend anyone you wanted, socially. And Goodpasture intended to take advantage of that, right now.

25

THE VIEW from the gazebo was exquisite. The back lawn of the Kohrs estate consisted of ten acres of rolling green lawn, sculptured hedgerows, colorful flowers, a fountain, and a goldfish pond. Leslie came often to the gazebo, just to enjoy the view, and to have a few reflective moments.

It had been a wonderful two weeks with the Kohrs, not only because Augusta Kohrs was a fine woman and had become a good friend, but also because Leslie had been allowed to spend as much time alone with her thoughts as she wished. When she wanted to talk, Augusta was there, but when she wanted to reflect, Augusta seemed to have a sixth sense which told her to allow Leslie her time alone.

Leslie had been giving a great deal of consideration to going back to England. She didn't really want to, but she was beginning to feel as if she had no choice. Charles Goodpasture expected her to marry him when she returned from her visit with the Kohrs, but Leslie was now convinced that marrying Charles would be the biggest mistake she had ever made in her life.

Leslie knew now that she was in love with

Quince Parker. She had been shocked and hurt by
the incident she had happened upon before leaving
Sweetgrass. The scene of Quince and that woman
was burned into her mind. And yet, there was
something else about that incident that she remembered as well, and that was the look on Quince's
face.

It was a look which couldn't be painted by an
artist, nor described by a poet, for it was a look of
such shame and sorrow that it bared his very soul.
This was not an indiscreet moment blundered into,
nor the action of a lustful seducer. It was a moment
of sorrow and tragedy, and over the last two weeks,
that image was foremost in her thoughts. Whatever
reason Quince had for seeing that woman it didn't
change a thing. Leslie loved him and she believed
that he loved her.

But how would she approach him? How would
she go up to him, and tell him that she loved him,
and that she didn't want to marry Charles, she
wanted to marry him? That was the problem she
had been struggling with for several days now.

"I thought you would be down here," a voice
said, and Leslie's musings were interrupted by
Augusta Kohrs. Augusta was wearing a long, white
lawn dress, and a wide-brimmed straw hat, liber-
ally decorated with flowers. She ran her household
in Teutonic style, sometimes resorting to her native
German language when angry or frustrated with
her servants. She did that, she explained to Leslie
with a smile, so that she wouldn't say something in
anger which would offend the people working for
her.

"I can blow off steam in German," she said, "and no one is the wiser."

"Hello, Augusta," Leslie said, smiling as the older woman approached the gazebo. "Isn't it a lovely day today?"

"*Ja*," Augusta said. She laughed. "I think you would sleep here if you could."

"Yes," Leslie said. "I really would. I've never seen a spot quite so lovely."

"You should see it in February," Augusta teased. "Then, I think, you would not believe it to be so lovely."

"I've not been out here for a winter, yet," Leslie said. "Are they very harsh?"

"Ach, the winters are terrible," Augusta said. "Last winter we had a blizzard, and on a nearby ranch a man froze to death, not one hundred yards from his house. The snow was so heavy he could not see, and he got lost in his own front yard."

"Oh, how awful!"

"*Ja*. But, I did not come to speak of such awful things," Augusta said, smiling brightly. "There is someone here I want you to meet."

"Oh?"

"*Ja*. He is a young man, come to buy the Herefords."

"Leslie laughed. "You mean Mr. Kohrs has managed to talk another rancher into raising Herefords?"

"You think this is not a good idea?" Augusta asked.

"As a matter of fact, I think it is an idea whose time has come," Leslie said. "And if I thought I would have any influence over Quince, I would tell him to buy Herefords."

"I think you are right," Augusta said. "So, you agree that the young man who is here to buy the Herefords is a smart young man. I will tell you that he is handsome, too, and he is without a wife."

"Without a wife? What does that have to do with anything? Augusta, you know I am engaged to marry Charles Goodpasture."

"You don't love him," Augusta said.

"What? Why would you say such a thing?"

"I can tell," Augusta said. "When you came, you were very troubled. You have spent many hours thinking about your troubles, and now you have decided."

"How do you know I have decided?"

"I know," Augusta said. "And I know that you have decided that you do not wish to marry Charles Goodpasture. Am I not right?"

Leslie sighed. "Yes," she finally said. "Augusta, I just can't marry Charles Goodpasture. I don't love him, and though there may be many things involved in choosing the right husband, I think love should be one of them."

"*Ja*. I think so too," Augusta said. "That is why I want you to see the young man who is here."

Leslie laughed. "Is he so handsome and smart that I will fall in love with him the moment I see him?"

"You are already in love with him," Augusta said quietly.

"What?" Leslie asked quietly, with a sharp intake of breath. "Augusta, who is here?"

"I think you know," Augusta said.

"Is it Quince?"

"*Ja.*"

"Augusta, no, I can't see him," Leslie said. "I wouldn't know—" Suddenly Leslie put her hand to her throat and stopped in mid-sentence, for there, coming across the lawn toward the gazebo, was none other than Quince Parker himself.

"Hello, Leslie," Quince said.

"Quince, what are you doing here?"

"I told you I was going to restock Three Crowns. I'm going to raise Herefords."

"Well, I can see you two have much to talk about," Augusta said, smiling broadly. "I'll just leave the two of you alone."

"No," Leslie said. "No, don't, you don't understand, I . . ."

"Let her go, Leslie," Quince interrupted. Then, more softly, "Please, I do want to talk to you."

Leslie turned away and walked across the gazebo. She found something fascinating in the shrubbery to look at, and she fixed her gaze upon the dark, green leaves, as Quince began to speak.

"Leslie, I was ten kinds of fool for going into town that day. I had no idea that I was going to be set up, Rosita's letter said only that it was very important that I come to see her."

"You got a letter from Rosita? Why? Was Rosita an old girl friend of yours, too?"

"No," Quince said.

"Then why would she send you a letter?"

"I was just as curious about that as you are," Quince said. "And I was curious as to why she would specify that I come at nine o'clock."

"She said be there at nine?" Leslie asked and

now she looked around at Quince, this time with a puzzled expression on her face.

"Yes," Quince said. "At nine o'clock. Why? Is that significant to you?"

"I guess not," Leslie said, though it was clear that she was thinking about something.

"Well, when I got there at nine, she offered to loan me some money to buy cattle. I wanted to be able to build Three Crowns back to the way it was, so I agreed to accept the money. That was when she invited me up to her room. She said the money was there."

"And did she give you any money?" Leslie asked.

"No," Quince replied. He looked at the floor, and his cheeks colored red in embarrassment.

"She, uh, threw herself at me. Leslie . . . I swear to you, I had no intention of . . . of *doing* anything in that room other than borrowing money, but . . . well . . . I have no excuse for my weakness. She . . . she made certain advances, and I was too weak, and too much of a damn fool to resist them."

"I have to admit that it was a shock to me, to be a witness to such a thing," Leslie said. "But something you said, makes me believe now that the whole thing was planned, and that we were both victims."

"You mean, you also believe we were set up?" Quince asked.

"Set up? Yes, I think that would be an appropriate description," Leslie said.

Quince smiled. "That's what Rufus said the night I returned. But what did I say that convinced you of the idea?"

"It was her insistence that you meet her at nine,"

Leslie said. "You see, Charles got the sudden idea that we should call on Rosita at nine-thirty, the delay perhaps to ensure that she had you in a compromising position."

Quince sighed. "I wish I could take a degree of satisfaction in the fact that you know what happened now, but I can't. All I can think of is how weak and foolish I was."

Leslie reached out and put her hand on Quince's hand. "Quince, you aren't the only weak or foolish one," she said. "For in my own way, I was just as big a fool with Charles Goodpasture."

Quince glanced up with a look of surprise on his face. "Leslie, see here, does this mean that you . . . I mean, could you possibly *forgive* me?"

"There is nothing to forgive," Leslie said. She smiled. "It was merely a misunderstanding, which has now been clarified."

"Oh, Leslie," Quince said, beaming happily. He put his arms around her, and she leaned into him, meeting his lips more than halfway as they kissed.

"Excuse me," a voice said, and as Leslie and Quince were locked in an embrace, they jumped at the sudden, and unexpected interruption. They looked around to see one of the servants. Though he had obviously seen them kissing, his impassive face was a study of non-involvement. "Dinner is being served," he said.

The servant turned then, and walked back to the house, leaving Leslie and Quince to return on their own. They looked at each other, then laughed together over being "caught" by him, and, hand-in-hand, walked across the lawn to join the others at dinner.

The meal was eaten in a very relaxed atmosphere. Leslie learned that Quince had bought several head of Herefords, and that they were being herded into pens to be loaded onto a special train which would arrive for them at the end of the week.

"Three Crowns is ready for them," Quince said. "The water system works perfectly."

"You've done a lot of work there," Kohrs said. He looked over at Leslie. "You are one lucky woman, madam, to have a foreman as efficient as this man."

"He isn't just a foreman," Leslie said.

"Oh?"

"He is a co-owner," she went on.

"No, Leslie, the ranch belongs to you," Quince said quickly.

"But the water improvements . . . and the cattle . . . belong to you. In my book, that makes this a partnership."

"In my book, too," Kohrs said, laughing broadly. "Though it is a strange partnership, with the ranch owner living on another ranch."

"I was visiting for a while," Leslie said. "As I visited here. But tomorrow, when I go home, I will go home. Back to Three Crowns." She smiled. "That is, if you haven't neglected the Bighouse while you've been doing everything else?" she teased.

"The Bighouse is ready for you," Quince promised her.

"Well," Kohrs said. "Now that we have finished our meal, shall we go into the parlor? I've arranged for some entertainment on this, our charming guest's last night."

"*Ja*," Augusta said. "I think that would be wonderful."

The parlor was Leslie's favorite of all the rooms in the Kohrs house. It was less formal, and consequently, much more comfortable than the others, though the entire house was comfortable, and even the most formal room was pleasant.

Indian rugs decorated the floor of the parlor and hung from the walls. There was also a rack of rifles against one wall, and the antlers of antelope and horns of buffalo were mounted on decorative plaques. There was a great, stone fireplace on one wall, and though there was no fire there now, Leslie could well imagine how cozy it must be on a cold winter's day.

"Now," Kohrs said. "We are about to listen to a guitar concert. Leslie, are you familiar with the guitar?"

"Yes," Leslie said. "Of course. Someone is always playing one around the ranch."

"Ah, but they only play chords to help them sing, am I right?"

"Well, yes. What else is a guitar for?" Leslie asked.

Kohrs laughed. "My dear, the guitar, in the hand of the right musician, is a concert instrument, as surely as is an organ. Wait, and you will see."

Kohrs nodded to a man Leslie had seen before. He was a Mexican, and he worked for Kohrs in some capacity, for she had seen him puttering around the grounds. But he looked vastly different now, as he was dressed in a beaded waistcoat and striped trousers. He picked up a battered guitar case and opened it.

The case may have been battered, but the guitar inside was exquisitely beautiful. The instrument was cherry red, giving way to soft yellow. It showed tender care, and the way the man handled it, gently and with respect, told the story of his love for the instrument. He strummed the strings lightly, moving through an intricate chord progression that rose from the sound box and wove a pattern of melody as delicate as a lace doily.

Leslie sat quietly, listening in delight. She was amazed that this sound was coming from a guitar. It was as if she were discovering something entirely new. She had thought herself familiar with the guitar, but had never really known it.

The man went through the chord progressions a few times, and then stopped. He hung his head for a few seconds, then started to play. The music spilled out, a steady, never wavering beat with two or three poignant minor chords at the end of phrases, but with an overall, single string melody, weaving in and out of the chords like a thread of gold woven through the finest cloth.

The sound was agony and ecstasy, joy and sorrow, pain and pleasure. It moved into Leslie's soul, and she found herself being carried along with the melody, now rising, now falling. Perhaps it was the moment, the quiet, the softly lit room, but Leslie had never been moved so deeply by music before. She sat spellbound for several seconds after the last exquisite chord faded away.

"Now," Kohrs said, quietly. "She understands."

26

"Now, REMEMBER," Augusta was saying. This Christmas, you are to come to New York with me. Don't say no, now, because I insist upon it."

"Yes," Leslie said. "Yes, I think I would like that. We would have a lovely time, I'm certain of it." Leslie was standing on the platform of the station, preparatory to boarding the train. The train had already come into the station, and was standing alongside now on the track. Little wisps of steam escaped from lines and valves beneath the cars, while ahead, on the track, the engine sat blowing off the pressure relief valves with great, puffing sounds, as if the engine were trying to regain its breath after the long run it had just made.

Leslie kept looking over the Kohrs' heads, into the faces of the crowd.

"Who are you looking for?" Kohrs asked.

"Oh, no one in particular," Leslie said.

Augusta smiled. "Don't take us for fools, Leslie," she said. "You are looking for Quince Parker, aren't you?"

Leslie laughed, a short, embarrassed laugh. "I suppose I am," she said. "I guess I hoped he would be down here to see me off."

"Now, dear, you know he explained all that," Kohrs said. "He has to tend to his cattle. The cattle train won't leave until Friday."

"Yes, I suppose so," Leslie said. "Still, I rather hoped . . ." she said wistfully, letting the sentence trail off.

"Well, don't hope. He is a practical man," Kohrs said. "And you should be glad, for it takes a practical man to get ahead in this world."

"Board!" the conductor shouted, and Conrad Kohrs guided Leslie over to the mounting step, and up into the coach.

"You must write to us now," Kohrs said. "We love to get mail from our friends."

The train began to jerk forward.

"I will write," Leslie said. "I promise you, I will write to thank you for the wonderful vacation I have had here."

"And remember that we shall go to New York for Christmas," Augusta said, as the train began to roll.

"Goodbye," Kohrs shouted.

"Goodbye," Leslie said.

"*Auf Wiedersehen,*" Augusta called.

Now the train was moving at a pretty good rate, and Leslie continued to wave to the Kohrs, while all the time searching the crowded station platform in a vain attempt to catch a glimpse of Quince.

"Miss, you can't stand between the cars," the conductor called as the train cleared the end of the platform, and Leslie, with a sigh, stepped inside. Kohrs was right of course. Quince did have too much to do. But still, it would have been nice if he had come down to at least see her off.

Leslie could feel a throbbing beneath her feet as the engine's pulsing rhythm was transmitted throughout the coaches. She walked down the aisle of the coach and showed her ticket to the conductor, who smiled at her. Then he escorted her to the Pullman car and opened the door to one of the compartments.

"This is your compartment, Miss," he said.

"Thank you very much," Leslie said. She stepped into the compartment, then closed the door behind her.

Inside there was a cushioned seat, a table, and a water basin. She sat on the seat and looked through the window. The train had not cleared the town yet, and she could see outside the window, the buildings of Main Street; the saloons and restaurants, already wearing their evening dress of lights, for this was a night train and darkness was beginning to fall.

There was a knock on her compartment door.

"Come in," she called, thinking it was the porter.

The door opened and closed before she turned around. Then, when she did turn around, she was shocked to see Quince standing there, smiling from ear to ear.

"Quince! What are you doing here? I thought you weren't coming back until Friday!"

"I have to go on ahead to make arrangements to get the cattle transferred from the railhead out to the ranch," Quince said. "I don't need to ride on the train with them, because Mr. Kohrs is sending one of his top men along to look after them."

"You mean Mr. Kohrs knew all along that you would be on this train?"

"So did Mrs. Kohrs," Quince said, still smiling. "We thought it would make a nice surprise."

"Oh, but how wonderful!" Leslie said. "But, I wish I had known. You have no idea how I looked through the crowd, hoping you were there."

"And angry because I wasn't?" Quince teased.

"Yes," Leslie admitted, laughing.

"I love you, Leslie," Quince said in a low voice.

The simple declarative statement, coming as direct as it did, in the midst of small talk and chatter, made her heart leap in joy.

They kissed then, a kiss of hunger and urgency, and it set Leslie's head whirling. She felt his tongue brush across her lips, gentle yet rough, demanding, enticing and commanding. Leslie felt herself go limp against him.

"Leslie, take off your clothes," Quince said huskily. "Take them off, I want to make love to you."

Leslie was a little surprised by the forthrightness of the request, but she complied, willingly, even eagerly. And, as she undressed, Quince secured the latch on the compartment and began removing his own clothes. Then, unashamedly nude, Leslie opened out the bed, and lay back to receive him.

Quince joined her on the small bed. He kissed her again and again, causing her to float in the bliss of sexual arousal. Her blood was hot, and there was a sweet aching in her loins, and her body trembled with fire under Quince's tender touch.

Quince moved over her, then into her. Leslie felt the most exquisite pleasure then . . . silken sensations which lifted her to the heights of ecstasy.

Leslie gave as well as took. Then she felt the building up of pleasures inside her, a tensing of her body, and, feeling herself approaching that magic moment, she abandoned all thought save this desperate quest for culmination. She rushed to the precipice, there to hang balanced precariously for several seconds. During that time of rapture her body became so sensitized that when she was propelled into the apex of ecstasy, she exploded like a rocket into fiery bursts of muscle-jerking spasms of pleasure.

It was totally dark outside by the time the last twitchings and tinglings had subsided, and Leslie and Quince lay together in each others' arms, she with her head on his shoulder.

They fell asleep that way, and she slept for several hours. She awoke once, and was at first surprised to realize that she was nude, and lying in Quince's arms. But memory returned quickly, and with it a warm, almost giddy feeling, and she nestled even closer to him, to be rewarded by his affectionate squeeze, even though he was asleep.

Beneath the bed on which she lay the wheels clicked melodiously against the rails. From her vantage point on the bed, she could see a silver moon hanging high in the midnight sky, and she watched the hills and trees passing by, and she wished there were some way she could capture this moment, to hold it locked forever in her heart so she could relive it any time she wished.

Leslie heard a knocking on the door, and she turned over, hoping the sound would go away. As soon as she turned, she realized that Quince was gone, and with that realization, she came quickly and fully awake.

The knocking persisted.

"Who is it?"

"Leslie, it's me, Quince."

Leslie sat up in bed, then noticed that she was still nude. She looked around for something with which she could cover herself, then she realized that such modesty after last night would be misplaced with Quince, so she walked over and pulled the door open.

"Well," Quince said, smiling in obvious delight at the sight which greeted him. "What have we here?"

"Obviously, we have a naked lady here," Leslie said. She looked at Quince pointedly. "And a fully clothed man."

Quince stepped in and closed the door behind him. "I can take care of that," he said, and, quickly, he began stripping out of his clothes.

"Wait," Leslie said, putting her hand out to stop him. "Quince, there is something I want—"

"Will you marry me, Leslie?" Quince asked, interrupting her.

Leslie smiled. "Yes," she said. "That's what I wanted."

"I've asked in every way that I know how," Quince said.

"Simple English would have been enough," Leslie said, and she pulled him against her, pressing herself against him, kissing him soundly on the lips. Quince returned her kiss, and she could feel the

texture of his lips on hers, and her mouth opened
hungrily.

Within a moment they were back in bed with
their naked bodies pressed together. Leslie gave
herself entirely to him, feeling once again the delightful wanderings of Quince's skilled hands, and,
under her gentle urging, he moved over her again,
and as he had last night, began making love to her.

Leslie could scarcely believe that she had been
so wanton as to invite him, to actually urge him, to
make love to her. And yet, astonishingly, she felt
neither shame nor guilt. She felt nothing but supreme joy, and as he loved her, she was lifted to
the dizzying heights of sublime rapture.

Later, with the pleasant weight of Quince lying
on her, Leslie turned her head toward the window,
only to see the houses of a town rushing by.

"Quince!" she shouted. "My Lord, we've come
into a town. Someone will see us!"

Quince looked toward the window, at the houses
and buildings of the town, and he began laughing.

"Don't laugh," Leslie said. "For heaven's sake,
pull the shade!"

Quince closed the shade, but he couldn't stop
laughing, and soon, even Leslie saw the humor,
and she joined him in the laughter as they dressed,
and prepared for breakfast.

The train arrived at Sweetgrass late that same
afternoon, and Charles was sitting in the carriage,
waiting. Andrew was perched upon the driver's
seat, steadying the horses against the noise of the
approaching train, and when it stopped, Charles
got out of the carriage and started toward it. He

was smiling, for he knew something Leslie didn't know. She had promised to marry him as soon as she returned, and even now, back at Mountain Shadow, a wedding party was in progress. The Episcopal priest, a full orchestra, and neighbors and influential people from three states were there, waiting on them.

Charles knew that Leslie didn't plan on getting married the *moment* she returned, but he figured by this method to pressure her into it. She would have no choice. She would succumb to the pressure and marry him, then, he would have everything under control, once more.

The smile on Charles' face left, the moment he saw Leslie detrain. For, coming down the steps behind her, and obviously with her, was none other than Quince Parker.

"Charles, hello," Leslie said.

"Hello, Leslie," Charles said. "Did you have a pleasant trip?"

"Yes," Leslie said. She looked at Quince and smiled. "I had a *very* pleasant trip."

"I see," Charles said coolly.

"Charles, I hope you can understand."

"Yes," Charles said, interrupting her. "I think I do." He sighed, then he smiled, weakly, as if finally surrendering to the inevitable. "I'll send your things back over to Three Crowns."

"Thank you," Leslie said.

"Parker," Charles said. "I'm sorry, but I'm just not a big enough man to congratulate you, or even offer you best wishes. But if you ever drop the reins, I'll be there to pick them up."

"Don't worry, Goodpasture," Quince said. "I don't intend to ever let her go."

"No," Charles said. "No, I suppose not." He turned and walked back toward the carriage, alone.

"You want me to get Lady Leslie's luggage?" Andrew asked, when Goodpasture climbed back into his seat.

"No, Andrew," Charles said. He looked toward Leslie and Quince for a long moment, and saw that they were so lost in their own world that they had already forgotten him. "No, just take me to Rosita's," he said. Then he added, "If she'll have me."

"She'll have you, Mr. Charles," Andrew said. "She'll always have you, you know that."

"I wouldn't blame her if she wouldn't," Charles said.

"Mr. Charles, what about all those people who are waiting out at Mountain Shadow?" Andrew asked.

"What about them?" Charles asked.

Andrew laughed. "You're right, Mr. Charles," he said. "What about them?"

As the carriage carried Charles down the street toward Rosita's, Quince made arrangements to hire a buckboard to drive the two of them out to Three Crowns. The buckboard could also carry Leslie's luggage, so it was more convenient than a buggy. Quince explained that he would have one of the hands return the buckboard to town, early the next morning.

As they drove toward the ranch, Quince filled Leslie in on all the plans he had for expansion. He was convinced now that Hereford cattle were indeed the cattle of the future, and, as he would be the first, major Hereford producer in Wyoming, he would have a distinct advantage over all other Wyoming ranchers.

"Not only that," he explained, as the team pulled the buckboard toward the large, red sun which was now dying in the West with a brilliant display of color. "But I've been in touch with one of the largest meat packers in Kansas City, and they have agreed to underwrite a railroad spur line."

"What does that mean?" Lesie asked.

Quince laughed. "Well, my dear, it means we are going to own our own railroad. We'll have a line that branches off the Union Pacific, right out to our ranch. We won't be losing pounds on the cattle with long drives to the railhead. We'll put them on, fat and sassy, in their own backyard, and when they get to Kansas City they'll weigh as much as they did when they left."

"Oh, Quince, it all sounds so wonderful," Leslie said.

"It's there, Leslie," Quince said. "You know I used to have a dream about something like this, but, well, to be honest, I thought I'd missed my opportunity. All the big cattle barons have made it in the last 20 years. I thought the opportunity was lost forever. But now, with Longhorn cattle on the way out, and Herefords on the way in, why, the new cattle barons will be the ones who had sense enough to start raising Herefords."

"The King is dead," Leslie said. "Long live the King."

"What does that mean?"

"Oh, nothing," Leslie said.

Quince smiled. "Your dad used to say things like that all the time," he said. "He'd make little comments that only he would understand, and you know, damned if sometimes I didn't think he enjoyed them more because of that."

Leslie laughed. "Yes," she said. "I can believe he would."

"I just wish he was here now," Quince said. "I wish he was here to see us." He looked over at Leslie, then he leaned over and kissed her.

"Well, now, looky here," a cold voice suddenly said.

Quince recognized the voice at once, and he looked up, just in time to see Emil Bates pull his horse onto the road in front of them. Bates had been hiding behind a cluster of boulders, waiting for them to approach.

"Bates!" Quince said. "What do you want?"

"Well, up until now, I thought all I wanted was to kill you," Bates said. He looked at Leslie. "But I might just want a little of this girl, too."

"Get the hell out of our way," Quince said, standing up.

Bates laughed, quietly, then the laugh fell from his face, and his smile faded. "When you get to hell, tell all my friends hello," he said. Then, as fast as the strike of a serpent, he pulled his gun and fired.

The bullet hit Quince high in the chest, and the weight of the impact knocked him out of the buckboard and onto the ground. He groaned as he fell, but once he hit the ground he was deathly quiet.

"*Quince!*" Leslie screamed, and she jumped out of the buckboard and ran around to look after him.

"Leave him be, girl," Bates said. "He's either dead, or he soon will be." He smiled, as evil a smile as Leslie had ever seen in her life. "But don't you be worryin' none about him. I'll take care of you. Yes'm, I'll take care of you, real good."

Leslie was so concerned for Quince, that she didn't get the gist of what Bates was saying. Not until she saw him right on her, with lust enflamed eyes, and his pants already unbuttoned, did she know what he intended for her.

"No!" she said. "No, get away!"

Leslie screamed, but her scream was choked back by his hand, dirty, and smelling now of gunpowder from the gun he had just fired.

From then on, things seemed to grow dim. The ground came up to meet her, and she knew that she had either fallen, or was knocked down. Shortly after that, she felt a rush of air on her bare legs, then a brutal, searing pain. She was vaguely aware of an oppressive weight, a sickening smell of sweat, fouled teeth, and lust. Then, mercifully, she passed out.

When Leslie came to much later, it was dark. The buckboard was still there, the team having stayed in place, and for just an instant, she wondered where she was and what had happened.

Then she saw Quince's still form, lying in the moon-splashed sand of the road, and she remembered.

"Quince!" she yelled. "Quince, oh, Quince, are you all right?"

Leslie pulled herself up to her hands and knees, felt a pain and nausea sweep over her, saw that her clothes were so badly torn that it was impossible to preserve any modesty, then she crawled over to look at Quince.

"Quince, oh, darling, don't be dead," she said. "Please, God, don't let him be dead."

Leslie put her head down to Quince's head, and then, with a surge of joy, she realized that he was breathing!

Leslie put her hand down in the dirt, then recoiled in horror, for the sand was gummy with blood, already coagulating. She turned him over, and in the moonlight, could see the spreading stain of crimson on his breast. She pulled off her silk blouse, which was itself torn, and made a hasty bandage. Then, with a strength she didn't know she possessed, she managed to drag him over to the buckboard, and then, onto it. She opened one of her suitcases then and there on the open road and in the dark, changed dresses so that she could cover her nakedness, then she climbed onto the buckboard and drove it the rest of the way home.

"Well," Rufus said, greeting her in a cheerful tone when she finally pulled up to the front of the bunkhouse. "If you aren't a sight for sore eyes!"

"Rufus, help me," Leslie said. "Quince has been shot and I've been . . . I've been . . ." but she was unable to finish. For with the completion of her journey, and the realization that someone else was here now to bear the load, the last ounce of her incredible strength left her, and she passed out, falling from the seat, right into Rufus's arms.

27

THE SOUND of the raising shades awakened Leslie, and when she opened her eyes she saw sunlight streaming into the room. She was in bed, dressed in a nightgown, and for an instant she felt the type of panic one feels when one suddenly discovers that they don't know where they are, or how they got there. Then, she remembered the terrible events of the night before.

"Oh," she said. "Quince! Where is he?"

"Quince is going to be just fine, Lady Leslie," a well dressed and distinguished-looking man said. He came over to sit on the bed beside her, and he pulled a thermometer case from his jacket pocket, then extracted the instrument itself, and started shaking it down.

"Who are you?"

"I'm Dr. Presnell," the man said. He started to put the thermometer in her mouth, but she pushed it away.

"Wait," she said. "Where is Quince?"

"He is in your father's old bedroom," Dr. Presnell said. "He's lost a lot of blood, but I got the bullet out, and I cleaned the wound. He's going to be just fine."

"Are you sure?"

"Yes, I'm sure," Dr. Presnell said, reassuringly. "The bullet didn't hit any vital organs, and there is no sign of infection."

"When can I see him?"

"Never, if you don't let me take your temperature," Dr. Presnell scolded.

Leslie leaned back and let the doctor put the thermometer in her mouth. He picked up her wrist and began taking a count of her pulse, as the thermometer did its work.

"I guess you went through quite an ordeal yourself, young lady," he said. "And the least I can do is make certain that you are all right."

Leslie looked at the bed in quick shame, and her cheeks flushed red, and tears sprang to her eyes.

"There, there," Dr. Presnell said. He reached up and brushed her hair from her eyes. "There's no serious damage done, except what may have been done up here." He touched her temple. "And whatever harm was done there, only you can cure. So my advice to you is to be glad that you sustained no worse injuries. And, if you are as strong a girl as Rufus seems to think you are, then you'll have no trouble at all." He pulled the thermometer out and looked at it, then smiled.

"How am I?"

"You are fine," Dr. Presnell said. "In fact, if you would like, you can get out of that bed right now, and start nursing Quince back to health."

"Yes," Leslie said. "I'd like that very much."

"I thought you would," Dr. Presnell said. "You can start by taking him his breakfast. He won't be hungry, but he has to eat in order to get his strength back."

"I'll have Rufus fix him a nice, clear broth," Leslie said.

"I'm afraid you are going to have to do that yourself, girl," Dr. Presnell said. "Rufus is gone."

"Gone? Gone where?"

"I don't know," Dr. Presnell said. "He stayed around until he knew that Quince was out of danger, then he said he had some business to take care of and he left."

"That's odd. That's very odd," Leslie said. "He has always seemed so loyal to Quince. Oh, well, I won't worry about that. I'll just get Quince's broth made."

"That's a good girl," Dr. Presnell said. He started closing his bag. "I'll look in on Quince about once a day, but, outside keeping his bandages clean, and feeding him enough to keep up his strength, there's little that needs to be done. And I'm sure you can do that."

"Thanks for everything, Dr. Presnell," Leslie said.

"Young lady, there are two people in this world I would have done anything for. One was your father, and the other is Quince Parker. Now your father is gone, God rest his soul, but you've come along to take his place. And, if what I hear is right, you've come to your senses now, as you've broken off with Charles Goodpasture, and you aim to marry Quince. Is that right?"

"Yes," Leslie said.

Dr. Presnell beamed. "Then there's no thanks needed," he said. "It's a pure joy just seeing you two get together the way Lord Kendrake and God intended."

Leslie laughed with him, then, after he let himself out, she dressed, and went to the task of making Quince's broth.

Quince was awake when Leslie came into his room some time later, carrying a tray with her. He smiled when he saw her.

"Leslie, thank God you are all right," he said.

"Me?" Leslie said. She laughed. "Of course I'm all right. I wasn't the one who was shot. You were. Now, tell me, how do you feel?"

"Well, I wouldn't want to go out and bulldog a steer right now," Quince said. "But I feel pretty good, considering. Especially since I see that you are all right."

"I'm fine," Leslie said. She took the cover off the tray, then stuck a spoon into the bowl of broth. "Now, open wide," she said. "You must eat."

"I'm not hungry," Quince said. "But, I'll confess to enjoying the nursing. You are a lot better than Rufus would be. Where is Rufus, by the way?"

"I don't know," Leslie said. "It's the strangest thing, but Dr. Presnell said he just left this morning. Now, why would he leave when he knows that we need him most?"

"He left? Leslie, did you tell him who attacked us?"

"Yes," Leslie said

"Oh, my God. He's gone after Bates."

"Quince, you can't be serious," Leslie said. "Rufus strikes me as a man who is far too intelligent to do something that foolish. After all, Bates is a deadly killer, and Rufus is only a cook."

"He's far, far more than a cook, darling," Quince said.

The bartender picked up the whiskey glass and saw that there was nearly an inch of whiskey left in it. He shrugged his shoulders, then removed the cap from the whiskey bottle and poured the liquor back into its original container. The man who had been drinking it wouldn't mind. He was upstairs right now, with Angie. Angie was a pro, all right. She could go to bed with anyone if he had her price. Even someone as cold-fish looking as this guy. He had given the bartender the willies, and he was just as glad that Angie had taken him out of here. He was a pale looking man, with sun-bleached hair, and eyes that were as flat and color-less as any he'd ever seen.

"I'd like a whiskey, please," a man said. He was a short, bandy-legged man, with a face a little like a road map. There was a sadness about him, but a dignity too. His clothes were nondescript, clean and well mended, but certainly not the duds of a vain man.

There was something about the demeanor of the man which arrested the bartender's attention. It could have been his eyes, cool and appraising, or his manner, confident and assured, or, just the way he wore his gun. It was slung low and kicked out, the way a gunfighter wore a gun.

The bartender started to pour whiskey from the bottle he had just returned the leftover whiskey to.

"I would prefer a new bottle, if you don't mind," the man said.

"Yes, yes, of course," the bartender said nervously. Something about this man made him uneasy, and as he started to pour, he saw that his hands were shaking badly.

"Maybe you'd better let me do that," the man suggested, taking the bottle from him. The man poured a glass and sat the bottle down. "There is a roan out front," he said, as if making conversation. "It has a white stocking on his left foreleg. This horse is ridden by a washed-out-looking hombre, no color in his face, or hair, or eyes. Do you know who I am talking about?"

"No," the bartender said.

The man took out a coin and put it in the bartender's shirtpocket. "He's dressed all in black," the man said.

The bartender's eyes darted toward the head of the stairs at the room where the colorless one had gone with Angie.

"I see," the man said. "Bates is up there, is he?"

"Bates?" the bartender said. "Emil Bates?"

"Yep."

"What do you want with Emil Bates?"

"I want to kill him."

The man said the words quietly, but within seconds it had spread over the entire saloon. Conversations, poker games, and just plain drinking stopped as all the patrons looked at this strange, bandy-legged man.

"What did you say, mister?" someone said.

The man looked toward the speaker and saw that he was wearing a badge.

"So, you are the sheriff?"

"I am. And I don't intend to stand by and watch you get yourself kilt. Not in my jurisdiction, I don't."

"You misunderstand, sheriff. I said I was going to *do* the killin', not get killed."

"Mister, I don't intend to let that happen either," the sheriff said.

"And I don't intend to let you stop me," the man said. He turned slowly, and with self-assurance, to look at the sheriff. "So, if you got 'ny ideas along that line, you may as well try 'em now, so I can get you out of the way."

"Let 'im shoot it out if it's a fair fight, sheriff," someone called.

"Yeah," another put in. "If it's fair, why stop it?"

The sheriff licked his lips nervously. He really didn't want to face down this man, and now, there seemed to be an honorable way out of it.

"All right," he said, looking around the room. "All right, I'm goin' to back out of this 'n let it go on as a fair fight. And I don't want anyone interferin'. Does everyone understand that?"

"We got you, sheriff. That's the way it ought to be done," someone said.

The piano, which had been playing in the corner and had stopped for the discourse, now began to play again. However, all eyes were on the top of the stairs, and all conversation directed toward the upcoming gunfight. Within a moment, the piano stopped again, and everyone in the saloon waited.

The waiting grew more strained, and the conversation soon petered out. Now there was absolute silence, and when someone coughed nervously, everyone turned to look at him accusingly. The bartender wiped the same glass until it began to squeak loudly, then, nervously, he put it down and picked up another. The pendulum on the clock swung back and forth, marking the passing of each second, and involuntarily, perhaps a dozen or so men looked at it as if it were very important to fix the time in their minds, the better for the telling of their stories, later.

Whiskey glasses were refilled as quietly as everything else, the drinker merely walking over to the bar and holding his glass out silently.

More people drifted into the saloon, but they were met at the door, and a whispered exchange told them what was going on. Most who wandered in, stayed, drawing on their beer or whiskey as silently as the others, and then waiting.

Waiting.

The tension grew almost unbearable. From the room at the top of the stairs there came the sound of a woman's moan of passion. There wasn't a man in the saloon who didn't know what was going on up there, but that which would have normally elicited peals of embarrassed laughter, brought only silence.

The woman who had moaned in passion laughed a bit later, and her laughter was joined by a man's. Then there was the sound of footfalls, as boots struck the floor. The door opened and Emil Bates came out of the room, talking animatedly to the girl who had gone in with him. They started for the steps, but when Emil reached the head of the steps, he noticed the deathly silence, and the eyes, staring up at him.

"What the hell is this?" he asked. "What's going on?"

The girl also sensed a danger, and she hurried back into the room from which they had just come.

"You don't cover your tracks very well, Bates," the bandy-legged man said, stepping away from the bar. "It was real easy to find you."

Bates saw him and smiled. "Well, if it ain't the cook," he said. "The little sawed-off, piss-ant, runt-ass of a cook. The one who held a rifle on me. What's your name, cook?"

"Rufus."

"Rufus?" Bates laughed. "Now, that's just a dandy name."

"Some folks call me Ruthless," Rufus said. "Ruthless Butler."

There was a collective gasp of shock from those in the bar."

"Did he say Ruthless?"

"I thought he was dead. I thought he was shot dead in Abilene."

"Not Ruthless Butler," another man said. "There ain't never been a man could hold a candle to him."

"You reckon *this* could really be Ruthless Butler?"

"If it ain't, I wouldn't want to be in this fella's shoes right now. If they's a man alive could take Ruthless Butler, it would be Emil Bates."

"So," Bates said, still smiling. "I've heard about you all my life. I often wondered what it would be like to go up agin' you."

"You are about to find out," Rufus said.

"I'm not knockin' the opportunity, you understand," Bates said. "But I'm wonderin' why. I mean, why after nobody has heard of you for all these years, have you come out after me? I sure as hell can't make your reputation."

"I'm not interested in a reputation," Rufus said. "I'm just interested in seein' that a friend of mine is never bothered by you again."

"Oh? And who would that be?"

"Quince Parker."

Bates laughed. "Now, what makes you think I can bother him anymore? He's dead!"

"No, he isn't," Rufus said. "He's still alive, and I aim to see that he stays that way. I figured that if you heard that, you'd try to finish what you started."

"Well, you figured right, old man," Bates said. "I'd finish him off, 'n might even enjoy that piece of baggage who was with him again."

"I'm tired of talking now, Bates," Rufus said. "Make your play."

"With pleasure, old man," Bates said.

Bates stared at him for a long moment, then his hand started for his gun, but Rufus had his own out and booming before Bates could completely clear leather. The gun slipped out of Bates' hand and fell to the stairs, then, tumbled and clattered loudly down each one, all the way to the floor.

Bates stood there for a moment, looking on in total surprise. Then he tried to take a step forward, lost his balance, and fell against the bannister. The bannister gave way, and he crashed through it, falling back first, through a poker table, and onto the floor below.

One of the men near the poker table walked over and looked down at Bates's prostrate form.

"He's deader 'n a doornail," the man said, looking at Bates.

"That was a fair fight, sheriff," another said. "You can't say it wasn't no fair fight."

"No," the sheriff agreed. "It was fair enough. Mister Butler, if you don't mind, I'd like to buy you a drink."

"I appreciate it, sheriff, but I don't have time to stick around," Rufus said.

"What's the hurry?" the sheriff asked. "I already told you it was a fair fight. There won't be any paper out on you."

"I appreciate it, sheriff, really I do," Rufus said. "But I've got to be going, just the same. You see," he said with a grin, "I've got me a weddin' to go to."